THE
SHATTERED
TRIDENT

ALSO BY RICHARD PHILLIPS

The Endarian Prophecy

Mark of Fire
Prophecy's Daughter
The Curse of the Chosen
The Shattered Trident

The Rho Agenda

The Second Ship
Immune
Wormhole

The Rho Agenda Inception

Once Dead
Dead Wrong
Dead Shift

The Rho Agenda Assimilation

The Kasari Nexus
The Altreian Enigma
The Meridian Ascent

THE
SHATTERED
TRIDENT

THE ENDARIAN PROPHECY
RICHARD PHILLIPS

Text copyright © 2019 by Richard Phillips
All rights reserved.

No part of this book may be reproduced, or stored in a retrieval system, or transmitted in any form or by any means, electronic, mechanical, photocopying, recording, or otherwise, without express written permission of the publisher.

Published by 47North, Seattle

www.apub.com

Amazon, the Amazon logo, and 47North are trademarks of Amazon.com, Inc., or its affiliates.

ISBN-13: 9781542007337
ISBN-10: 154200733X

Cover design by Shasti O'Leary-Soudant

Printed in the United States of America

I dedicate this novel to my wife and lifelong best friend, Carol.

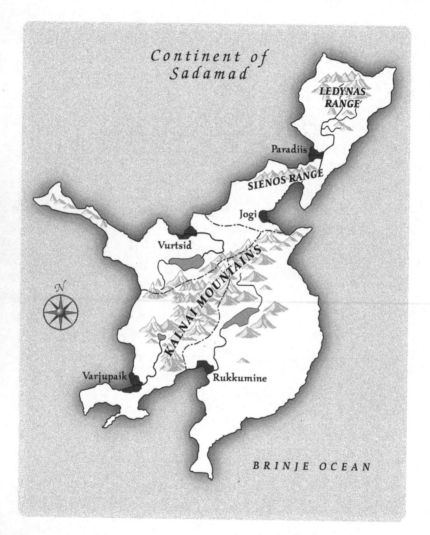

Endarian
Continent

Uostas   KINGDOM
Lika River   OF
              ENDAR

Northeastern
      Plains

Erzen River

Endar Pass

Gauga River

Northern
    Plains

Banjee River

Lagoth

N

GLACIER MOUNTAINS

Sul River

Hannington

Mo'Lier

Val'Dep

Coastal Range

Endless Valley

Areana's
  Vale

MOGEV
DESERT

Rork

Borderland Range

Rafel's
Keep

KINGDOM
OF TAL

Far
Castle

Rake River

Coldain's
Keep

PART I

Magic is of three forms: time, life, and mind. And each form branches thrice, forming nine magics in all.

In the grip of what I once believed a noble ambition, I gathered the nine fingers of focus, forging them into a weapon of staggering potential. But this trident of magnification filled my mind with such wretched temptations that I have dismantled the thing before it unmakes me.

Thus have I sent my sons and daughters to secrete six of these mummified fingers within the far reaches of the Continent of Sadamad. The other three have I hidden on the Endarian Continent, that they may never again be so combined.

—From the *Scroll of Landrel*

1

Kragan sat at the edge of the red and black lines etched into the stone floor, staring at the she-vorg seated cross-legged at the spiral's center. The warrior was lit by the three candles arranged in a triangle around her, the flickering flames casting a trio of shadows up the chamber's walls to waver on the granite ceiling. Over the months since he had merged his mind with that of Kaleal, the primordial Lord of the Third Deep, Kragan had grown to like this new seven-foot-tall body with bronze skin, golden eyes, fanged mouth, and fingers tipped with sharp, retractable claws. A vast improvement over the stunted human body the magic wielder had last occupied. His slitted pupils widened with an anticipation that tensed his muscles, threatening to burst the seams of his leather armor.

Charna, the she-vorg who commanded Kragan's vast army, stared sightlessly toward him, her black hair cascading down onto the bronze chain mail that draped her torso. Her lupine jaws jutted an inch from a vaguely human-looking face. The squareness of her chin reflected the aggressive nature that defined her even in the midst of the trance.

When Kragan spoke, his low voice rumbled through the chamber. "Shall we begin?"

"Yes, my lord," said Charna, although her eyes remained unfocused.

Ever so carefully, he created a magical channel from the mummified ear in his left hand to Charna's right ear. Before the Endarian time-shapers had created the time-mist barrier that wreathed the Endarian Continent, this branch of life-shifting magic had been Kragan's most powerful ability. Now, isolated from the source of his power, which lay across the Brinje Ocean, he could barely even manage this minor transference. But it would serve its purpose.

A low moan escaped the she-vorg's throat. Her right ear shriveled as life essence was pulled into the Zvejys ear that Kragan held. The ear plumped and warmed in his hand until it felt as it had all those centuries ago, when he had cut the organ from the head of the body that had once been his own, back on his home continent of Sadamad. With a deft movement, Kragan drew the ceremonial dagger from its belt-sheath, leaned forward, and cut Charna's now-shriveled right ear from her head, feeling the spray of warm blood on his knife hand. A heavy odor wafted to his nose, leaving a faintly metallic taste on his tongue.

After setting the knife on the stone floor, he pressed the Zvejys ear against the bloody hole on the side of Charna's head, wielding his magic to funnel the life energy from a caged rat to heal her wound. Ignoring the rat's agonized screeching, Kragan watched as the Zvejys ear knitted itself in place, stopping the flow of blood that ran down Charna's neck and onto her armored shoulder.

Kragan leaned back, picked up the dagger, wiped it on a dirty wool rag, and returned the weapon to its sheath at his side. Then, with a sharp clap of his hands, he awoke the she-vorg from her trance.

The warrior blinked twice, and her grimace became a scowl that she quickly suppressed, her iron will a testament to the self-control that had long ago earned his respect. Charna reached up to touch her new ear, comparing it to the feel of the other. Once again a scowl tweaked the corners of her mouth as she arranged her blood-matted hair to hide the deformity.

"So now we will be able to talk from a distance?" she growled as she climbed back to her feet.

"Only if I open a channel between us. But you can always sense the direction back to me. Those abilities will be important when we begin our assault on the Endarian citadel next week."

Charna spit at the mention of the foes she hated almost as much as Kragan did.

"Can't wait," she said, then turned and walked from the chamber, her long strides carrying her rapidly down the hillside toward the encampment in the valley below.

Kragan glanced down at Charna's shriveled ear lying in a puddle of crimson, gracing himself with the thought that he would soon be standing in rivers of Endarian blood. Only fifty leagues now stood between him and his vengeance.

A familiar voice rumbled in his mind, that of Kaleal, whose body Kragan now shared.

"Are you certain she will come?"

"The tiles are lined up as I have arranged them," said Kragan. "Our attack on Endar will bring a response from High Lord Rafel. He will seek to aid his former lover, Elan, the queen. And Carol will accompany her father's legion to Endar Pass. It will happen as Landrel foretold."

Kaleal's laugh escaped from Kragan's throat as the primordial broadcast his next thought into Kragan's mind.

"The Scroll of Landrel leaves the outcome of that encounter in doubt."

"Landrel failed to foresee what we have become," said Kragan. "As one, you and I shall shatter this world and Landrel's prophesied witch along with it."

"You sent hundreds of those who called themselves the protectors against her, and yet she destroyed them all," said Kaleal. *"If we are to overcome her,*

I must forge the wards that can protect us from her mind magics, of which elemental sorcery is but one branch. That can only be done in one place."

Kragan knew where this discussion was leading him—to the throne room from which Kaleal ruled the four elemental planes as Lord of the Third Deep, a place that Kragan had visited only once before, a place where he had endured awful suffering to secure his alliance with Kaleal. A shudder spread from the base of his neck, raising gooseflesh down his arms and up into his scalp.

He could return to that realm with Kaleal only by performing the ritual that would grant the primordial lord supremacy over their shared mind and body. That meant submitting to possession, along with all the horrors that would accompany it. But the thought of the danger Carol Rafel posed overcame Kragan's reluctance.

Remaining in the cross-legged posture he had maintained while forging his link to Charna, Kragan stared at the pool of vorgish blood, tendrils of which had crawled toward him. He inhaled deeply, held his breath for several seconds, and slowly released it.

Kragan closed his eyes and muttered his question. "After you create the wards, you will return me to this world and reinstate the arrangement we both agreed to?"

"Yes."

Although this was what Kragan wanted to hear, the anticipation in Kaleal's voice filled him with trepidation. Nevertheless, Kragan let the tension flow from his body. And as he did so, he felt the world dissolve around him.

—᙮᙮᙮—

Kragan felt his mind pushed into the background as Kaleal took control of their body. Although all of Kragan's senses still functioned, he could not so much as twitch a finger. He was merely along for the ride. Kaleal stepped to a heavy, iron-bound door, twisted the handle, and shoved. It swung outward to reveal a narrow stone stairway that spiraled downward, its steps worn by the passage of many feet, the granite walls almost scraping his broad shoulders. Kaleal descended with the sure strides of long familiarity.

The stairway ended, and Kaleal entered a dimly lit chamber, its high ceilings supported by tall, fluted columns. In the great hearth on the far wall, an eternal flame bled its red light into the mist that swirled almost to Kaleal's knees. Kragan felt his eyes drawn to the throne across from the fireplace. The red wood of the chair had the texture of scabbed flesh. Bas-relief faces distorted in pain crowded together along the surface, portraits that seemed to move as he approached.

The sight of that chair and the tortured souls forever enslaved within it pulled forth the memory of the pain that Kaleal had inflicted on Kragan within the chamber. He could almost hear the ghostly cries emanating from the wood.

Kaleal paused before a massive golden kite shield mounted on the stone wall to the throne's right, its metal, rubbed to a mirror finish, reflecting Kaleal's firelit figure. Then the primordial turned and seated himself on the throne. As he settled into place, the agony of the thousands of souls that Kaleal had imprisoned within the chair filled Kragan's thoughts.

Kaleal fed upon their torments, drawing power and focus from his seat of authority. With a flick of his right hand Kaleal summoned a piece of delicate white cloth from the mantel above the roaring hearth. A vivid memory blossomed in Kaleal's mind, pulling Kragan into that dreamscape along with him.

—◊◊◊—

The primordial lord stood in his throne room facing Carol Rafel, who wore only a white lace nightgown. Kaleal moved closer, his hungry eyes devouring her body as she watched. A smile flitted across Kaleal's lips as he reveled in the foreboding he sensed within this young woman. She imagined herself strong enough to dare confront him here, within his nexus of power. Such arrogance carried a heavy price.

"You are the one of whom the Endarian Landrel foretold. I am Kaleal."

Her beautiful face tightened in a mask of concentration, and a wall of steel bars materialized between them. Kragan reinforced his mental vise on her mind, achieving a link so strong that he could hear her thoughts and feel her emotions, a rush that left him salivating with anticipation of all to come. He held out a hand, flicking his finger upward. A sudden gust of wind whipped up her gown. As Carol moved her hand to push the flimsy covering back down, she lost her focus and the bars disappeared.

"Girl, in moments you will beg me to take you, even though you know that to make love to me is madness."

Kaleal's eyes narrowed, and a wave of desire assaulted Carol, leaving her squirming beneath his gaze. Her breath came in ragged gasps. He projected a vision into Carol's mind of his strong arms encircling her body.

Kaleal moved in until his body lightly touched hers, his fingertips softly stroking a path up her stomach. As he bent his striking face to look directly into her eyes, Carol's knees sagged. She struck out at him, but somehow her slap became a caress, her arms moving up and around the primordial's neck of their own accord. As her hands touched his smooth skin, a wave of passion surged through her body, robbing her of the strength to remain standing. Kaleal swept her up in his arms and carried her toward an ebony-colored divan.

He felt Carol struggle to get hold of her feelings. She knew that to have sex with a being from the elemental planes damned the human soul to eternal imprisonment and would leave Kaleal in control of her earthly form.

Kaleal laid her on satin. Thin veins of red meandered through black cloth, veins that pulsed with a vitality matching her pounding heart. The primordial's hand stroked lightly, barely touching her skin, leaving her gasping and squirming beneath his touch. Carol began to shake uncontrollably. He leaned over her, gently caressing ankle and calf. Her gown had risen until more than half her thigh showed. His ravenous eyes sucked her in, his hot breath searing bare skin.

The primordial moved her hand to his breast, guiding it to stroke his chest. Carol's eyes widened and began to water as she fought with every ounce of her strength to deny the feelings that assaulted her.

Kaleal's lips brushed her neck, and she felt her hands move over his chest. He reveled in her horror as Carol realized that he had released them. Carol's mind tried to lock the experience into a part of her mind where she would not remember it. And his knowledge of such thoughts further excited Kaleal.

The primordial moved slowly atop her, his hand slowly raising the hem of her gown. Kaleal then shifted his attention to the upper part of her nightgown. Peeling it back from her shoulders, little by little, he revealed the firm curves of her heaving breasts.

Lowering his head, he kissed her throat softly, the contact sending an electric thrill through her with each exceedingly light touch. He moved lower, working ever so slowly down her silky throat. A low moan escaped Carol's parted lips.

"Easy now," Kaleal purred. "The pleasure that only I can deliver is worth eternal damnation."

Kaleal felt her burst of will as Carol forcibly shifted her thoughts to a man whose name she spoke aloud.

"Arn."

Kaleal seized upon the image that formed in her mind, covering his face with his hands. When he lowered them, Arn, the assassin known as Blade, stared back at her.

In this guise, Kaleal leaned in. She kissed him, running her arms around his neck and into his curly brown hair. A wave of emotion stronger than the primordial's desire suddenly took hold of her.

"I love you, Arn," she gasped, clasping him to her. "I have always loved you."

With that admission, a new strength of will blossomed in her mind. She loved the real Arn, not this impostor. Releasing her arms from around his neck, Carol shoved him away.

Kaleal snarled, transforming back into his true form. The dark slits within his golden eyes widened as his lips curled back to reveal fangs.

"So you reject my passion. Then know pain."

As Kaleal's clawed fingers touched the shoulder of her nightgown, Carol's anger crystallized. Above Kaleal, the ceiling supports gave way, crushing the primordial to the floor beneath tons of falling stone. He tossed debris aside in an attempt to rise, but she conjured steel chains that strapped him to the ground. Kaleal fought desperately to break free. The chains thickened and held. Carol fastened a steel collar around his neck and bolted it to the stone floor.

For a moment the woman stood over him. Then she faded from the primordial's realm, leaving Kaleal clutching the scrap of lace that he had torn from her nightgown as she pummeled him to the floor. The magical chains with which she had bound him disappeared as well. As he climbed back to his feet, squeezing the garment fragment in his right fist, Kaleal's bellow of rage shook the stone walls. The sound died away to a low growl that devolved into a disgusted hiss. The Lord of the Third Deep had just endured humiliation at the hands of a novice wielder of magic.

He had never sensed such raw, untamed prowess within any other being, not even within the long-dead Endarian wielder, Landrel. The prophecy that Landrel had penned all those millennia past spoke of this woman. Even though much of the scroll's message remained obscured by ciphers that Kaleal had been unable to unravel, its contents had filled him with concern.

Kaleal walked to the golden mirror, placed his hands on the wall to either side, then leaned forward until his forehead touched the chill metal surface. How had he allowed himself to underestimate this acolyte? Kaleal had squandered the perfect opportunity to destroy the threat that the woman presented, all because he had lied to himself, denying the seed of worry that Landrel's prophecy had planted within his primordial soul.

Deep within his breast, Kaleal felt that seed sprout green tendrils of dread.

—⌇⌇—

Kaleal's memory evaporated, leaving Kragan shocked at what he had seen. This had been Carol's introduction to the elemental planes. Unlike any other aspiring wielder Kragan had heard of, she had been brought into the presence of the Lord of the Third Deep by the Ritual of Terrors. By all rights, her mind should now reside with the other lost souls, trapped within the scabbed wood of the throne atop which Kaleal now sat.

Kragan turned his attention to the piece of Carol's nightgown that had pulled Kaleal back into the memory that haunted the primordial. Ever so carefully, Kaleal shifted the lace to his left hand and plucked a single strand of brown hair from the cloth. He held the hair up so that it shone with the light of the hearth flames.

"This will have to do," said Kaleal, his low voice rumbling above the sound of the crackling fire.

Kragan watched in fascination as yellow tree sap bubbled into the palm of Kaleal's left hand. Extending a claw, he sliced a two-inch piece of the brown strand, made a slit in the sap, and carefully embedded the hair within. Pulling upon the energy he drew from the souls trapped within his magical throne, Kaleal concentrated. Kragan saw the sap flow, closing around the strand and hardening into a transparent amber pendant that had a hole at one end to allow it to be strung on a necklace.

Setting the newly fashioned pendant aside, Kaleal set to work creating four others, each unique in shape. But the longest piece of Carol's hair went into an amber that measured a handspan in length. Kragan felt Kaleal's excitement grow, as did his own, knowing as he did that he would wear the largest of these warded pendants into battle against Carol. He would reserve the other four for the most important of his army's magic wielders.

Having completed his spellwork, Kaleal rose from his throne, strode to the stairway, and climbed back into the natural world.

—⁂—

Kragan opened his eyes, his lungs expelling an involuntary gasp of relief that Kaleal had released control of this body, honoring their arrangement.

He stared down at the five amber pendants in his right hand, feeling their soft glow spread into the golden skin of his palm. They tingled, causing his clawed fingernails to extend. Kragan rose and walked outside to stare into the gathering twilight.

Summoning Dalg, an Earth elemental he favored, Kragan began to transform the cavern he had created. As the stone and detritus flowed, the cliff wall re-formed, restoring the original landscape. As he turned to look at the smattering of fires in the valley below, his gaze shifted toward the moonlit white peaks that sheltered Endar Pass. If he could have teleported this horde to his objective and begun the battle tonight, he would have. But to someone who had survived millennia, the extra eight or nine days needed to march his army to the citadel were nothing more than the buzzing of a gnat in his ear.

He sniffed the night breeze. The smoke from his army's campfires filled his nostrils, pulling forth a vision of Carol Rafel's battered form impaled on a pike as the Endarian palace burned and crumbled.

A snarl curled his lips, saliva dripping from his inch-long fangs. Before he let his prophesied nemesis die, Kragan would savor the taste of blood.

2

Lorness Carol Rafel pulled her dapple-gray mare Storm to a halt on a ridgetop amidst a clatter of hooves from the horses of her three companions. She sat in the saddle a half league to the west of the narrow gorge that formed the only entrance to her home within the cliff-lined valley of Areana's Vale. The other riders accompanying her stopped nearby. To her left rode Carol's Endarian half sister, Kim, and Kim's hawk-faced human husband, John. Carol's husband, Arn, the notorious assassin whom the people of Tal had nicknamed Blade, sat astride his ugly horse just to her right. Having been married for only two days, Arn refused to stray far from Carol's side.

In the aftermath of the battle for Areana's Vale, Carol found herself in the disconcerting position of being simultaneously respected and feared by the people she had helped save. Due to the way she had placed herself on the high pinnacle overlooking the uppermost of High Lord Rafel's three forts, the magic she wielded had been visible to the civilians those walls protected.

Carol didn't feel like a hero. She had only done what was necessary in order to prevent every man, woman, and child in the vale from being slaughtered, raped, or enslaved.

Her situation was not as difficult as Alan's. Her brother's reputation had grown to epic proportions based upon his exploits in leading the women of the walled fortress of Val'Dep to fend off thousands of attacking vorg warriors. The trouble with reputations was that they tended to be double edged. Some had spread the rumor that Alan was the legendary Chosen of the Dread Lord, destined to attract the greatest warriors who had ever lived but cursed to have nine out of every ten who fought alongside him die in battle. The fact that this was utter nonsense didn't prevent the people from believing the tale. Thus most of Rafel's warriors feared to be placed under Alan's command.

Turning her attention back to the task at hand, Carol scanned the western horizon. As she stared out at the foothills that gradually gave way to the Great Valley many leagues to the west, she felt the cold breeze whip her long brown hair out behind her. She shivered despite the warm buckskin pants and brown leather jacket she wore.

Suddenly Kim rose in her stirrups and pointed.

"Look there," Kim said. "It is as I thought. Do you see it?"

Carol redirected her gaze farther north. At first she saw nothing out of the ordinary. Then the farthest hill began to darken as a gray mist crawled over it, billowing forward at unnatural speed.

"That's a time-mist," said Kim. "From its shade, it's an accelerating rychly mist. The slowing pomaly mists are much lighter. My brother, Galad, approaches. My sense of his nearness grows with each moment."

Carol turned to look at Kim, whose mocha skin, brunette hair, and six-foot stature emphasized her half-human nature when she was compared to the taller, ebony-skinned people of pure Endarian blood. Concern etched itself on Kim's features, and the feeling infected Carol.

"Whoever is coming," said Arn, his hand moving to the haft of the black knife he had named Slaken, "is in a hurry."

Carol watched Kim tilt her head in concentration. That look reminded her of when Kim had linked their minds together, the half sisters sharing a lifetime of memories as they combined their magical abilities to save a possessed little girl's life.

Carol gently reached out to touch Kim's thoughts, following Kim's tenuous connection with her brother and sensing the aura of desperation that surrounded Galad. The idea to use her mind magic to create a direct psychic link to Galad occurred to her but was not possible in this case. Only an Endarian family bond or mystic abilities that branched from time magic could penetrate a time-mist boundary. Since both of Carol's magics, the mental control of elementals and the manipulation of animals or people, were branches of mind magic, penetrating the mist was out of the question.

So she settled back in her saddle and summoned Putimas, forcing the air elemental to create a shimmering plasma shield around the waiting group of riders. Kim's startled glance contained a trace of anger that Carol would erect such a shield in advance of her brother's arrival.

Carol leaned in her saddle to place a hand on Kim's arm, speaking words of reassurance.

"It's not Galad who concerns me. His haste may mean that he's being pursued. If so, we should be ready to take action."

Kim's expression softened, and she redirected her attention toward the approaching mist. And as Carol stared at the billowing fog that raced across the leagues that separated them, the biting breeze seemed to grow colder.

—◦◦◦—

Prince Galad strode into the Great Forest. His color-shifting uniform picked up the tints and textures of his surroundings as he moved. As he passed from sunlight into the shadows of trees that rose to touch the heavens, the time-mists that he channeled wreathed the corridor through which he traveled. Whereas he would have normally stopped to admire such arboreal splendor, the length of his journey and the depth of his need drove him to hurry forward.

He had made the long trek southward from Endar Pass within a rychly mist, while also leaving a balancing pomaly fog trailing behind. Many weeks had passed within the rychly zone, but in the normal world, only a couple of days had gone by.

His sense of his sister grew stronger as he advanced. Princess Kimber was near, indicating that he was approaching his ultimate objective. His mother, Queen Elan, had set him upon the desperate mission to seek out Kimber's father, the human high lord who had requested Elan's aid during the Vorg War three decades ago. This time it would be Elan seeking a boon from High Lord Rafel and Carol, his human daughter, the magic wielder foretold within the ancient Scroll of Landrel.

The thought of his mother brought forth the memory of the conflict that had almost cost him her love. Throughout his boyhood, his mother had pushed him into the study of time-shaping, having identified within her son an exceptional ability to channel the time-mists. But Galad had wanted only to become a mist warrior.

The mist warriors fought within the murky tendrils of fog that the time-shapers sent forth to disrupt and confuse attacking armies. Operating in the mists was a difficult skill to acquire and being such a warrior had its costs. Fighting within the fogs of time posed tremendous challenges, since a person could see or interact with others only when time moved at the same pace for all parties. It was easy to become disoriented within the mists, moving from a tactically advantageous region into one where you were at a disadvantage—one of the reasons so few elite mist warriors existed.

The time-mists were of two types, rychly and pomaly, two ancient terms from the long-gone era of Landrel. The passage of time slowed within the pomaly mists and accelerated in the rychly mists, each balancing the other. Passing from a slower mist into one within which time moved faster was like fighting your way out of thick mud. The reverse was true as one exited a rychly mist, stepping into a slower zone, pressing oneself into mud instead of out of it. If the time difference between mists was too great, passage between them became impossible. Thus any time-shaper who supported mist warriors created complicated flows that contained relatively gentle gradients. Learning to recognize those gradients took a long time to master. And because the time-mist warriors preferred to traverse the rychly mists, where time passed more quickly, they aged at an accelerated rate . . . another reason for the scarcity of the special warriors.

So when Galad had come of age, he'd chosen to abandon the path his mother had set for him in order to live the life he craved, eventually rising to command an elite mist warrior brigade of his own. Weeks ago, he had led that brigade to its destruction against Kragan's army. Although Elan had not blamed him for that defeat, Galad had not been so lenient with himself. This mission offered him the opportunity to give his people a chance and, perhaps, to earn redemption.

For hours he traversed the mighty forest, his sensitive nose taking in the tang of the giant evergreens as his feet felt the spring of the needles that covered the ground. The sense of his sister pulled him forward. When Galad reached the end of the woods, he crested a rocky ridge and paused to step through the lighter-colored mist where his rychly zones ended.

As he stepped forward, pressing himself through the numerous transitions that would take him gradually from a zone where time passed much faster to the natural state of the world, he forced himself to exercise the caution such transitions required. Each time he stepped into a new mist, that area cleared as the one he had left behind fogged over. Feeling the pressure of the final passage, he saw the vast expanse of rocky hills that led upward toward the snowcapped Glacier Mountains to the east. He gazed upon a group of four riders atop a ridge a quarter league ahead. When he focused his gaze he noticed a shimmering in the air around them, reminding him of a desert mirage.

Even at this distance he recognized Kimber; her husband, John; and Blade. That could only mean that the woman who sat on her gray mount beside Blade was Lorness Carol Rafel. Quickening his step to match his racing pulse, Galad stretched his legs into an easy run that carried him up the slope toward the spot where the riders waited, letting the mists he had channeled dissipate behind him. Soon he would have to weave those mists in vastly greater amounts.

—⁂—

Carol marveled at the tall Endarian running up the hillside toward them, his waist-length black hair flowing out behind him as his clothing shifted colors, making it difficult to distinguish his body from the terrain and foliage he moved through. But his elegant saber glinted in the sunlight. The dark fog behind him dissipated as he approached the companions.

With a gasp Kim dismounted and raced forward as Carol dismissed Putimas, erasing the shield the elemental had created. When John dismounted to follow Kim, so did Carol and Arn, leaving their horses to stand as if the dropped reins tied each of them to a rail. On the hillside below, Galad swept Kim up in an embrace that lifted her from the ground as her arms encircled his neck. The look of joy that transformed Galad's stern face spread a warm glow through Carol's chest.

John halted several paces from the siblings. Carol and Arn stopped beside him, allowing Kim and Galad the space their reunion deserved. When Galad released his sister and stepped back, his face settled into the stern, noble countenance that seemed its natural state. He walked forward to clasp hands with John and Arn, his manner one of cool acceptance rather than warm regard. Considering that John and Arn had spent a winter in Endar Pass, where Queen Elan had presided over and blessed John's marriage to Princess Kimber, Galad's coolness to these two surprised Carol.

Galad shifted his gaze to her, astonishing her when he took her hand. His eyes locked with hers, filling her with a trepidation that chilled her soul.

"Lorness Carol, on behalf of Queen Elan of Endar, I exhort you to return the favor that my mother granted your father during the Vorg War. I kneel to beseech an audience with High Lord Rafel that I may present my mother's plea. She requests an alliance against Kragan the thaumaturge and his vorg army that even now approaches Endar Pass. I ask this boon in the name of my sister, Princess Kimber, Queen Elan and High Lord Rafel's daughter. For she is your sister, just as she is mine."

Galad's words left Carol momentarily speechless. Then she placed her right hand on his shoulder.

"Please, Galad," she said, "dispense with the formality. Call me Carol."

"Very well. Much as I wish we had time for pleasantries, I need to meet with your father immediately."

The Endarian's anxiety radiated from him in waves such that Carol spun toward her mare, swinging into the saddle, as did her companions. Picking up a trot, she led the way down the eastern side of the hill, noting that Galad with his loping stride had no trouble keeping pace with the horses. Having seen the grace with which Kim ran, Carol was not surprised by the fleetness of her much taller brother.

She rode up beside Arn and leaned over in the saddle to touch his arm.

"Please ride ahead and inform my father of Galad's request for an urgent meeting."

Arn glanced at her, nodded, and urged Ax into a run. As she watched his black form race toward Areana's Vale to inform the high lord and Earl Coldain of Prince Galad's arrival, Carol felt a storm gathering just beyond the horizon.

—⟋⟍—

The beat of Ax's hooves on the stony ground, the chill air rushing through his curly brown hair, and the sight of the towering cliffs that formed the sides of the narrow gorge that guarded the entrance to Areana's Vale sent a thrill of anticipation through Arn. Only a week had passed since the combined might of Rafel's legion, the horse warriors of Val'Dep, and the freshly arrived army of Tal had destroyed the foul horde of the priesthood known as the protectors. During those few days Arn had attended the funeral of his friend Ty, witnessed Earl Coldain swear fealty to Rafel, and watched as the two leaders prepared their combined legion to rain vengeance on Kragan, the magic wielder responsible for the destruction of the kingdom of Tal and the deaths of thousands who had perished within this gorge. And with the high lord's blessing, Arn had married the love of his life, the most forceful woman he had ever known, Carol Rafel. A league into that narrow rift, he saw the still-smoking remains of the westernmost of Rafel's three forts and slowed Ax to a trot. The acrid smell of smoke combined with the lingering odors of the many who had died wrinkled his nose and stung his eyes. A hundred soldiers stood guard as others worked to clear away the debris, loading it onto wagons pulled by teams of oxen. With a nod the captain of the guard waved Arn through. Thus the assassin passed through the wreckage of the lower two forts and across the drawbridge that led into Rafel's partially intact upper fortress.

He glanced up at the pinnacle of rock that had long ago separated itself from the sheer cliffs that formed the opening into the broad valley of Areana's Vale. Arn halted Ax as a storm of emotions elevated his pulse. A week ago, Carol, supported by Kim's life-shifting magic, had stood fast atop that high perch as she contested against the hundreds of magic-wielding priests who sought to pull her down as battle raged below.

A thickness in Arn's throat caused him to swallow hard. Arn had not been here to support his wife during that awful struggle. Rafel had sent him out from the vale on a mission to infiltrate the army of the protectors and use his assassin's skills to kill as many of the foul priests as possible, reducing the number of wielders who could challenge Carol. But in response to the tug of his intuitive sense, Arn had abandoned the task his adoptive father had set him upon and thus abandoned his beloved to fend for herself.

If not for the self-sacrifice of Ty in blocking the trail that led to the summit of the pinnacle atop which Carol had stood, she would not have lived for Arn's return. But the bodies Ty sundered on that narrow path had cemented his status among the horse warriors of Val'Dep. Having previously fought alongside Ty, they had dubbed the bare-chested ax-master Dar Khan, the Dread Lord, prophesied to return from the land of the dead to select the man who would become the warrior known as the Chosen.

Arn cared little for the myth. What mattered was that his friend had given his life so that Carol might live on. And in doing so, Ty had indirectly saved Arn's life as well.

The sight of Captain Hanibal, his red hair whipping about his shoulders in the swirling breeze, pulled Arn from his reverie. The captain shouted orders to a group of soldiers working to restore the upper fort and then, catching sight of Arn, turned to meet him.

"Blade," Hanibal said, using the nickname that Arn detested, his glance taking in the foam of sweat at the edges of Ax's saddle blanket.

"Where is High Lord Rafel?" asked Arn.

Hanibal jerked his thumb toward the high lord's council chamber in one of the buildings that remained standing along the fort's eastern wall.

"He and my father are holding a war council with Earl Coldain."

Arn nodded and turned Ax toward the indicated building.

Hanibal's voice called out in annoyance. "Battle Master Gaar said to let no one disturb them."

Ignoring the captain's call, Arn crossed the courtyard, dismounted, and tied Ax's reins to a post outside the entryway. He opened the heavy redwood door without knocking, drawing startled looks from the three men seated at the far end of a long table, backlit by a roaring fire in the hearth. But as Rafel saw who had made this sudden entry, the irritation faded from his face, replaced by a look of concern that mirrored Arn's.

The high lord rose to his feet, almost tipping over his chair.

"Arn? Why aren't Kim and Carol with you? And John?"

Arn approached the high lord. "Carol is on her way, along with the others. She sent me ahead to inform you that Prince Galad has arrived bearing dire tidings and Queen Elan's desperate request for your aid."

Arn watched the muscles in the warlord's face tighten at the mention of the mother of his half-Endarian daughter. Rafel had gone more than thirty years without knowing of Kim's birth.

He motioned for Arn to join them at the table, and Arn seated himself beside Battle Master Gaar. Arn slowly withdrew Slaken from its sheath at his side, setting the black knife on the table in front of him. He saw the surprised looks from the other men but ignored them. As his right hand released the haft of the weapon that shielded him from all magic, he felt Carol's mind caress his. Knowing that she was now seeing through his eyes and that she understood precisely where this group awaited her arrival, Arn returned Slaken to its sheath and shifted his gaze to the still-standing high lord.

"Carol and the others are inside the gorge, about a quarter league from this fort. She is bringing Galad here."

Rafel merely nodded, having witnessed the full extent of his daughter's magical prowess during the recent battle, but Coldain regarded Arn skeptically.

"How do you know this?" the earl asked.

Arn shifted his attention to Coldain. The lines in his face had deepened since his son, Garret, had delivered the news that Kragan had sacked Coldain's Keep, killing the earl's wife and kidnapping his two young daughters. When Arn looked into those cobalt eyes, he could see within them a fire for vengeance that matched that which had long raged within his own breast. That look, combined with Coldain's unkempt hair and beard, showed a wildness that seemed barely contained.

When the door opened to admit Rafel's barrel-chested son, Alan, all eyes turned toward the young man. His recently shaved head, which emphasized the thickly muscled neck that sloped into his shoulders, still startled Arn. Alan's decision to shave his shoulder-length auburn locks in favor of this harsher look had come shortly after Ty's fiery funeral, a testament to the fact that Alan felt he did not deserve the mane that had matched Ty's blond hair in length. The lack of hair emphasized the scar that ran from his forehead through his left eyebrow and down his left cheek.

With Ty's crescent-bladed ax strapped to his back, Alan approached his father. Behind strode Alan's closest followers, the witty young ranger Bill Harrison, the wiry female knife fighter Katrin, the peg-legged weapons master Kron, and the aptly named swordsman Quincy Long. The four had also shaved their heads, as had each of the hundred warriors who had pledged themselves to Alan.

Bill had detailed the events of that recent day when Alan had held the fortress wall of the horse warriors' mighty stronghold, Val'Dep. His forces outnumbered ten to one, Rafel's son had led the women of Val'Dep in a furious counterattack that had repelled a vorgish horde until Earl Coldain and his army had arrived to put an end to the siege. The survivors of the battle for Val'Dep had proclaimed Alan the Dread Lord's Chosen, a demigod of war destined to attract the mightiest heroes to fight alongside him.

Arn shifted his gaze to Alan's four closest companions. To them, and the rest of those who chose to embrace the challenge, danger was the spice that gave life meaning. Quincy, the newest of these devotees, towered a head above Alan, his lanky body radiating a caged energy that seemed barely contained. He gripped and released his longsword's pommel, a habitual action that marked the man as distinctly as his great height.

"Let me guess," said Rafel as he motioned for his son and his companions to be seated. "Carol summoned you."

"Yes," said Alan. "I expected her to be here already."

Arn considered setting Slaken aside once more to allow his wife to reestablish her mental link but discarded the notion. She would be here soon enough.

When Carol arrived, she ushered Kim, John, and Galad into the meeting room. The Endarian prince took in the room's occupants at a glance, then stepped forward as High Lord Rafel rose from his chair. Galad dropped to one knee before Rafel, and Arn noted the surprise on the older man's face.

Kim moved forward as well.

"Father, I present to you my brother, Prince Galad of Endar."

The high lord recovered his equilibrium. "Rise, Prince Galad. This is no royal court. At the moment it is little more than a war camp. I hear that you bring troubled tidings from Queen Elan."

Rafel clenched his jaw at the mention of the queen.

"I do, indeed," said Galad, who seated himself in the chair opposite Rafel.

Once seated, the prince leaned forward, leaning on his elbows and peering at the high lord over steepled fingers. When he spoke, Arn could feel the chill in his voice.

"My mother has sent me to ask for your help, just as, three decades ago, you came to Endar Pass requesting hers. Our plight is desperate. As we sit here, Kragan's horde moves through our mountains, only a few days' march from Endar Pass."

"What?" Rafel's shock at the statement rang in his voice. "Then all is lost. It would take several weeks to march my twenty thousand soldiers from here to Endar Pass. Does the queen believe that she can hold off the army for that long?"

"No."

Arn watched Galad slowly shake his head in a gesture that expressed both desperation and self-doubt.

"That is why she sent me," Galad continued, "in the hope that I can speed your legion's journey through the time-mists I wield."

This statement pulled a gasp from Kim, who sat beside John, across from Arn.

"But surely," she said, "even you cannot safely channel that much time-shaping magic."

Galad turned his black eyes on his sister, and Arn saw them soften. "If our people are to have any chance, then I must try, assuming that High Lord Rafel is willing to come to our aid."

Coldain, clearly no longer able to contain himself, pounded the table with a fist, directing his words at Rafel. "I have sworn to cut Kragan's heart from his chest and free my daughters from whatever foul bondage he has forced upon them. Within this vale, my legion stands ready, hungering for vengeance against those who destroyed our homes and families. The drums of war call to us."

"And we shall answer that call," said Rafel, rising to his feet. Rafel turned to address Battle Master Gaar. "I want you to issue a warning order that we will march before dawn tomorrow. All commanders are to assemble with us here at sunset to finalize our plan of action. Be prepared to recommend how many soldiers we will leave behind to secure Areana's Vale. I also want to leave behind two of our wielders, one for the vale and one to augment the defenses of Val'Dep."

Gaar nodded and strode rapidly out of the meeting hall.

Having risen to his feet beside Carol, Arn felt the call of the shadowed blade strapped to his thigh. Only then did he realize how tightly his right hand gripped Slaken's haft. The look of dread on Carol's face told him she had noticed his unconscious reaction. Her expression did not surprise him. Despite knowing that her father and Coldain intended to hunt down Kragan, she had hoped for a longer honeymoon before the horrors of war once again swept them into the maelstrom.

As he looked into her brown eyes, Arn felt his own heart sink. By the deep, he had longed for that same reprieve.

3

Glacier Mountains—Southwest of Endar Pass
YOR 415, Late Spring

A tremor began in Galad's fingers and worked its way up his arms and into his spine, movements that he struggled to hide from Carol, who sat astride her dapple-gray mare nearby. Throughout the weeks that Rafel's legion had made the long march to Endar Pass, Galad had felt the strain of channeling the time-mists for such a large force. Now that the legion had made its way from the north end of the Endless Valley and onto the much narrower paths that led through the Glacier Mountains toward Endar Pass, the columns stretched for more than a league from front to rear. A single thought kept him from collapsing.

Almost home!

He had accomplished that which even he had thought impossible. As less than a week passed in the outside world, he had brought Rafel's host the hundreds of leagues that separated Areana's Vale from southern Endar.

With a shock Galad realized that in the midst of this sudden weakness he had allowed the trailing part of his rychly mists to dissipate, separating a tenth of Rafel's legion from the rest by more than a league, leaving an entire brigade of two thousand isolated and vulnerable.

Galad gritted his teeth in concentration, attempting to widen the channel through which he funneled the mists, seeking to reach back for those with whom he had lost contact. But as he did so, the drain on his strained reserves escalated, squeezing beads of sweat from his brow. The rychly mists extended, flowing down the canyon toward the vulnerable brigade, the difficulty of his summoning compounded by the necessity of creating a balancing amount of slowing pomaly mist.

Something snapped within Galad's mind, sudden convulsions dropping him to his knees.

The entire channel collapsed.

Pain seared the fingers of his left hand, gradually spreading up into his wrist. Through a red-limned haze, he watched his fingers wither and flake away as the hand decayed into bone and then fine dust that sifted away on the breeze like smoke. He tumbled forward, smashing his nose on the rocky ground.

No. He would not give in to the allure of the comforting darkness that threatened to snuff out his vision. He had come too far to allow himself to fail to deliver this legion to his mother, mere leagues from the entrance to Endar Pass. With every ounce of will he could muster, Galad attempted to climb back to his knees, only managing to curl into a fetal ball before his battle came to its bitter end.

He expelled one last gasp, quivered, and lay still.

—⚏—

Kim turned in surprise as Galad dismissed the accelerating rychly mist within which he had wrapped the twenty-one thousand soldiers of her father's legion. And as the balancing white pomaly mists also dissolved away, they left her staring up the winding trail that led toward the cliff-lined entrance to Endar Pass, blinking to adjust to the sudden brightness as the sun appeared through the dissipating fog.

But when she heard Galad's tormented moan, she knew that his release of the time-mists had been involuntary. His sudden pain filled her mind, making her stagger and almost fall. Two stumbling steps later, she gathered herself and rushed to the side of her brother. The sight of his missing left hand, the stump wrapped in mummified skin that looked a thousand years old, made her gag . . . that and the dust that hung in the air, smelling of an ancient tomb that had just been cracked open.

Working quickly, she tried to accept his injury into her own hand in an attempt to channel the energy of nearby trees and plants through herself and into him. Nothing happened. This was no injury. Having remained in the rapidly condensing rychly mist, Galad's appendage had died and decayed a millennium ago, returning to the dust of ages.

Kim dropped to the ground beside Galad, gathering his limp body into her arms, relieved to feel his warm breath on her neck as his hair draped her right arm. Blinded by the tears that welled from her eyes, she felt Carol kneel by her side, speaking words that Kim's distraught mind could not interpret. The knowledge that Galad would live failed to console her. Her brother had damaged himself in a manner that would affect his psyche. The finest of the Endarian mist warriors would wield his bow no more.

And as she rocked her wounded brother back and forth in her arms, Kim could do nothing to mend him.

—⁓—

The sight of Kim holding Galad, her failure to respond to Carol's words of concern, and Carol's glance at his withered stump of a wrist generated within her a sense of foreboding. The distant squall of vorgish war horns pulled Carol to her feet. Magic crackled from her fingertips as her mind ensnared the air elemental Lwellen, plucking him from the plane of air into this world.

Her father's stentorian yell reverberated along the ranks of his marching legion, his command echoed by signal flags along the winding line of soldiers. And the lead elements of Rafel's legion reacted as only well-trained veteran troops could.

Leaping astride Storm, Carol maneuvered the mare off the main trail to a position where she could see the steep slopes of the ridgeline along which they had been moving. A large force of vorgs and men in similar uniforms raced along the opposite hillside to block Rafel's way forward. The advance guard of Kragan's army had arrived at the junction between canyons simultaneously with Rafel's legion and were revealed only by the dissipation of Galad's time-mists.

The confusion in the ranks of the vorgs made clear that, despite the fact that they must have noticed the influx of the roiling mists that filled the canyon, they had been just as surprised by the sudden appearance of Rafel's legion as Carol was to see the enemy force. She turned to look for Arn, but he was nowhere in sight. Her knowledge of her husband's uncanny intuition told her that it had spurred him into action even as Galad had fallen.

A quarter league ahead, the leading elements of Rafel's legion charged forward to attack the foremost of the vorg warriors. Among those, Carol sensed a wielder summoning a fire elemental and blocked the flames that sought to engulf a group of Coldain's cavalry, calling forth her own lightning to strike at the source of the fireball.

Her opponent deflected her lightning into a nearby group of vorg troops. Carol sensed her magical adversary as if through a thick haze, the image of a statuesque, slender she-vorg forming in her mind along with the name Silap. What shocked Carol was that Silap met her gaze, her sneer revealing long canines that matched the cruelty in her pale eyes.

Carol focused on those eyes in an attempt to force her way into the mind behind them. Her failure to bridge that boundary startled her.

Something far stronger than Silap blocked her attempt. Carol tried again and again with no better results, her frustration mounting with each defeat. Instead of giving up, she turned her attention to the source of that power, finally settling on the amber pendant looped around Silap's throat. Within that bauble a glow illuminated a short strand of brown hair that triggered an unpleasant memory.

It was as if she were staring at one of the faces carved into the throne upon which Kaleal sat when Carol had first encountered him during her Ritual of Terrors. That traumatic experience had granted her access to the mind magics.

She had defeated Kaleal then and had done so again when he tried to possess Arn in Misty Hollow. So how could a Kaleal ward have the power to block her mind? And how had this wielder in Kragan's army come to possess such an artifact?

Silap attempted a fireball spell, but Carol redirected it into the vorgish warriors that rushed to reinforce those engaged by Rafel's lead elements. The ease with which she redirected the new attack made one thing clear: the amber pendant was solely a personal defensive ward and did nothing to enhance Silap's other arcane talents. Still, Carol's inability to launch a magical attack against the wielder troubled her.

Carol urged Storm up the steep slope to the left of the main trail, seeking to get a better view of the battle ahead. As Carol entered a copse of pines that blocked her from view of the troops moving a hundred yards below her, her mare scrambled over loose shale, lost its footing, and fell, throwing Carol clear and sending her tumbling down the hillside. As she reached out for the air elemental, Ohk, to arrest her fall, the back of her head slammed into an exposed root. For a sickening moment, the world spun around her. Then, as it slowly spiraled into nothingness, Carol failed to muster the will to care.

Lord Alan Rafel sat astride his bay warhorse, staring across the unexpected tableau that lay before him. The time-mists had dissipated around the two thousand soldiers that formed Rafel's rear guard, including the mounted company Alan commanded, a group of sworn followers whom Commander Hanibal had derisively named the Forsworn. Up ahead, the bulk of Rafel's legion had simply disappeared, leaving the brigade isolated.

"Where in the deep did the rest of our legion go?" asked Kron, who had pulled his horse to a halt beside Alan.

Alan turned to look at the weapons master, who sat atop his special saddle with one stirrup modified to accommodate his peg leg.

"It's as if the time-mists swept them away from us as they rounded that last bend in the canyon," said Alan.

Bill and Katrin edged their horses closer. Alan had become accustomed to the shaved heads of all the others who had pledged themselves to his service, but Kat was the exception. As he looked into her green eyes, he could not deny that her baldness accentuated her beauty. Or perhaps it was the frightening intensity of the woman that so attracted him to her. Like Bill and most recently the swordsman Quincy, she had assigned herself to Alan as his personal bodyguard whether he liked it or not.

Bill's lilting voice pulled Alan's attention back to their present situation.

"Seems to me that our legion has a poor regard for its rear end."

That comment brought a derisive snort from Quincy. "Whatever the cause, I strongly recommend that we do our best to catch the others."

A hundred paces away, a signal flagman made a sequence of motions that drew Alan's attention.

"Ah, a summons," said Bill. "Perhaps Commander Hanibal misses you. I cannot wait to hear what he desires of the Chosen and his band of lovely followers."

Alan ignored the jibe, turning instead to Kron. "The company is yours in my absence. Ready them for a forced march."

"Yes, Chosen."

Alan nudged his stallion with his heels, sending the big animal trotting along the front line of troops toward the brigade commander's distant guidon. Seeing his approach, Hanibal rode out to meet him, his flaming hair whipping around his head in the stiff breeze.

Hanibal pulled to a stop beside Alan, gesturing up the canyon along the broad trail made by Rafel's legion's passage.

"I have received word of a vorg battle group up ahead," said Hanibal. "I want you to position your company well out to our front as my advance guard. If you encounter the enemy, press the attack so that we can identify the true size of the force. If you cannot break through their lines, then hold until I can bring the rest of the brigade to bear against them."

"As you wish." Alan could not bring himself to address as sir the man he had routinely beaten in every contest of arms, despite being four years Hanibal's junior. But Alan's father had promoted Hanibal to a higher position of leadership, and in Rafel's legion, military rank took precedence over noble birth.

"One more matter," said Hanibal. "My scouts have examined the tracks left by the main body of Rafel's legion. That trail is hours old. We have to assume that High Lord Rafel is several leagues ahead of us. This fight will be ours alone."

"What of your wielder?" asked Alan. "May I count on her services?"

"No. Lektuvu stays with me. I cannot afford to risk her forward of our main lines."

Alan squelched the urge to reach out and throttle the man. For Hanibal to deny him the indirect support of the brigade's only wielder showed how little the commander cared for Alan and those who had pledged themselves to his service. To his left Alan saw Katrin's right fist tighten on the haft of her long knife as his mood infected her. But she caught his sharp glance and relaxed her grip.

He merely nodded at Hanibal, then wheeled his horse and galloped back to where his company had formed up before Kron. Despite knowing that his rival would not greatly care about sending Alan and his company to their demise, Alan found his heart pumping with exhilaration. Finally, after all these weeks of marching through the damnable rychly mists that blocked most of the surrounding world from view, he would taste battle once again.

Alan's Forsworn company had grown with volunteers until it now numbered well over a hundred, organized into a skirmishing formation with a half dozen scouts spread out well to the front of the main body. Ninety-one mounted soldiers formed a spear point behind which Alan's three dozen mounted archers followed, completing the combat wedge.

Alan moved to his place at the head of the column of horse soldiers. He paused to survey his troops, letting the pawing of hooves, the champing of bits, and the rattle of weaponry splash over him, its prebattle rhythm exhilarating. He gave the order that put the company into motion, rapidly rounding the bend that put the rest of Hanibal's brigade out of sight behind them.

They had traveled almost a league when Alan spotted one of his outriders riding hard back toward him. Charlie Franks pulled his horse to a sliding halt, scattering pebbles and throwing up dust.

"What is it, Charlie?" Alan asked, having freed his crescent-bladed ax from his back.

"A vorg column is moving through the canyon up ahead. They haven't spotted us, and it looks like we're about to get lucky."

"How so?" asked Alan.

Charlie's blue eyes narrowed, his face tightening in anticipation. "It's a supply train, Chosen. We seem to have found the trailing edge of a much larger force. I counted seventy ox-drawn wagons stacked high with tents and supplies along with a half dozen ballistae. The vorgs and several hundred human soldiers are moving along our path."

For the first time all day, Alan grinned.

"Okay. Charlie, ride back and inform Hanibal that I am initiating an attack on the vorg combat supply train. Tell him he's welcome to join the action if he can catch up. But I won't wait for him."

"Yes, Chosen."

As Charlie galloped past the rest of the company to disappear down their back trail, Alan rose in his stirrups, his yell carrying to the entire company.

"At the gallop. Forward!"

Putting words to action, he urged his big bay into motion. Whirling his ax above his head, he gave the signal for the combat run. And behind him, every member of his company readied themselves for battle.

—⁓—

Carol groaned as gentle hands cradled her head. Kim's features swam before her eyes, and Carol blinked to clear her vision. But as her sister bent over her, Carol felt a warmth flowing from Kim's hands into her body. Or perhaps they pulled the pain and chill from Carol's throbbing skull. With the return of her eyesight, she saw a wound open on Kim's head, soaking her hair in blood. Although the Endarian life-shifter's face tightened into a grimace, no moan escaped her lips. Kim's eyes maintained a faraway look of concentration. And as the surrounding plants withered and died, Kim's wound faded away.

With a barely audible gasp, Kim lifted her hands from Carol's face and leaned back against the young pine that she had just drained of life. The gentle movement her body imparted to the tree sent a shower of brown needles raining down upon the two women.

Carol understood why. Kim's life-shifting magic was most powerful when transferring energy between similar types of living beings. While she could heal a person by exchanging her own health for the other's wound, it took significantly longer to channel the life essence of plants to restore herself. And during that interval, she suffered.

Carol reached out and placed her hand on Kim's. "Are you all right?"

"I just need a moment."

A sudden worry blossomed in Carol's mind, and this time she did manage to sit up.

"The battle," she said. "What has happened?"

The fatigue on Kim's face shifted into concern. "Our soldiers have broken through the vorgs to link up with an Endarian regiment. For now, the vorgs have retreated to await reinforcements."

"That's wonderful. Why the anxious look?"

"The dissipation of Galad's time-mists somehow separated Hanibal's brigade from the rest of the legion. We don't know how far behind they are. Alan's company is with them."

A new worry struck Carol. "Where's Arn?"

"Arn volunteered to go back to find the others and lead them the rest of the way to Endar Pass."

"Alone?" Carol asked, dreading the answer.

"Yes."

Carol struggled to her feet, an effort that left her shaking. She knew why her father would grant his assassin's request. Arn's knife would protect him from sorcerers while he made use of the skills that had earned him the alias Blade.

She stepped out onto a rocky outcrop to look back down the canyon they had traversed. With the withdrawal of the vorgish force, only the long lines of Rafel's legion were visible, much of it still concealed by the nearest bend in the canyon. Ox-drawn supply wagons were now making that turn, accompanied by columns of infantry marching alongside.

She dismissed the hope that her father would send a large force to search for Hanibal's brigade. Rafel's first duty was to get the bulk of his legion into Endar Pass so that they could be incorporated into the Endarian defensive plan. Only then would he consider a mission to aid the stragglers. Alan and the others were on their own . . . unless Carol could help them.

She needed to find a bird into which she could transfer her consciousness. She scanned the sky, failing to catch sight of any avian creatures floating on the breeze or roosting in the pines. Fighting the desire to scream, she abandoned her search and returned to Kim.

Carol knelt beside her sister, wincing at the blood that matted her hair. Kim's wound had closed, but the sight caused Carol to put a hand to the back of her own head, finding it similarly coated with blood. Giving her sister a gentle shake, Carol roused Kim from the slumber into which she had slipped.

"I'm sorry to wake you," Carol said as Kim's eyes fluttered open, "but we cannot remain here. We need to find Father and enter Endar Pass at his side. Queen Elan will be expecting to see you among the early arrivals, and we shouldn't disappoint her. Galad's disfigurement will come as enough of a shock."

To Carol's surprise, Kim's face hardened, and she climbed to her feet.

For the first time since she had been revived, Carol looked around carefully. Although Kim's horse was tied to a nearby tree, there was no sign of Storm. Placing two fingers to her lips, Carol issued a shrill whistle that echoed across the canyon. Moments later she heard hoof-beats, and the dapple-gray mare trotted from a nearby copse, stopping to nuzzle Carol's hand.

Reaching into her pocket, Carol withdrew one of the sugar lumps she kept there, then held out her palm to let Storm's sensitive lips gather it into her mouth. Then, as Kim mounted her horse, Carol swung up into her own saddle. The sudden movement delivered a wave of dizziness that took several moments to pass. Seeing Kim's questioning glance, Carol nodded, then urged Storm forward at a trot, following Kim northeast along the column of soldiers toward the entrance to Endar Pass. And as she and her sister made their way toward the front of the column, a troubling feeling draped her.

The complications that they had encountered as they neared their destination were not a good omen for what was to come.

—⁓—

Kim rode toward her homeland's southern entrance, her trepidation growing as she passed along the columns of soldiers making their way along the narrow road that wound up the steep canyon wall. The last time she had returned to Endar, she had experienced the anticipation of not only seeing her beautiful homeland after a long and dangerous trek, but also of introducing her three new friends to her mother.

Over her trying months of travel in the company of Arn, Ty, and John, who had rescued her from vorg slavers and fought their way through a plethora of enemies to bring her home, Kim had grown fond of Arn and become enamored with Ty's witty banter. But she had fallen in love with John. The human's devotion matched Kim's own. She remembered the pride she had felt when John had asked her mother for Kim's hand in marriage, a wish that Elan had granted.

This homecoming felt altogether different. Kim was returning from having just escaped one siege only to become embroiled in another. As horrifying as it had been to endure the threat of losing her newly discovered father and sister in the recent battles, what filled her with dread was the thought of losing her husband.

Angry at herself for allowing selfish worry to consume her, Kim turned her attention to the winding trail and the soldiers who stepped aside to let her and Carol pass. There was work yet to do if they were to reach Endar Pass.

4

Endar Pass
YOR 415, Late Spring

Having left Ax with Rafel's grooms, Arn made his way southeast along the steep, forested canyon, paralleling the legion's trail away from Endar Pass. Clad in tan buckskin boots, trousers, and shirt, he carried a pair of throwing daggers in his boots, two more strapped to his thighs, and Slaken belted at his left side. Arn had let his brown hair grow out during the weeks of travel through the time-mists so that it almost reached his shoulders. But for Carol's sake he had kept his face closely shaved.

He heard the vorgs and men of Kragan's army moving along the walls of the deep canyon before he saw flashes of them through the dense undergrowth. They tromped forward, uncaring of the rocks or shale that clattered downward from their passage, confident in their numbers and in the magic users who accompanied them. If anything, they sought to bring themselves to the attention of their enemies, hoping to draw the Endarians from their mountain fortress to engage them. But they did not expect to be infiltrated by a lone assassin.

Arn slowly shook his head. It was ever thus.

Slaken burned his hip, spreading its bloodthirst through Arn's body, calling his hand to draw the knife from its sheath. Arn felt that longing concentrate within his right hand. His fingertips tingled as if he had just awoken from sleeping atop the arm, a sensation familiar yet somehow different from what he was accustomed to. For the thousandth time, the knowledge that something within him was changing built tension in his shoulders until he had to stop his hands from balling into fists.

As a five-year-old child, he had peered through a knothole in the wooden box within which his mother had hidden him before a wielder bound her to a wall to let a she-vorg rip her throat out. Throughout his troubled childhood, Arn's nightmares had terrified him. A startling number of those dreams had foreshadowed events that he later encountered.

When Rodan, the king of Tal, had gifted Arn the arcane blade that he now wore at his side, the dreams had diminished. But since the day when Arn had set Slaken aside to save Carol from errant spell casting, his dreams of what might be had returned with a vengeance.

Arn shifted his attention to the faint internal voice that had called to him since childhood. He allowed it to pull him toward the target that posed the biggest threat to his current mission. A biting wind swept down from the glacier-capped peaks to the east, bending the pines before it and whipping Arn's cheeks. Through the trees he saw men and vorgs lean into the arctic blast, looking as if they were trying to shrug down into their armor.

He moved with a stealthy ease that enabled him to pass through a juniper grove without rustling a branch or rolling a stone. For two hours he worked his way down the canyon, staying in the dense brush, forced to stop, time and again, to allow large numbers of soldiers to move past him. The nature of the enemy force changed as Arn penetrated the follow-on support units. The rattle of ox hooves on stone accompanied the crunch of wagon wheels, drowning out the mumbled complaints of marching soldiers. A new smell replaced the tang of pine, the odor of hundreds of unwashed, sweat-soaked bodies wearing ragtag clothing and mismatched armor.

A different wagon drew his gaze. This one had a high canvas supported by three iron hoops. A fresh gust whipped the back flap open just enough for Arn to confirm that the interior held no supplies. It was decorated as a mobile living space for an important occupant. Not for a military leader, rather for someone who needed lush accommodations to facilitate study or meditation. The space confirmed his earlier conjecture of the presence of at least one wielder within this contingent of troops.

A sudden commotion rippled through the enemy warriors, bringing the wagons to a halt. The warbling sound of a vorgish war horn caused some of the soldiers who accompanied the wagons to turn and rush back in the direction from which they had come, while others milled about in confusion as the distant sound of fighting echoed up the canyon.

Arn crawled into a dense thicket and wriggled his way forward until he gained a view of the battle being waged in the canyon just southeast of his overlook. Cavalry soldiers charged into the midst of the surprised vorgs, who struggled to block their path to the supply wagons. Mounted archers supported the assault that had thrown the vorgs into a state of panic. Many vorg warriors retreated directly into their own forces, racing to reinforce them.

The horse warriors were clearly Rafel's troops, but the sight of their shaved heads identified them as Alan's company, the Forsworn. At the head of that onslaught, Alan wielded the great crescent-bladed ax that had once belonged to Ty. Alan's thickly muscled arms whirled the weapon with such force that it cut through shield and armor to spray blood into the wind. Other vorgs crumpled beneath the flying hooves of Alan's bay warhorse.

The Forsworn pushed on as opaque tendrils of fog flowed down the walls of the canyon to swallow the combatants in an impenetrable haze.

Arn shifted his scrutiny back toward the wagons, where the vorg commander had organized a group of several hundred warriors into defensive lines between the mist-shrouded battle and the supply wagons. There, atop a rocky outcrop, stood a female vorg, her clawed hands raised above her head as the wind whipped her ocher cloak. Below her, ranks of vorg archers unleashed a storm of arrows into the fog, not caring whether they hit friend or foe within the roiling obscuration.

The sight pulled a light gasp from Arn's lips. There was no magical response from Lektuvu, the wielder Rafel had assigned to Hanibal's brigade. Why had Alan initiated this attack without such support? Carol's wild younger brother was about to get himself killed.

With a knot twisting in his stomach, Arn drew Slaken from its sheath and crawled from the thicket. At a dead run, he raced through the trees toward the she-vorg wielder's escarpment, serenaded by the screams of the dying.

—⚏—

Alan smashed the vorg's shield with a single blow of his ax, embedding the blade in his enemy's sternum. One moment Kat, Bill, Quincy, and Kron fought alongside him. In the next, vapor condensed around them, reducing his vision to arm's length. Blinded, he pulled his warhorse to a halt, afraid to swing his ax for fear of dismembering his own followers. An arrow grazed his left arm, and his horse stumbled sideways, two bolts sticking from its chest and neck. Alan leapt free of the saddle as the bay sank to the ground.

A body crashed into him, and he saw Kat stop her own blade just short of his throat. Her eyes widened in shock just before a running horse struck Alan, sending him rolling into a pile of dismembered carcasses. Clawing his way back to his feet, he arose, covered in gore and stinking of offal. If he didn't lead his warriors out of this murk, they would all die.

He saw the vorgish arrows stuck in the tree he had unconsciously leaned against. Their feathered ends pointed the way back to the archers who had shot them.

Alan reached down and grabbed a kite shield from one of the dead vorgs at his feet. Lifting it high in front of him with his left arm, he launched himself in the indicated direction, using it to batter his way through the confusion. His yell boomed out of his chest with such volume that it overwhelmed the other battle cries and shrieks of pain and terror around him.

"To me!"

Without bothering to see who or what he knocked aside, Alan concentrated on maintaining his forward momentum, ignoring the gashes he suffered along the way. He bashed onward, his repeated call echoing through the gray brume, a beacon for his companions.

And with each heaving breath, he hurled his mental curses at Hanibal, who had denied him and his Forsworn any protection from this foul magic.

—⚬⚬⚬—

The muddle within the vorg columns was heightened by wagon drivers whipping their oxen forward, away from the combat to their rear, while men and vorgs surged to reinforce the rear defenses. Due to the narrowness of the main trail along the steep canyon wall, these competing forces got jammed up, a situation that a tipped-over wagon made worse.

Arn moved within the mayhem as if he were a member of Kragan's host, but his target stood well back from the fighting, atop a rocky outcrop two dozen feet above the track that served as the road. The she-vorg wove her hands in a pattern that the air elemental she had summoned replicated, churning new fog banks into the melee to replace those the wind dispersed.

When Arn reached the base of the ledge where the wielder invoked her magic, he swerved off the trail, driving Slaken's point into the throat of one of the two vorgs who guarded the trail that led up. The dying one's companion swung his sword, but Arn ducked inside the blow, burying Slaken into the exposed armpit and then hurling the body into three more vorgs who lunged to stop him. As his pursuers toppled to the ground, Arn turned to see the wielder turn her attention to him.

Fire rippled through the air in a fountain that parted around him, funneled directly into the vorgs behind Arn. The stink of burning hair and cooked flesh accompanied their guttural screams. The ocher-cloaked wielder's yellow eyes widened in shock that Arn was still alive. Arn drew a throwing dagger and hurled it. The weapon tumbled through the air and then stopped two feet from her throat.

That did not surprise him. The attack was the distraction that allowed Arn to close the gap that separated them. He charged through the luminous energy bubble that enclosed the wielder and slit her throat. Then, with a shove, he hurled her corpse onto the startled soldiers below the outcrop.

—⚒—

The suddenness with which the fog blew away startled Alan. One moment he had been hammering his way forward with the kite shield and the next, crystal-blue skies opened overhead. He squinted into the bright sunlight, tossed the shield at a vorg that stood with its back to him, then split its head with his ax. He turned in a tight circle, thrilled to see that Kat, Bill, Quincy, Kron, and at least fifty of his company had charged to his side atop their mounts. The change in the weather reinvigorated Alan's followers. The startled vorgs and human soldiers from Kragan's horde broke and ran toward the lines of their own troops in a defensive posture fifty paces to the northeast.

Alan gave chase, and the mounted members of his company bolted past him, his archers unleashing their arrows as they rode. Alan's stentorian yell rose above the thunder of hooves.

"Run them down!"

He pushed himself, reaching the enemy lines only moments after his riders had crashed through the formation. Pikemen had impaled several of the horses, throwing the riders clear. Those who remained in their saddles rained bloody death with ax, sword, and spear.

Alan charged into the thickest group of vorg soldiers, his ax howling through the air. A human soldier attempted to club him with a war hammer, but Alan caught the man's wrist with his left hand and squeezed. He felt the bone shatter and saw white splinters jut out through the fellow's skin as the hammer dropped to the ground. Alan's ax ended the soldier's squall.

When their enemies broke and fled, a flash of yellow drew his eyes to the base of a nearby rocky promontory. The bloody cape draped a broken corpse that had formerly been a wielder. Atop that ledge, a familiar figure fought to hold the narrow trail that led up to it. The economy of motion with which the lean man employed his knives and sideslipped attacks revealed his identity, even from behind.

Blade.

"Burn the wagons," Alan yelled, sending his mounted riders racing ahead to kill wagon drivers and light the fires.

But he did not follow, turning instead to race toward the trail leading up to the ledge where Arn battled. The first of the wad of soldiers clustered at the base of the narrow trail fell to his ax, spraying blood over his startled companions. Rather than let the man fall, Alan caught him by the throat with his left hand, lifting him high and hurling his body into the vorgs who spun to meet this new assault. The bellows in Alan's chest heaved with exertion as he cleaved a trail of destruction up toward Arn. The assassin cut down the last two of their enemies as Alan reached the top of the outcrop.

Alan scanned their surroundings, seeking out new threats but finding none. He and his blood-soaked brother-in-law stood alone atop the cliff. In the canyon below, the two dozen or so of his company who had lost their horses stalked the battlefield, finishing off Kragan's soldiers while others treated their own wounded. The rest of the routed vorgs and men had fled in panic, deserting the wagons filled with supplies, the nearest of which had started to burn.

He shifted his ax to his left hand and stepped forward to grip wrists with Arn.

"Thank you," Alan said, nodding down toward the dead wielder. "The deep would have taken us all had you not killed her."

"And now you've returned the favor."

A new movement drew Alan's gaze toward the southwest. Rounding the distant bend in the canyon rode the lead elements of Hanibal's brigade. The captain sat astride his black stallion accompanied by Lektuvu, a petite wielder with spiked blonde hair, resplendent in her billowing silver robe. Behind the two hundred mounted cavalry came hundreds of infantry and archers. They did not rush but poured into the canyon at a steady march. Doubtless Hanibal's scouts had informed him of the outcome of the skirmish and he had arrived to seal the victory.

The heady rush of battle drained from Alan's limbs, replaced by a depressing sense of dread as his thoughts turned to the losses his company had endured within the murk that had enveloped them. From this height he watched his followers retrieve the bodies of their fallen comrades and lay them out near where the wounded were being treated. Of his original 133, he could see that fewer than a hundred remained alive, and some of those would probably not last the day.

His body felt thick, as if the heaviness of his muscles overwhelmed his strength to carry them. Once again he had led those he commanded into battle against overwhelming numbers, this time without any defense against the wielder such a large force was almost certain to have. Alan could tell himself time and again that this was Hanibal's fault for denying him the magical resource he had requested, but in the end the soldiers' welfare was always the unit commander's responsibility.

The thought thrust Alan into one of the many memories that haunted his dreams.

A sword sliced open Alan's cheek, but he paid no notice, his whirling ax severing the arm that held it, continuing in its great arc to remove the head from the body to which the limb had been attached. A low moan arose from those who stood before him. Trapped by those behind, they could not retreat before the blood-covered demon whose ax swept them from this world into the next.

Alan's muscles bulged with exertion and his breath now came in mighty gulps, but still he pushed forward. As he reached the upper entrance to the chasm, the last two men turned and ran toward their horses. Two arrows whispered over his shoulder, catching the first as he tried to mount and sending the second tumbling from his horse.

Alan glanced back to see Bill, weak with blood loss, lowering his bow and dropping to one knee, a knee that slowly gave way beneath him. Alan grabbed the ranger in one arm and carried him back down the chasm toward where he had left George. The old veteran sat at the lower entrance to the chasm among the corpses, a thick arrow jutting from his upper chest. He raised his head to look at Alan, who set Bill gently against the wall next to George.

Seeing the question in Alan's eyes, George spit a red wad from his mouth and said, "I nailed the last one to a tree down there as he let loose this shaft. I was just a hair slow."

The veteran chuckled softly, a sound that took on a gurgle toward the end. He spit another wad of red phlegm against the wall.

"Ah, George," Alan said, a sudden wave of exhaustion and sadness assailing him.

"Don't you die on us now," said Bill, himself pale from blood loss.

"Too late, son," said George.

Then he turned his head toward Alan, and a broad grin split his face.

"I'm just glad I got to see this day, glad I got a chance to be a part of it. Alan, I swear to the gods I have never seen the like of what you did here. Your father would burst with pride. I wish I was going to be around to tell him, to see his face."

With one last effort, the veteran thrust out his arm, catching Alan's wrist in a strong grip. "You get Bill on back safely, okay?"

"I will, boss. You have my word on it."

The ranger smiled one last time and sank back against the wall, dead.

Alan screamed his frustration to the wind, then collapsed back against the cliff wall. George Dalton, dead. Harry Budka, dead. Jim Clemens, dead. Sam Jacobson, dead. Only Bill Harrison remained alive, and he clung to life tenuously.

Alan felt Arn's hand clap him on the shoulder and roused himself from his stupor.

"See to your soldiers," said Arn. "I will meet with Commander Hanibal. High Lord Rafel sent me to guide his brigade into Endar Pass."

Alan slung his ax over his back, gripped wrists with Arn once more, then strode back down the trail toward his wounded. This time he would let the assassin meet Hanibal. Right now, Alan did not trust himself to greet his commander.

—◊—

Ten leagues south of Endar Pass, Kragan stood atop a windswept ridge, staring at a sunset that burned the western horizon in scarlet. He listened to Charna's report of the advance guard's dual engagements with High Lord Rafel's legion near Endar Pass. Kragan's army commander and loyal friend made no attempt to soften the news of how badly his advance guard had been routed on this day's battleground. But she seemed shocked by his reaction to the news.

Kragan clasped his hands to his chest. He met her eyes, finding within them the wrath that she had expected him to feel.

"Be at ease," he said, the growl in his voice one of anticipation. "Landrel's Scroll predicts that Rafel will lead his legion into Endar Pass to fight alongside the Endarian queen. And his spell-casting daughter shall be at his side in the cataclysm that I shall rain down on them. It is precisely what I need to happen."

"But we have given Rafel a taste of victory. It will bolster his soldiers' confidence."

"So much the better when we supplant that emotion with despondency. After two days' march we will make camp outside Endar Pass. There you will take the twenty thousand men we conscripted after my conquest of Tal and place them at the head of my army. Make sure the Talian conscripts know that their women and children in the comfort camps at the rear of our columns will be killed should those soldiers disappoint me. When we begin our assault, we will see how the high lord and his daughter react to butchering their fellow countrymen."

"As you command," said Charna.

"As for Earl Coldain's twin little girls, I want them displayed on the battlefield in chains."

The rumble at the back of his mind told Kragan that Kaleal very much approved of this plan.

5

Endar Pass
YOR 415, Late Spring

Carol rode the final stretch that led into Endar Pass beside Kim, John, and Rafel, escorted by a dozen Endarian scouts wearing color-shifting uniforms, the mottled greens, browns, and grays blending with the pines, shrubs, and stones that formed their background. The narrow road, barely wide enough for the wagon that carried Galad's unconscious form, exited the forest to carve its way along the face of rocky cliffs. The thought of how Kim's brother had overtaxed his time-shaping talent worried her. Might he have damaged the mental conduit through which he channeled the time-mists?

She turned her attention to the leagues-long column of mounted and marching soldiers that formed her father's legion. They moved up toward a crevice between twin peaks that had once been a single mountain, split asunder by some gargantuan force in ages long forgotten. A lone, gnarled pine maintained its precarious perch on the bare rock face.

Carol leaned in her saddle to look into the depths of the gorge that yawned below. She caught a brief glimpse of the sun glittering off a mist-shrouded stream in those depths.

As she rounded a final bend, a sheer cliff closed off the canyon. Far above, the river leapt from beneath a vast glacier that had carved its way through the peaks. It plunged over the edge of the precipice to fall several thousand feet to the floor of the canyon below, creating the veil of mist. The trail disappeared behind a plume of water. The sight pulled forth an eerie feeling, as if she were about to make passage into a numinous world. The Endarians who led the way forward paused for several seconds as they entered the mist, so that Carol and her companions were forced to pull their mounts to a stop lest they run into their guides.

"Is that the sole entrance to Endar Pass?" Carol asked her sister.

Kim shook her head. "No, although it is the only way into the pass from the south. There are several routes into the pass from the Endarian lands in the north."

The Endarian guides disappeared into the swirling fog and Carol followed, aware of the mist pressing against her body as if it resisted her entry. Then the feeling passed, and rider and mount were moving naturally again. Once through the murky boundary, Carol looked around in surprise. The way forward had cleared, although the mists swirled around her and her companions so that they could not make out their surroundings. Her long familiarity with the time-mists that Galad had wielded on their journey told her the true nature of the haze. Still, the otherworldly feeling raised the gooseflesh on her arms.

As the riders emerged from the miasma, a valley descended before Carol, dropping between forested ridges until it came to the edge of an azure lake. Mountains surrounded the lake, sending tree-covered fingers of land out into the water. Sandy beaches stretched along the lakeshore. High on the slopes above, groves of white aspen replaced the pines. These in turn gave way to glacier-covered mountains.

The country grew ever lovelier as they approached the lake. The trees had an unusual palette of blue and green needles, along with a hint of yellow near the heath. Wildflowers bloomed within meadows, glowing in the brilliant sunlight in hues of white, purple, and blue.

As the riders descended the ridge, Carol studied her immediate surroundings. Thousands of Endarian soldiers manned defensive positions, while many times that number stood ready to fortify any breach in those front lines. The sight of the ivory fortress and the walled city it protected covered the island at the lake's center.

The gleaming white walls rose hundreds of feet into the sky, brilliantly colored pennants flapping from the tops of four towers. A single bridge of the same white stone crossed a wide expanse of water, connecting the south shore to the island fortifications. Warriors lined this span, standing erect along both sides of the bridge. The castle battlements were fully manned, the archers and warriors watching Rafel's approaching legion.

"Beautiful, isn't it?" said Kim.

"Breathtaking," said Carol.

"By all the gods," said Rafel, "it swells my heart, just as it did when I first entered this enchanted place three decades ago."

Kim raised her arm, pointing toward the column of soldiers escorting a pearlescent carriage.

"Mother approaches."

Carol caught the worry in her half sister's voice and glanced back at the covered wagon wherein Galad slumbered. Although Kim had not been able to restore her brother's withered hand, she had funneled enough life energy into him to ensure that he would recover from the exhausted state resulting from his attempt to channel too much time magic. Now he just needed sleep.

Their Endarian guides signaled a halt, and Rafel yelled the command that his flagmen echoed down the column, which was still emerging from the distant mist-veiled passage.

The royal guard parted, and as the carriage came to a halt, Rafel swung down from his saddle, as did Carol, Kim, and John. They handed their reins to the high lord's grooms and strode forward to greet the Endarian ruler.

The carriage driver opened the door and lowered the steps before moving aside. Queen Elan descended, resplendent in a turquoise gown that matched the color of the lake that surrounded her fortress city. Her dress swirled in the gentle breeze as her eyes shifted from Kim to Carol and then lingered on Rafel, her lips hinting at a smile.

Rafel knelt, bowing before the queen as John and Carol mirrored his movement. Kim stepped forward to embrace her mother, who returned the hug, kissing her daughter on the cheek. When Elan released Kim, she signaled Kim's husband to stand and smiled at him. Then she stepped to Rafel and gently lifted his chin with her right hand.

"Rise, my unforgotten love," she said, her midnight eyes glistening.

Rafel rose to his feet to stare up at the taller woman. Taking her extended hand, he kissed the back of it, his bearded face appearing pale and weathered against the queen's ebony skin.

"My queen," Rafel said. "Through all the years of our separation, you have never wandered far from my thoughts."

"It seems but a blink of the eye," said Elan, her soft smile widening. "Although those streaks of gray in your hair and beard tell me differently. Thank you for answering my entreaty."

"I would come to your aid even if I owed you no debt."

Releasing Rafel's hand, Elan turned her attention to Carol, signaling for her to rise.

"Hello, Carol. You look exactly as Landrel drew you all those centuries ago. It is a pleasure to welcome you to our home, which I have had the great fortune to rule these last few decades. Perhaps, with your help, this demesne shall endure for many more."

Carol felt a rush of warmth color her face but kept her voice steady. "Gods willing."

The queen turned back to Kim, concern etching her fine features.

"Where is Galad? Why did he not come to greet me?"

Kim pursed her lips, her unease palpable. "Mother, I am sorry to tell you that Galad has been injured."

"What?"

"He will live, but he has lost his left hand. He is resting in the back of the wagon."

Elan turned toward the indicated wagon, astounding Carol with how quickly she could move in the lengthy gown. Rafel hastened to lift the canvas flap, allowing the queen to peer inside.

Her breath caught in her throat, then hissed out.

"That is a time-shaping wound," Elan said, turning back to Kim. "When did it happen?"

"I was riding near him this morning," said Carol. "One moment he appeared to be fine. Then the time-mists dissipated and Galad collapsed."

"He must have overtaxed himself trying to extend the mists," Kim interjected, tears welling in her eyes. "I felt him fall, but by the time I reached his side, his hand was gone."

Elan placed a hand on her daughter's shoulder, although her gaze had returned to her unconscious son, lying faceup atop a pallet in the back of the wagon.

"Such wounds cannot be mended," Elan said. "Not even by a life-shifter of your skill. We are fortunate that the collapse of his time-shaping channel did not kill him. I hope that the loss of his hand is the only deep injury he suffered."

"I healed his other trauma," said Kim.

Elan turned back toward the group, her brow furrowed. "It is his mind that concerns me."

Carol was worried about the same thing.

The queen shifted her attention back to the high lord. "Let us return to my palace. There I will convene a war council so that we may best determine how to incorporate your legion into our defensive plans."

Elan walked back to her carriage, climbed inside, and was driven away, accompanied by her royal guard. As the vehicle made its way toward the ivory bridge, the sound of pounding hooves pulled Carol around. A rider leaned low across his horse's neck as he raced along the column toward them. The messenger pulled his mount to a halt a dozen feet from where Carol stood.

"High Lord," he said, "I have been sent to tell you that, after a minor skirmish with the enemy, Commander Hanibal's brigade has rejoined the rear of your column."

"What of Alan?" Rafel asked.

"Lord Alan and Blade are with them."

A wave of lightheadedness almost caused Carol to lose her balance as relief inundated her. She steadied herself before the others noticed.

"Very good," said Rafel. "Ride back and summon Hanibal, Alan, and Arn to my side."

The high lord strode to where his battle master and Earl Coldain stood, a dozen paces away. Carol watched as he instructed his two subordinate leaders to gather key commanders. Their Endarian escorts would guide Rafel's leaders to the palace. She looked over her father's shoulder, her vision drawn to the sight of Elan's chariot and royal guard crossing the ivory arch of the bridge that provided passage from the lakeshore to the fortress beyond.

Her scrutiny strapped her chest with a warring mix of dread and anticipation. The confrontation with Kragan that Landrel had predicted millennia ago scuttled through the mountains toward her. Soon human, Endarian, and vorgish blood would stain those shining walls crimson.

—⁂—

Carol blinked and squinted as her eyes readjusted to the sunshine, which seemed much brighter than when she had passed through the fog-filled bastion entry a few moments before. In fact, the sun seemed slightly higher in the sky than it had been just a moment ago. She looked around. The thick outer walls of the fortress arced away behind her, gradually curving inward. Kim, John, and Rafel stood near Queen Elan. Several other Endarians stood just behind these three, but Carol turned toward Arn, who had just dismounted alongside Alan and Hanibal.

Carol ran forward and threw her arms around Arn's neck in a hug that he heartily returned. She released her embrace of her husband and turned to her brother, taking his face in her hands as she studied his blood-matted scalp and armor. The ax strapped to his back gleamed in the brilliant sunlight, having been cleaned of gore.

"You're hurt," she accused.

"Flesh wounds, Sister, thanks to that husband of yours," Alan said, his tone dark. "But I lost many good warriors today."

Hanibal sneered. "Perhaps if you had waited for me to reinforce you instead of succumbing to your thirst for glory, most of those lives could have been saved."

She saw the muscles in Alan's neck bunch. Carol whirled on the commander, her face flushed with the same fury she had seen in her brother's eyes.

"Were you on the scene?"

Hanibal straightened.

"No, Lorness. But I observed the aftermath."

"Then save your comments for your battle report. My father will be the judge of this."

Carol felt Arn's hand on her shoulder as he stepped up beside her. But his chill gaze was locked on the redheaded commander.

"Take care to get your facts right," said Arn. "You were not there, but I was."

Hanibal bit his lip, then clapped his fist to his chest in a salute to Carol. "Please excuse my careless words, Lorness. The loss of dozens of men under my command has loosed my temper and my tongue. By your leave?"

Carol managed a curt nod. Hanibal accepted the dismissal and walked away. With a deep breath, she willed her anger away, ignoring how Alan's stare bored into the captain's retreating form.

She took Arn's hand and led him to the place where Elan waited. Arn had told her how this graceful queen of Endar had once threatened his life, an act for which he harbored no bitter feelings. Elan had ignored the guidance of the Endarian High Council and tasked Arn with helping Princess Kimber find and protect Carol Rafel, the one whom Landrel had prophesied would destroy Kragan.

When they reached the royal party, Arn sank to one knee before the queen, his head inclined in respect, a movement that Alan mirrored.

"It is good to see you again, Majesty," said Arn, "although I would have preferred that the circumstances be different."

"Please rise. We have no time for such formality."

Carol watched Elan study Alan as he raised himself to stand beside Arn, the queen's eyes widening at the power that radiated from his burly frame.

Rafel stepped forward. "Majesty, this is my son, Alan."

The queen's serious face softened. "Lord Alan. I see much of your father within you."

The queen then turned and walked across the park toward one of the many gardens, accompanied by her guards, with Carol and the others trailing. Flowers had been the central theme of the park, but as they approached the palace facade, water became the dominant feature. Waterfalls, lily ponds, fountains, and geysers produced a lilting melody that Carol found hypnotic.

This gave way to steps a hundred feet wide, leading up a terraced embankment to the wide palace doors. The walls of the palace were of the same white stone as the outer fortress, although the doors and other fixtures were of wood, intricately carved and inlaid with scenes of animals, trees, and mountains. These carvings had been painted so that the scenes appeared lifelike. The group passed into a ballroom decorated with delicate tapestries. The far wall was glass and looked out over an inner garden completely enclosed by the palace. At the center of the ballroom, a set of stone steps spiraled upward. The queen moved away from these toward the spot where two of her guards opened a pair of twelve-foot-tall double doors.

Carol stepped inside a room that pulled a soft gasp of awe from her lips. The floor was covered in a turquoise carpet with an elaborately embroidered sun at its center. Whereas she had seen many flying buttresses, those in this hall came in fours, each group supporting arches that held up a ceiling laced with the constellations of the night skies. A jade throne sat atop a terraced dais, elevated two paces above the floor in this otherwise unfurnished hall.

She approved. There would be no lounging in the queen's audience chamber, a feature that was clearly meant to keep the monarch's meetings short and to the point. Carol assumed that the Endarians gathered a dozen paces in front of the queen's seat of power were members of the High Council. However, there were many other Endarians within the chamber. From the variations in their uniforms, she surmised that some of the attendees must be leaders from other regions of the kingdom.

Elan took her seat on the green throne, and Rafel's group moved to an empty space on the right side of the high councillors, completing the arc of those marshaled before her. Leaving her husband's side, Kim ascended the dais to stand at her mother's right hand, making the vacancy on the queen's left all the more obvious. Arn had told Carol that during his lengthy stay in Endar Pass, Galad had counseled his mother not to trust the motives of the infamous assassin. Thankfully, Elan had ignored the advice. Whatever Galad's disagreements with his mother, the queen's quick glance toward the empty place beside her throne told Carol that his absence had left her shaken.

The fleeting frown melted from Elan's face as she looked out over the leaders before her. She signaled with her right hand, and an aged

Endarian strode forward, stepping up onto the lowest of the three tiers that formed the royal dais. He turned to face the crowd.

"For the benefit of those of you who are new to this land, I am High Councillor Failon. Queen Elan has tasked me with ensuring that everyone in this audience has the same understanding of the perilous nature of the situation in which we find ourselves."

As Failon uttered these words, Carol noted the slouch in the old man's shoulders.

"With the arrival of High Lord Rafel's legion, our numbers have swollen to just over forty-three thousand warriors. Our scouts put the number of Kragan's horde at more than five times that. Only eighteen hundred of our mist warriors remain alive and able to fight."

This sent a low muttering through the assemblage. Carol had the disconcerting feeling that the news was about to get worse.

"We have received reports that Kragan's wielders are scattered throughout his multitude, meaning that they number more than a hundred. For our part, we have a grand total of fifty-six casters, three of whom are Rafel's users of elemental mind magic, including Carol, the one Landrel prophesied would confront Kragan in the coming battle."

The old Endarian's chocolate eyes settled on Carol before he continued. Beside her, Arn's right hand gripped Slaken's haft so hard that the sinews in his forearm bunched.

Failon continued. "Our combatants will also be supported by fifty-one life-shifters, three dozen of which have recently arrived from the north. They will be joined by twelve time-shapers, assuming that Prince Galad can still exercise his talent."

A movement within the crowd caught Carol's attention, and she watched an Endarian woman clad in gray step forward, holding up a palm to interrupt the briefing.

"My queen, the people of the Tundral Plains are well aware of the dread that encroaches upon us. That is why I stand before you to present their demand that you rescind your edict banning the use of our most devastating form of life-shifting."

A stunned silence descended on the audience chamber. The shock on Kim's face filled Carol with alarm. What in the deep was this woman talking about?

Queen Elan rose to her feet and descended from the dais to stand before the representative who had initiated this confrontation, her turquoise gown in stark contrast to the other's dull gray trousers and loose-sleeved blouse.

"Nagol, how dare you confront me with such a demand as we prepare for war? Necrotic life-shifting is an abomination."

"In this time of dire need, your abhorrence of one of life magic's natural branches has no place in Endar. We must dispel the time stone that holds one of the fingers from Landrel's Trident and give it to our most powerful wielder of necrotic life-shifting, that it may amplify her magic. If we are to have any chance to save the kingdom, we must unsheathe the weapon. Half of the High Council agrees with me."

The muscles in Queen Elan's jaw tightened and her eyes flashed.

"As long as I am queen, necrotic magic will have no place in Endar."

Necrotic magic! As a teen, Kim had drained the life from the Endarian teen who had attempted to rape her. Despite having acted in self-defense, Kim had almost been condemned for using the forbidden talent.

For several long seconds, Nagol stood before the queen, her arms folded in defiance before the dumbfounded onlookers. A tear trickled down her left cheek. When she spoke, grief filled her voice.

"I am sorry, my queen."

With a sudden movement, Nagol uncrossed her arms and lunged at Elan, light glinting from the knife she wielded. Arn's hand blurred into motion. His spinning dagger flashed through the air and buried itself in the back of Nagol's neck, transforming her thrust into a limp collision that sprawled the queen to the floor beneath her. Carol sprang forward, collided with Alan, and would have fallen had Arn not caught her.

Pandemonium erupted within the chamber. Carol caught a glimpse of the nearest of Elan's royal guards as he grabbed Nagol by the hair and flung her lifeless body off his bloodied queen. The twin doors swung open and more guards flooded the room, separating Elan and Kim from the milling throng. Carol saw one of the guardsmen help Elan to her feet and usher her from the chamber, accompanied by Kim and a half dozen other guards.

Amidst the shouts and cries, Arn pulled Carol to an open space beside one of the pillars, where she struggled to gain control of her quickened breathing and heartbeat. She saw her father arguing with one of the royal guards, Alan and Coldain at his side.

That an Endarian had attempted to assassinate Queen Elan within her own palace had stunned Carol so badly that she was having difficulty organizing her thoughts. She had always believed that the meritocracy that was the kingdom of Endar was above acts such as this. What she had just observed put the lie to one of her fondest beliefs.

Her eyes shifted to the would-be assassin. Nagol lay sprawled on her right side, her head turned toward Carol, the tip of Arn's dagger extending through the front of her throat. The side of Nagol's head lay in a pool of blood. But her eyes were open wide, as if she were staring at the man who had killed her.

How could this have happened at a time and place where every moment of preparation was of critical importance?

Could this somehow be Kragan's work?

6

Kragan mounted the invisible platform that the air elemental Ohk had created to allow him to observe the tens of thousands of Vorg soldiers and human conscripts jammed into the steep canyon, halted just before the tunnel entrance to Endar Pass. Behind him, the bulk of his army lay hidden beyond a bend in the gulch.

He looked down at his clawed hands, watched the sinews shift beneath the paper-thin golden skin of his seven-foot, quasi-feline body. Even Kragan's closest advisers still quailed in his presence, all save Charna. The commander of his army continued to be the closest thing to a friend that Kragan had ever allowed himself. He respected her utter lack of fear, one of many traits that Kragan admired, even though he occasionally found Charna's candor irritating.

The time approached when he would extend those talons to clutch Carol Rafel's delicate throat. Before that happened, Kragan had to tire the woman prophesied to destroy him.

Kragan studied the sheer cliff that blocked the end of this ravine and the roaring waterfall that plunged from the heights to form a widow's veil that hid the mist-shrouded Endarian passage that led through those walls and into Endar Pass. Towering several thousand feet above the place where that stream began its plummet, the glacier that had once carved these canyons rose toward the high peaks, its craggy surface threatening to calve icy death on the tiny creatures who dared confront it. Up there, winter never surrendered its bitter grip. And within that ice lay the undecayed corpses of those who had attempted to conquer nature.

But Kragan had no intention of having his army scale those heights. Nor did he plan on funneling his troops through the time-mists the Endarian wielders had channeled into the tunnel beyond that waterfall. Through his mind link to Charna, he commanded that she order the lead elements to blockade that opening so no one from inside Endar Pass could sneak out to infiltrate his forces.

With steady strides, Kragan descended from his elevated perch and stepped behind a rocky outcrop that could not be observed from the water-cloaked entrance to Endar Pass. Locking three earth elementals that he favored in his mental vise, Kragan spread his arms wide.

"Dalg, Zemlja, Kamen! I task you."

—⁓—

Kim strode into the High Council Chamber and took her seat at her mother's right. The queen had bathed, washing the blood from her body. Now she wore a lustrous emerald gown, her bare right arm showing no sign of the wound from the assassin's blade. But as Elan's eyes shifted from one high councillor to the next, accusation coruscated from the others.

Thirteen of the fourteen council members were present, including the queen and Kim. Only Galad's chair sat empty, on Elan's left. The inward-facing chairs formed a circle, with the queen opposite the carved door that was the room's lone exit. Kim knew them all, although her extended absence had left her unaware of their current agendas.

Nagol's words to the queen replayed themselves in Kim's distressed mind.

In this time of dire need, your abhorrence of one of life magic's natural branches has no place in Endar.

What Kim saw in the faces that met the queen's eyes told her they were thinking the same thing. The representative from Endar's northwestern Tundral Plains had secretly gathered the support of half of the High Council members for the authorization to use necrotic life-shifting during Endar's battle for survival. Elan faced two forms of assassination on this day, only one physical in nature. The outcome of the political attempt to pull down the queen was yet to be determined.

"I declare this meeting of the High Council in session," said Elan. "There has been a challenge to my continued rule, a challenge that several within this room support. I call upon you to speak now so that we may jointly decide who will lead our people during the coming battle and beyond."

Her mother's pronouncement hit Kim in the gut so hard that a gasp escaped her lips.

"Mother, no! There is no reason . . ."

Elan held up her hand, cutting off Kim's outburst.

"Proceed," Elan said.

Directly across from Elan, a slender Endarian man rose from his chair, his narrow face set in grim determination. That Sersos was the first to accept the challenge surprised Kim. Ten years her senior, he was still one of the youngest councillors and had always displayed caution in both speech and manner.

"My queen, I believe I speak for the others assembled here when I say that I had no knowledge that Nagol planned to attack you."

"I made no such accusation," she said.

"Yet, despite my abhorrence of her action, I support her reasoning. All weapons maim and kill. For you to deny our life-shifters the use of their most powerful weapon displays astonishing timidity at the very moment when Endar needs audacious leadership."

Before Kim could respond, Devan, a female councillor whose long white hair framed her raven face, rose from the third chair on the queen's left. She smacked her hands together as if she wished her slap could strike Sersos on the face. Her look amplified the violence of the sound to such an extent that Sersos took a half step backward.

"How dare you, someone who has never seen the horrors of war, make such an accusation against one who led our people to victory in the Vorg War alongside Lord Rafel and the army of Tal. You know not of what you speak!"

"But I do," said Kelond, a middle-aged mist warrior whose leadership skills had elevated him to the High Council. "And I stand with Sersos. In the conflagration that encroaches we cannot have a leader who has grown weak in the knees, unable to make the grim decisions that the Scroll of Landrel demands."

"You!" Kim said, standing and pointing a finger at Kelond. "You betray the queen whose support elevated you to this council. Would that I could rescind my vote in your favor."

Kelond ignored the princess, keeping his hard gaze locked on Elan as a murmur crawled through the group.

"Let all who support Sersos and me stand."

To Kim's dismay, five other high councillors scattered around the circle rose to their feet, though with less conviction than Kelond had demonstrated.

"So, Elan, it appears that you are queen no more. We represent a majority of this council."

"No, you do not," said a new voice that sent a thrill through Kim's body. Galad stood tall in the doorway. "Despite our past differences, I attest my allegiance to my mother, the queen. A tie does not a majority make."

A mist enshrouded Galad, flowing around one side of the circle of chairs as a light-gray fog coalesced near the door. A half breath later, Galad emerged from the murk to take his seat at Queen Elan's side, his mummified wrist in plain view. Seeking to calm her stuttering heart, Kim composed her face, followed her brother's example, and resumed her seat. Expressions of emotions from outrage to shock etched the faces of the seven high councillors who stood as they surveyed the seven who remained seated.

Queen Elan broke the silence, her voice steady and calm, as if she were presiding over a dispute between minor tradesmen.

"By the vote of this council, my authority stands confirmed. I will hear no more talk of using the fragment from Landrel's Trident to amplify necrotic magic. That relic's last use was by Landrel himself, and it corrupted his bloodline. He placed his love for his dying son above his duty to the Endarian people. Landrel channeled the life essence of a female wolf and her pups into his son, knowing full well the danger of what he was attempting. In doing so, he mingled the characteristics of Endarians and wolves, dominant traits that became inheritable. Through the use of this forbidden form of magic, Landrel created the vorgs and spawned all the wars we and the humans have fought against them. He is responsible for the horde that seeks to destroy this citadel of freedom."

Kim's mother lifted her chin ever so slightly. "No. We shall fight this battle with the same honor our people exhibited during the Vorg War. This meeting is ended."

Despite the frustration Kim saw in the expressions of those whose effort to appoint a new leader had failed, they bowed to the queen and exited the chamber alongside their fellows. Only Kim and Galad remained behind.

Galad slumped back in his chair, the effort he had expended having drained him. Kim watched the calm slip from her mother's face, replaced by woe. A wretched chill made Kim want to return to her room and crawl under the covers, letting sleep expunge the grief from her soul.

"Mother," she said, "what has happened to produce such discord within the council while I was gone? Is it the threat that Kragan presents?"

Elan lifted her eyes from the stump of Galad's wrist, ran a hand from her forehead to her chin, and turned back to Kim. A barely audible sigh issued from her lips.

"Landrel caused this rift."

"You refer to the piece of the trident that Nagol mentioned?" asked Kim.

"That is part of it. But this dispute began weeks ago when Failon discovered a hidden cipher within the words of the scroll. It is just a small part of what the master historian believes is a much larger subtext within Landrel's prophecy. He has tried to identify other coded fragments but has thus far failed."

"How could a minuscule part of Landrel's prophecy introduce such turmoil within our realm?"

Galad roused himself, leaning forward in his chair to address Kim.

"I should have warned you, Sister. If I had not been so fixated on my assignment to bring High Lord Rafel's legion and Carol to aid our people, I certainly would have. But I had no inkling that the growing sedition would come to a head during the few days that passed in the normal world while I swaddled us within the rychly mists."

"Imminent peril amplifies strife between otherwise judicious individuals," said Elan. "Sadly, the menace we face produces enough desperation for some to advocate the use of dread powers. That magic can be enhanced by the piece of Landrel's Trident that lies encased in a time stone within my throne room."

"What does the cipher say?" asked Kim.

Elan's hesitation was brief, but Kim sensed her mother's concern that imparting this knowledge could invoke discord between the two of them. Kim glanced at Galad, who grasped the stump of his left wrist. He did not meet her questioning gaze.

"Kimber, I am afraid that I cannot tell you that," said Elan.

The answer stunned Kim. "Cannot or will not?"

Elan rose from her chair and turned to look down at her daughter. The sadness in her mother's eyes sapped the ire from Kim's heart.

"My answer to that question would be tainted with my own personal view. Despite his vote to maintain my rule, your brother disagrees with me at a fundamental level. You must decide how to interpret this small portion of Landrel's cipher on your own, just as Galad has. Consult with Failon and draw your own conclusions."

Then Elan turned and walked from the High Council Chamber, escorted by Galad and six of her personal guards who had been waiting just outside the doors, leaving Kim to ponder her mother's words. Kim sat as if she had been transformed into an obsidian carving. Talk to the old historian as war gathered on their doorstep, perhaps less than a day away? Madness.

Kim shook her head to clear the negative thoughts, forced herself to rise, and walked out of the room. It was time to ready herself for tomorrow's battle.

PART II

And there shall come a day when Endar's fate hangs in the balance, the outcome subject to the slightest nudge. Death shall stride the battlefield unnoticed. The thrust he delivers shall be both an end and a beginning.

—From the *Scroll of Landrel*

7

Endar Pass
YOR 415, Late Spring

Alan sat astride the unfamiliar white charger that he had chosen to replace the animal the vorgs had shot from beneath him during the recent battle. Far off to the south, Rafel rode a bay warhorse at his army's front and center. He faced southwest, the direction from which the enemy would enter Endar Pass. A rider behind the high lord carried his battle standard, a silver dagger on a black background, which fluttered in the frigid breeze.

Carol and Arn sat atop their mounts a half dozen paces behind Rafel. Alan could see the air shimmer around his sister as if the elementals she had summoned were readying themselves to do her bidding. Her flickering web of power looked warped, failing to extend into the area on her right where Arn straddled Ax.

Alan lifted the far-glass from his saddlebag and raised it to his right eye to study the layout of Rafel's forces. Battle Master Gaar commanded the division on Rafel's left, with Hanibal's brigade on Gaar's right flank. Earl Coldain commanded the division on Rafel's right flank, Alan's company having been reassigned from Hanibal's command to Coldain's.

Sweeping the glass to the southwest, Alan took in the forces arrayed across what was soon to become a battlefield. He had been astonished that his father's twenty thousand were being held in reserve along the southwestern lakeshore instead of being incorporated into the Endarian frontline defenders. Far forward of Rafel's lines, thousands of Endarian archers and warriors were positioned to block the horde that would soon pour from the mist-filled tunnel that formed the route into Endar Pass.

Kragan would not fail to identify this lonely opening as a trap, filled as it was with a time-slowing mist designed to separate each rank of the enemy from those who followed. But there was nothing the wielder could do to circumvent that passage unless he wanted to brave the deathly cold and crevices of the towering glaciers above. The Endarians had planned for that contingency. A much larger Endarian force lurked higher up on the forested ridgeline, ready to counterattack any survivors of such an endeavor.

Alan's thoughts spun to yesterday's attempted assassination of the queen. The attack had disrupted the war council. Although Elan had not been seriously wounded, Nagol's words and actions had resulted in such a lengthy delay that the Endarians and Rafel's leaders had managed only an abbreviated, postmidnight war council. With Kragan's army staging just outside the Pass, the queen had decided that there was not enough time to integrate Rafel's legion into her front lines.

Katrin's calm voice caused Alan to lower the far-glass. The woman had ridden up between his horse and that of Bill Harrison.

"Chosen. I have validated that each member of this company understands your final battle instructions. Your Forsworn stand ready for combat."

"What is our final troop tally?" Alan asked.

"One hundred and seven."

Alan cocked his head. "That includes the five too injured to ride."

"An Endarian healer has returned Quincy and the others to combat duty, Chosen," said Katrin.

"Excellent. Which life-shifter do I have to thank for this?"

Katrin's lips shifted into a tight line.

"The princess."

Kat wheeled her horse and trotted back to take up her position beside Kron.

Bill smirked, the ranger edging his horse close to Alan's as he leaned over, a conspiratorial gleam in his brown eyes.

"I think you may have tweaked a jealous bone."

"Ridiculous," said Alan, although he had noticed Kat's sudden attitude shift. "Kim only has eyes for her husband."

"I don't think Kim's eyes are what put a kink in Kat's reins."

Alan felt a frown form before he could stop it. By the deep, Bill had a knack for poking him in a weak spot, much as Ty had. That thought triggered a distant memory of the Kanjari warrior.

Ty stood in the clearing, his hair and body slick and dripping with the blood of the vorgs whose bodies lay strewn around him. His crescent ax bled down from the blade along the handle so that no metal or ivory was visible. Only Ty's eyes shone through the crimson.

The horseman who had fought beside Ty was a familiar-looking warrior of Val'Dep, his beard gathered into bloody twin braids. The fellow's companion lay dead at his feet.

Suddenly the horseman dropped to one knee and bowed his head toward Ty. "Dar Khan."

Alan had not been familiar with the words, but the horseman's manner indicated that he considered himself to be in the presence of royalty. No, that wasn't right. A god. The man had seemed to think that Ty was some blood-drenched god of war. And as Alan had shifted his gaze to Ty, he could not really blame the man for believing such a thing.

Alan shook his head to clear the vision and lifted his far-glass once again.

"Pay attention to the task at hand," he said to Bill, irritated that his words were relevant to himself.

Bill turned away, but the breeze carried his soft snicker to Alan's ears.

Just then, a rumble shook the ground, causing Alan's mount to rear and paw the air, almost unhorsing him. He nudged the animal with his heels, bringing its front feet back to earth, and regained control. Smoke billowed from the sheer mountain cliff to the west, and Alan redirected his far-glass to that spot.

"Spawn of the deep!" he hissed, a chill spreading through his chest.

What he saw was not smoke. Instead great gouts of earth and stone erupted from three places a hundred feet above the valley floor. The collapsing soil and stone flowed in triplet dirt rivers, forming ramps down from the cliff wall. Men in tattered armor surged down the hillside by the thousands, a half league north of where the Endarians had positioned themselves to block the entrance to the valley. Kragan had created his own tunnel in order to turn the defenders' northern flank.

Storm clouds boiled into the sky above them, rushing south toward the astonished Endarian soldiers. The sound of Rafel's battle horns caused Alan to rise in his stirrups and unlimber his crescent-bladed ax from where it and a round shield were strapped to his back. Cavalry doctrine frowned upon carrying a shield, since the thing's bulk made horse soldiers awkward in the saddle. But due to Alan's recent experience of having his horse shot from beneath him, he had ordered each member of his Forsworn to carry such a defense. He had also instructed his followers to leap from their mounts once they closed with the milling throng of enemies rather than present themselves as targets to be dragged down one by one. Once they were on the ground, shields would be additional weapons as they cut a path through Kragan's horde.

All along the front lines, flag-bearers echoed the high lord's command. Instead of the charge that Alan had expected, Rafel ordered his legion forward at a double-quick march, focused on keeping his legion together during the league-long advance toward the forming enemy. As he adopted Rafel's controlled pace, Alan glanced behind him, pleased to see that his Forsworn already had arms at the ready, be it sword, hammer, ax, or bow.

Far ahead, a round hole formed in the clouds, allowing a shaft of sunlight to strike a large group positioned forward of where Kragan's army had begun to deploy into combat ranks. The sunbeam clarified as the air around this collection of people transformed into a lens that gave Alan and the rest of Rafel's lead element a perfect view of those Kragan had pushed forward to meet them. Horror blossomed in Alan's gut as he recognized many of the people. These were the men whom Kragan had conscripted into service after his conquest of Tal.

Alan retained many fond memories of growing up in Rafel's Keep. As his eyes scanned the faces of the front ranks of Talian conscripts, a lump formed in his throat at the thought that he would soon be killing those whom he had formerly vowed to protect.

The shaft of light narrowed until it illuminated two large vorgs mounted atop the hideous werebeasts that were a cross between a horse and a wolf. And each vorg clasped a young blonde child seated in front of the saddle.

Oh gods! Earl Coldain's little girls.

From Alan's right front, the earl's enraged scream split the air. A new battle-flag command rippled along the line of his troops. Coldain signaled for his cavalry to charge, a command at odds with that which Rafel had given. Coldain's mounted assault would leave his five thousand infantry soldiers and the rest of Rafel's legion behind.

Even though Alan knew that this attack was a terrible idea, he and his Forsworn were under Coldain's command. Leaning forward in his saddle, he lifted his ax high and kicked his charger into a dead run. His battle yell merged with the cries of hundreds, only to be drowned out by the thunder of hooves pounding earth and stone.

—⁓—

Carol rode Storm beside Arn, the horses trotting in tandem toward the hillock that overlooked the enemy force flooding into Endar Pass from the west, almost unopposed. Having little experience using earth elementals, she had not imagined the scope of what Kragan and his wielders would accomplish on this day. Since Carol had not been able to see their powers at work, she had not been able to block their magical tunneling.

She eyed the gathering storm clouds, sensing the air elemental and lightning master Lwellen moving within those vapors. Semitransparent reds, blues, yellows, and greens shifted through the air that surrounded Carol as she shackled the minor elementals that would give her warning of any incoming arcane attacks.

Perhaps it was the static electricity in the air that sent a tingle along her skin. Or maybe it was her vision of the looming clash of magical forces that set her teeth on edge. Her father's curses pulled her gaze to where he sat on his mount, pointing northwest. Carol looked in that direction, unable to believe the sight that confronted her.

Earl Coldain's cavalry, five thousand strong, had broken away from the rest of the army. The soldiers leaned forward in their saddles as their horses raced toward the distant lines of Kragan's horde, their lances, axes, swords, and hammers angled toward the enemy force.

She couldn't understand it. What could have made Coldain defy her father's orders? The maneuver exposed Coldain's flanks. Even if the earl's cavalry managed to penetrate Kragan's front lines, they would find themselves surrounded, separated from the support that the rest of Rafel's legion would have provided.

Overhead, the storm clouds that had boiled up to block the sun parted just enough to allow a single shaft of golden light to spear downward, illuminating two vorgs mounted atop shaggy werebeasts. Carol felt a lump form in her throat as she saw whom they held in their arms.

She snared Nematomas, forcing the elemental to lens the air so that Carol could see the young girls better than through a far-glass. The twins' eyes glistened with moisture, their tears cutting trails down their dirty cheeks. Their ragged clothes were barely recognizable as matching pink dresses.

Wrath burned the thickness from Carol's throat as its heat spread from her chest into her temples. Kragan was using Coldain's daughters to bait him into a homicidal frenzy. And the wielder's plan had succeeded. For a moment Carol considered killing the two vorgs, but she could not do so without hurting the children held against their chests. And even if she could, the girls would fall and be trampled or ravaged by riderless werebeasts.

Fireballs streaked outward from Kragan's lines toward the charging cavalry, and Carol quenched them, leaving trails of steam that the chill wind dissipated as the horse soldiers galloped through. Then she saw the heavens open above Kragan's soldiers, pounding them with hailstones the size of lemons, a sudden barrage that must have been summoned by Vanduo, Coldain's azure-robed wielder of water elementals. But the storm did not target Kragan's front lines, lest it injure Coldain's daughters.

The two vorgs with the small captives turned their mounts and galloped back through forward troops to disappear within the follow-on forces. And as they did, Vanduo's hailstorm died. Carol refocused her air-lens, trying to see where the vorgs were taking the girls, but she lost them in the crush of enemy soldiers.

As Coldain's cavalry closed to within a hundred paces, the waiting army raised a forest of pikes, the butts of those spears anchored against the ground. Many of these fell under the volleys of arrows launched by the earl's mounted archers. Arrows darkened the sky as Kragan's archers answered, sending horses and riders tumbling across the ground to be trampled by their comrades.

Carol focused her vision on the pikemen, sending fire racing through their ranks, driven by a summoned gale. Sudden recognition broke her concentration. She knew some of these people. Cevas, a heavyset bald man who had owned a popular tavern in Hannington, stumbled forward as if he could no longer bear the weight of his armor. And there was Harl, the black-bearded blacksmith who had stayed behind with his family in the town below Rafel's Keep. He had made horseshoes for Shamir, the mare who had been a gift from her father. Now Harl rolled on the ground as fire consumed his beard and body. The sight sickened her.

She was killing people whose only crime was to have been captured and forced to serve in Kragan's army.

Her horse continued to trot toward the distant engagement. Carol scanned the mountainsides that formed the western wall of Endar Pass. Kragan's force had emerged a half league north of where the Endarians had concentrated their defenses. She estimated that several thousand vorgs had arrayed themselves behind thousands of conscripts from Tal, ready to kill any of the Talian slave-warriors who refused to fight against their brethren.

She considered launching magical attacks into these follow-on forces, but they lay in the direction in which the two vorgs had disappeared with Earl Coldain's daughters. Although she knew that she was falling into Kragan's trap, she could not bring herself to risk killing the two little girls. The fury that percolated through her blood made her temples throb with frustration. Targets had spread themselves across the battlefield before her, but the thought of killing more of her former friends and countrymen made her stomach heave.

She glanced at her father, his face an inscrutable iron mask as he directed a third of his cavalry to fill the gap created by Coldain's ill-conceived charge. Though his expression revealed nothing, Carol knew her father was seething.

There was little doubt that Coldain's five thousand cavalry would be surrounded and annihilated before the bulk of Rafel's troops could reach them. The knowledge that Alan's mounted company was with Coldain pulled forth a new dread from Carol, putting a quiver into her right hand and causing her to clench it almost as tightly as her left hand gripped Storm's reins.

Carol felt lightning gather within three separate clouds, but she redirected the triple spears away from Coldain's horsemen and the waiting enemy, cutting swaths through the ranks of Talian pikemen and archers. She shoved aside her revulsion as Coldain's cavalry crashed through the enemy lines.

Rising and falling in her saddle in rhythm with the trot, Carol moved closer to the high lord, feeling Arn ride up on her left. Right now she did not need his protection. What she needed was to find Kragan, to gain the focus required to penetrate the warding his strange amulet provided.

Where in the deep was he hiding?

—∞—

Slaken burned Arn's side through the thick leather sheath, its thirst for blood infecting him. Charna was out there, somewhere within the foul horde that poured into Endar Pass through its unnatural tunnels. Galad had described the commander of Kragan's army, leaving no doubt in Arn's mind that this was the she-vorg who, along with an unknown wielder, had butchered his father and mother.

Since that day, Arn had used every resource at his disposal to find Charna. Then, months ago, he had recognized her as he, John, and Ty rescued Kim from vorg slavers. Arn had come so close to killing the she-vorg, but she had slipped through his grasp twice.

After they tied their horses to a nearby pine, Arn stood atop the rocky hillock where Carol had positioned herself to best observe the combat. His view of the distant battle, toward which Rafel had his army moving at a double-quick march, bothered Arn. It wasn't just that fellow countrymen from Tal were busy massacring each other. Nor was it the way the vorgs waited in reserve for the battle initiated by Coldain's charge to work itself out.

Something else tweaked the small voice at the back of his mind.

What was out of place here?

Less than a quarter league now separated Rafel's legion from the battle. Within a handful of minutes they would enter the fray, hopefully in time to save some of Coldain's cavalry. As worried as the high lord must be for his son, he would not compromise his battle lines to save Alan. For good reason had the warlord earned his legendary reputation as a combat leader. His leadership was about to be further tested, since the friendly troops already locked in combat would prevent Rafel from making use of his archers prior to the assault.

Once again the call of his intuition distracted Arn, this time pulling his eyes to the Endarian lines a league to the southeast. With surprising speed the Endarian commanders had adjusted their formations, which now maneuvered to protect their northern flank from the vorg units that swarmed around them, attempting to encircle their enemies. The Endarian tactics seemed sound, yet the voice in Arn's mind had become a shriek. His eyes were drawn southward, toward what was now the Endarian rear.

High up on the slope, three hundred paces below the snow line, a cliff gave way, sending an avalanche of rocks bounding down the mountainside. The leading edge of the rockslide hit the rear of the Endarian forces, which had turned to confront Kragan's attack from farther to the north. The roiling earth swallowed hundreds of the warriors before they could flee its deadly path. Confusion swept the Endarian ranks as commanders struggled to reassert control.

Beside him, Arn saw Carol cry out, but the sound was lost in the deep rumble that shook the ground over which Rafel's army sprinted to Coldain's aid. Kragan's plan crystallized in Arn's mind. The northern assault by the Talian conscripts and the blatant display of Coldain's twins had been a feint, designed to divert Rafel's legion and disrupt the Endarian defenses.

As the landslide came to a halt, Arn saw through the rising pall of dust something that thickened the blood in his veins. Over the detritus left by the avalanche, thousands of vorg and human warriors poured out through a hole where the cliff had broken away.

—⁂—

Kim stood beside Galad on the battlefield, the queen having assigned her to be the master life-shifter supporting Galad's newly formed brigade of two thousand mist warriors. She wore the same color-shifting uniform as the rest of the Endarians on this front line.

The formation's shift in direction had been a rapid maneuver to reorient the force toward the threat that had appeared a league north of where the Endarians had anticipated fighting. From within the mountain wall that formed the western boundary to Endar Pass, thousands of men and vorgs emerged, threatening to turn the Endarian northern flank. That would isolate all of Endar's forward-deployed soldiers, cutting off any retreat to the fortress city within the lake.

In the distance, storm clouds roiled overhead, summoned by Kragan's wielders. The scent of ozone wrinkled Kim's nose. Fireballs arced across the sky only to ricochet off some unseen shield to engulf the enemy's own fighters. Her lips curled into a bittersweet smile. Carol was out there, supporting the sudden charge of thousands of Rafel's cavalry. But the knowledge that John fought alongside Rafel instead of being with her brought a dampness to Kim's eyes.

She understood. As princess, she had to be with her people during this fight. Although John had wanted to accompany her, he would be at a loss within the complicated mists that Galad would wield during the coming struggle.

South of Galad's mist warriors, twenty thousand of Endar's finest formed up behind his brigade, ready to deal death and destruction to Kragan's invading host. And Kim, along with the other life-shifters spread throughout this army, would heal as many of the wounded as possible, then send them back into harm's way.

Kim shifted her thoughts to the mental preparation that would enable her to be ready to take on the wounds of others while she performed the much slower healing that required her to funnel life from the abundant trees and other nearby plants into her own body. She would even draw the living energy from the tiny creatures that gave fertility to the soil. The vision of transforming this lovely place into a dead zone threatened to break her resolve.

She felt the ground shake as a dreadful rumble spun her around. High up on the mountain, just south of where her people's army held the field, the cliffs collapsed, sending a river of stone and earth plummeting down the steep hillside and into the rearmost ranks of the Endarian formations.

"No!" Kim heard her own scream as if from a great distance, so intense was her shock at seeing so many of her countrymen swept from the land of the living.

Through the thick cloud of dust that partially masked the southern slope, she saw the dim shapes of vorgs charging down the hillside toward the breached Endarian rear guard. A new fog flowed across the rearmost of the Endarian troops as one or more of the time-shapers worked to slow the onrushing enemy. Although it would not stop the attackers, those mists would provide a temporary shield from magical attacks. Since no elemental magic could cross a time-mist boundary, a wielder would have to enter the same area of time's passage as the Endarians in order to affect them with her spells.

She knew that time-mist defenses would not allow the queen's army to reorient itself to effectively meet Kragan's main assault. These Endarian defenders were not mist warriors, and attempting to maneuver such a large fighting force within time-mists would only heighten their confusion.

"Stay beside me," said Galad, his right hand squeezing her shoulder.

New time-mists spread outward from her brother. But almost as quickly as he disappeared in the haze, Kim felt herself emerge into the rychly zone as the mud of normal time sloughed off her. What she had left behind disappeared in pale fog while the mist she stepped into cleared as it enveloped her.

The speed with which Galad extended the mists startled her, his entire brigade appearing in a matter of seconds. To observers who watched from spots where normal time reigned, it would look as if the fog had swallowed Galad's troops. But to Kim and the others already within Galad's channel, his warriors emerged into the clear daylight of the hastened region. And that clearing extended east before turning back to the south.

Galad drew his sword from its sheath on his back, yelled a command, and broke into a run. Although she was hard pressed to keep up with her taller brother, Kim managed it, loping alongside him as he headed east along the path he had created through the rychly area. Considering the trauma of his recent maiming, Kim found his determination infectious.

He led her and the others across meadows and through forestland that separated the lake from the tunnel that was the southwestern entrance to Endar Pass. They looped wide of the Endarian formation before turning back to the southwest, toward Kragan's latest burrow through the mountains.

Of all the Endarian time-shapers, only Galad had displayed the ability to sense what was going on inside the mists that shrouded other timescapes. Her mind connection to her brother allowed her to pick up what he was seeing within those churning vapors. His intent became clear. Galad was going to thrust the knife edge of his brigade into the vorgs who had turned eastward in an attempt to encircle the Endarian army.

As they approached the fog bank that marked the end of Galad's rychly wielding, he halted and ordered his signal flagman to bring the brigade into assault formation in front of him, bows at the ready. Kim saw her brother reach back over his shoulder as if to grab an arrow from the quiver he no longer wore with the left hand he no longer had. The chagrined expression that flitted across his fine features almost caused her to reach out to comfort him. But the grim mask that he had worn since the accident returned, stopping her gesture before it began.

Kim took a quick look at the thick copse within which Galad had deployed his mist warriors, sensing the life that flowed through the trees, bushes, grasses, and soil. In mere moments she would find herself bathed in the agony of the wounded she would work to save. This time there would be no gradual trickle of life essence to make the healing process bearable. She would need to channel as much life magic as possible if she was to help Galad enable the bulk of the Endarian force to withdraw.

She sucked in a deep breath of chill air as Galad released the mists, letting them dissipate as his two thousand warriors reentered normal time and fired. They launched a dozen volleys, cutting a swath through the onrushing enemy. New mists flowed out from Galad as he used a combination of rychly and pomaly clouds to separate groups of Kragan's warriors from their compatriots and to maneuver his own troops to destroy the vorgs and brigands so isolated. Galad had managed to avoid engaging Kragan's wielders. In the midst of this close combat, the mist warriors exchanged bows for long swords and sabers.

And as Galad's soldiers fell, Kim moved among them, transferring her health to the wounded as she accepted their injuries into her own body. She could not restore a severed limb, but the healing of the wound shriveled part of her body until she could steal enough health from her surroundings to repair the damage inflicted upon herself.

Protected by a cadre of Galad's elite, she roamed the killing field. And wherever she went, the surrounding vegetation and soil beneath withered into dust.

She could not heal anyone within those areas she had already drained of life. She forced herself to keep moving, despite the endless torment that threatened to curl her into a whimpering ball. Each time she worked her magic, she sickened. The life essence of the foliage was too different from that of people or animals to allow for an efficient exchange.

A scream built inside Kim, but she refused to release it. On this day she would make Galad and her mother proud.

—m—

Galad was well aware that his left hand was no longer attached to his forearm, but the missing appendage felt as if it were on fire. Perhaps the sheer volume of the time-mists he was channeling was now chewing its way through the phantom limb in an attempt to consume the remainder of his disfigured arm. The prince angrily forced the distraction into the background of his thoughts, just as he did with the other minor wounds he had taken.

A glance at the princess left him shamed that he was taking notice of his own weakness. His sister was withstanding unrelenting torment as she absorbed the more serious wounds suffered by mist warriors. Her subsequent self-healing took longer. But instead of sympathy, anger rose up to clench his throat, anger at his mother for banning Kimber's use of necrotic life magic. And Galad was angry at Kimber for abiding by those restrictions.

A vorgish hand, glowing with summoned magic, fought its way through the mist wall. Galad's sword removed it at the elbow, then sliced through the neck that followed a snarling head into the rychly zone. And all around him, his mist warriors prepared to fight off the enemies who would trail their dying wielder.

—ɯ—

Alan leapt from his horse, an action that the members of his Forsworn replicated. His ax cut a glittering arc through the air, hissing like a snake as it sliced through the foes who had once been his countrymen. At the tip of his company's diamond-shaped combat formation, he pressed the attack, with Bill just behind him on his left while the scythe of Katrin's knives and Quincy's swift sword arm protected his right flank. Just to their rear, John strummed his bow so fast that its taut string acquired the pitch of a musical instrument as he placed his arrows through the shifting gaps between Alan's Forsworn fighters.

Each man who fell before him fertilized the fury that ravaged Alan's soul. The target of his wrath was not these innocents who had been press-ganged into this foul horde, rather the wielder who had spawned the war.

A fireball arced through the stormy sky toward him but was deflected as if someone had swatted it to the ground amidst the enemy troops. Alan had seen the results of Carol's immense will during the days of battle against the army of the protectors. Although he did not doubt that these wielders had abilities far beyond those of the evil priests, he would wager on his sister against all of them.

Kragan, however, was a different beast altogether.

For a moment the sea of soldiers who faced Alan parted just enough to provide a glimpse ahead. Two hundred paces to his front, entire companies of Earl Coldain's cavalry had been slowed to a walk by the sheer mass of foes crowded shoulder to shoulder against them. Although they forced their way forward, enemy arrows, spears, and ensnaring nets toppled an ever-increasing number of the mounted soldiers from their horses. Kragan's Talian conscripts hacked at the legs of Coldain's warhorses, sending them and their riders tumbling into the maelstrom. The horses' screams mingled with the howls of the wounded and the moans of the dying, forming a chorus so deafening that neither the clash of weapons and armor nor the thunder that rumbled overhead could drown them out.

It was toward the nearest of these isolated and surrounded groups that Alan led the men and women who had pledged their lives to him. The fanatical loyalty with which his Forsworn fought had been augmented by the weeks he had drilled them in tactics during their journey through the time-mists to reach Endar Pass.

Already those who fell back before the onslaught of Alan and his shaved-headed Forsworn betrayed the panic that his furious assault bestowed upon them. And as Alan's company cut its way forward, drenched in the blood of its foes, trepidation infected the Talians who witnessed their comrades' retreat.

Alan fell into a rhythm with shield, ax, and body. Bash, slash, advance . . . until he was walking on the bodies of the dead. To his right Kat dodged a sword thrust, taking a cut high up on her left shoulder as she sideslipped the strike to bury her dagger in the soldier's neck.

Less than fifty paces now separated Alan's fighters from an isolated group of hundreds of Coldain's cavalry. At their center rode Coldain's sixteen-year-old son, Garret. Kragan's fighters who found themselves between the two Coldain forces tried to escape to either side but were jammed up against their own troops as Alan's company hammered into them from behind. Seeing the panic induced by the bald and blood-soaked Forsworn, Garret Coldain signaled a new charge, and his horsemen surged into the enemy, who now fought against others of Kragan's horde blocking their escape.

A new sound penetrated the bedlam and pulled Alan's gaze to the southeast, the deep tone of Rafel's war horns signaling an assault. Lightning splintered the sky, ringing like sheet metal beneath a thousand blacksmiths' hammers. Fireballs bounded across the battlefield, chewing fiery paths through Kragan's Talian conscripts. And all the while, Alan worked his ax and shield until his sinews threatened to burst through his skin.

Having linked up with the half of Garret's three hundred who had been unhorsed, Alan yelled a command that shifted his company's diamond formation into a wedge. Coldain's men fell in behind, protecting his flanks and rear. And at the tip of this spear, Alan hurled himself into the foes upon whom fate had unleashed him.

—⟨⟨⟨—

John, having run out of arrows in his quiver, had slung the bow his father had so lovingly made over his head and shoulder. He now held his blood-coated saber in his right hand. The slender blade whistled through the air as gore from the enemies that Quincy Long cut down splattered his face, stinging his eyes and making it difficult to see. The blade's failure to make contact informed John of his miss.

The clatter of steel on steel and the cries of the dying for loved ones that they would not live to see again almost drowned out the rumble of thunder as magical forces fought for control of the storm clouds above. John pawed at his face with his left hand, restoring a blurry red view of his surroundings just in time to parry the spear thrust that would have impaled him. He lunged forward, his counterthrust piercing the man's stomach. His opponent dropped his spear, clasping both hands to the bloody hole in his gut in a failed attempt to keep his entrails inside.

Although the saber was not his weapon of choice, John was not unfamiliar with its use. But as he watched Alan and the tight knot of Forsworn around him wield their weapons, he felt like a neophyte. Quincy made expert use of his great height and reach, moving with a grace one would never expect upon first meeting the swordsman. Near him, Alan whirled the crescent-bladed ax that had once belonged to Ty with an unrelenting fury that split shields and bodies, his brawny chest threatening to split the chain mail shirt that draped it.

John took a cut on his right thigh that caused him to stagger backward, gasping at the pain that blossomed. He parried the bearded warrior's next thrust but failed to keep the man's sword from inflicting a deep cut on his left shoulder. John swung his blade in an arc toward the man's neck, only to have his opponent catch the blade in a notch atop his round shield. John heard the saber snap at the same moment that he felt it.

The enemy lunged forward, driving the tip of his sword into the center of John's chest with such force that it split the protective chain mail, stopping only when it encountered the linked chains that covered John's back. Agony such as he had never known exploded in John's upper torso. He barely felt the boot with which the bearded one kicked him free from the impaling sword. As John's back and head slammed into the ground, he gasped, feeling a bloody froth form on his lips as his chest spasmed in an attempt to get air. The sword had penetrated his right lung. He was drowning in his own blood.

He coughed and spit out a wad of phlegm. As the warrior who had stabbed him engaged a new target, John experienced a weird clarity as images, sounds, and emotions flashed through his brain.

Once again he saw Kim standing on the slaver's auction stage in the border town of Rork as Charna issued the winning bid. He watched a half-human, half-vorg bandit try to claim the bounty on Arn, identifying him as the wanted assassin Blade. John had not watched the ensuing fight, instead using the mayhem to help Kim escape.

Scene after scene of the subsequent months played out in moments. He saw himself, Kim, Arn, and Ty flee into the west, reexperiencing their capture and escape from nomads of the Mogev Desert. He watched the adventures that had transformed the trio of men into a band of brothers. But John had more than befriended Kim on the journey to return the princess to her homeland. He had fallen in love.

A haze crept over his vision as their wedding played out in his mind. The ceremony had taken place in the white citadel that towered in the azure lake's center. They had said the words of devotion as he gazed into her face. Her skin illuminated by the brilliant sunlight, her eyes glittering with moisture, he had leaned in to kiss his wife. Never again would he hold her close or taste her lips.

As his vision faded to black, John coughed again, feeling tears flood his eyes and trickle down his cheeks. He would not be able to tell Kim he loved her one last time.

8

Endar Pass
YOR 415, Late Spring

Kragan stepped through the opening that one of his earth elementals had created into the cloud-shrouded gloom within Endar Pass. He wanted to be closer to the distant fight, but that could not happen yet, not before Carol Rafel was nearing exhaustion. For now, he would use another method of viewing the conflict.

A moment's concentration activated his magical link to Charna, enabling him to see the battlefield through the commander's eyes and hear the combat through her ears, one of which had long ago belonged to the body within which Kragan had grown to manhood.

"Yes, Lord Kragan?" Charna's query sounded in his head.

"Show me the battle."

Charna shifted her head, and the distant view of the northern branch of Kragan's twin attacks swam into view. Through her Kragan summoned a magical lens to enhance the view of the hell into which he had thrust the Talians. Rafel's legion had formed the Endarian reserve force, but Kragan's feint far to the north had forced the high lord to commit his soldiers much earlier than he would have liked.

Rafel's attack was unorthodox. Several thousand of his cavalry had charged into Kragan's soldiers, throwing those twenty thousand poorly trained conscripts into disarray. No surprise that the rabble whom he had collected during his sacking of Tal put up a fight. While Rafel's legion was a disciplined throng, Kragan's threat to the families of his overmatched recruits would ensure that while some would try to defect, most would give their all.

The main body of Rafel's legion joined the battle, transforming the confusion within the ranks of the press-ganged Talians into desperation. The sight of brother killing brother kindled a warmth in Kragan's soul. Even the great Rafel had been unable to control Earl Coldain's wrath at the sight of his daughters held by a pair of vorgs.

Charna pulled her gaze back to where she stood, overlooking Kragan's army's main attack into the Endarian southern flank. All along the steep slopes, combat raged. Thousands of vorg warriors poured from the two nearby passages that Kragan's magic had burrowed through the mountains. This attack should have already encircled the Endarians, cutting them off from any attempt to fall back eastward to their stronghold in the lake. But they had swathed their troops on the southern flank in time-shaping fogs that blocked all external magical attacks.

Something about the way the southernmost of those miasmas swirled and flowed seemed too familiar to Kragan, something that curled his lips, baring his fangs. These mist warriors were commanded by the same time-shaping warrior who had delayed Kragan's army on its northward march toward Endar.

It was time to put that irritant to rest.

"Press your attack farther to the south," he told Charna. *"Draw the mist warriors away from the bulk of the Endarian army and destroy them first."*

"That risks allowing the Endarian main body to retreat."

"Only if our attack stalls. Put a dozen magic wielders in the front lines so they may be ready to cast spells as soon as they penetrate the time-mist boundaries. You have fought against that master time-shaper. When he falls, so will his mist warriors. Bring me his head."

9

Endar Pass
YOR 415, Late Spring

From the corner of his right eye, Alan saw the bearded warrior's thrust that impaled John. With a bellow of rage he wheeled around and charged, just as his new target kicked John off his sword and turned to meet Alan's onslaught. Dropping his own shield, Alan shifted to a doublehanded grip on the carved ivory handle of Ty's crescent-bladed ax.

As the bearded one raised his shield, the ax screamed through the air, splitting the round steel barrier, removing the man's left arm at his shoulder. The warrior's mouth opened in a shriek that Alan's next spinning blow ended as his ax cut the man in half at the waist.

Another enemy hesitated to fill the gap left by his dismembered companion, allowing Alan a quick glance at John's body. The archer Alan had liked since first meeting him in Areana's Vale lay faceup, his black eyes staring sightlessly at the churning sky, froth filling his gaping mouth. But it was the sight of the dirty tear streaks down each side of John's face that put a knot in Alan's throat.

One more hero who'd had the misfortune of being assigned to Alan's command had suffered the curse of the Chosen. Alan noted where John lay and rejoined the fray, fatigue vanishing as a fresh elixir of bloodlust flooded his system.

Today he would carve John's name into Kragan's horde.

—⚏—

Garret Coldain, astride his roan stallion, glanced over at his father. Earl Coldain's grizzled beard was beaded with the sweat that ran down his face and matted his shoulder-length brown hair. Miraculously unwounded, the earl led the few hundred of his cavalry who had survived the mounted charge to reach his twin daughters. The sight of Elena and Erica held by those mounted vorgs had stoked the fire in Garret's breast that had smoldered there ever since he had found his mother's bound and burned corpse in the remnants of Coldain's Keep.

Kragan had destroyed the Coldain family's fortress home, inadvertently launching the earl's tawny-haired son on a quest to find his father and inform him of Kragan's murderous deeds. He surveyed the combat that raged all around the faltering cavalry charge. The riders now found themselves surrounded. Garret realized that none of them would survive this day's fight, but at least he would give his all for his sisters.

Lightning crawled across the sky, illuminating a swarm of feathered shafts that descended from the clouds. Taras, his father's heavyset chief wielder, had broken his neck when his horse fell a few minutes ago, and there was nobody to shield them from the rain of arrows. The air hissed as horses and riders fell all around Garret.

A wet *thunk* followed by a slurping sound brought his head around. His father faltered in the saddle, an arm's-length shaft protruding from his throat, blood spurting from the wound in great gulps. Earl Coldain fell, and, despite rushing toward his father, Garret was unable to catch him. Garret leapt from his stallion to kneel beside his father's still-twitching body. He never felt the arrow that struck him behind his left ear, dropping his corpse atop that of the earl.

—⟋⟍—

Carol stood atop the rocky knoll that provided an unobstructed view of a goodly portion of the battlefield. To her west and south, glacier-capped mountains framed the killing ground that spread out before her. However, the forest and undulating terrain obscured the bulk of the Endarian army. But nothing hid the collapse of the southern cliffs, the resulting avalanche, nor the rush of vorgs and foul beasts that poured down those slopes toward the rear echelon of the Endarians.

"Dear gods!" she said, her chest feeling as if it had been strapped with iron bands. "Kragan is trying to separate us from the fortress."

"Yes," said Arn. "And they will succeed unless Rafel's legion can intercept them. It may already be too late. I don't think he can see what's happening to our south from where he's engaged the enemy."

Having lost sight of her father, Carol searched the murky sky for the carrion birds that always sensed battle and was rewarded with the sight of dozens of them circling beneath the lowering clouds. With a deep breath, she centered and established a mental link to one of the black-winged creatures, feeling the now-familiar juxtaposition of senses.

The battlefield swept far below her. Hunger filled her with need as she looked down on the dying men and animals that her host and its companions would soon gorge themselves upon. Exerting her will, she angled the bird toward the distant banner that marked Rafel's position on the battlefield. Then she saw him. Just as Arn had surmised, her father was focused on destroying the portion of Kragan's army that his legion had engaged. From where he sat on his mount, giving commands that his signal flagmen relayed to his subordinate commanders, a wooded ridgeline blocked his view to the south.

Although she had never established a direct mental link to her father, she did so now, knowing that it was likely to come as a shock to him.

"Father."

She felt him start in surprise but continued.

"This northern attack is a ruse. Kragan has opened other passages through the mountains along the Endarian army's southern flank. He seeks to encircle us."

She transmitted the view of the chaotic engagement almost a league to the southeast of where Rafel's soldiers now fought. Though her mind magic had astounded him, his reaction came with the clarity and swiftness that had built his reputation. Without bothering to address her, Rafel ordered the bulk of his legion to face about, leaving a rear guard to block the Talian conscripts while the rest of his force sprinted southeast toward the azure lake and the distant white bridge.

Carol released the connection to her father's mind, her sharp avian eyes drawn to the spot where several hundred of Earl Coldain's cavalry and supporting foot soldiers fought their way toward a much larger group of their comrades. Alan's small company of Forsworn stood out as much from the evident terror of those who faced them as from their bald, blood-splashed pates. The group fought with a fury that bordered upon insanity. At their front, Alan cut his way forward, dominating the surrounding battleground, a bull hurling aside the wolves who dared face him.

She felt an electric charge well up overhead, its counterpart forming on the ground just behind Alan. Carol ensnared Lwellen, overpowering the wielder who had previously controlled the air elemental, shifted the attractive ground charge, and released the lightning bolt on its unfortunate summoner.

The collective gasp that zipped across the field of battle wasn't an actual sound. When someone dies violently, the effect upon those who depended upon him is palpable. And when that person is a mighty leader, the number of those so affected is manifold. Carol did not see Earl Coldain fall with an arrow through his throat, but the effect upon those who observed it cascaded to their compatriots far faster than the news of their lord's death could have spread.

She sensed that shock in the minds of those far below her and traced the source of the combination of despair and glee that radiated outward through friend and foe. It drew her bird's eyes to the site of the tragedy at the heart of Coldain's command. The warlord who had been her father's loyal friend since the Vorg War lay on his back, his last feeble heartbeat spurting blood from the arterial wound. In a flying dismount, Garret landed to kneel at his father's side. Before she could act, another bolt buried itself in the young lord's skull, draping his corpse atop that of his father.

"No," she whispered, the spectacle having jolted her back to her own body.

"What is it?" asked Arn, who had stepped in to support her as she stumbled.

Carol fought off the despair that threatened to dissolve her self-control.

"Earl Coldain is dead. As is his son."

She looked into her husband's brown eyes, seeing the inner conflict against which he struggled, knowing its source even though Slaken prevented her from magically sensing his thoughts and emotions. She placed her right hand on his arm and gave it a gentle squeeze. Although she shrank from what she knew she must say, Carol forced out the words that tore a hole in her heart.

"I need you to go."

Arn's eyes widened and he took a half step backward, as if she had struck him. The sense of loss that accompanied her hand falling away from his arm tightened her throat.

"You cannot stay with me, wasting your talents as my personal bodyguard. Kragan has warded himself in such a way that I am unable to penetrate his protection. I fear that neither magic nor force of arms will prevail against this enemy. I need you to be the Blade that life has made of you. Find Kragan. Kill him."

She stepped in, placing her hands on the sides of Arn's neck, and softly kissed him, hoping that it was not for the last time. As she released her husband, two more words slipped from her lips.

"For me."

—⁓—

Arn watched Carol swing up onto Storm's back and handed her Ax's reins. Where he was about to go was no place to take the best horse he had ever owned. And the ugliness of the brute would draw unwanted attention. Three years had passed since he had liberated Ax from Charna's band of vorgs, but she would remember that horse should word of it reach her ears.

"Watch for my mind with yours," said Arn, his words causing Carol to arch an eyebrow.

"You know that I cannot. Despite how our minds have shared a strong bond before, Slaken blocks my ability to connect with you or even sense your presence."

"Every few hours," said Arn, "I will find a place to set Slaken aside so that you can contact me. If I am to work my way to Kragan within the short time that remains, I will need your ability to see through the eyes of the vultures in order to find him."

"I will watch for you," she said.

Carol leaned down in the saddle to kiss him, and he tasted salty tears at the corners of her mouth. But when she straightened in the saddle, her face was set in a stoic mask. For the first time he could remember, Arn found himself at a loss for words. He knew that she was correct to set him back on the path that destiny had paved for him. Yet to watch his wife turn and urge her mount and Ax into a canter toward the high lord's distant battle flag left him with an empty hole where joy had made its home.

Arn turned back to face the west, where the remnants of Coldain's cavalry and Rafel's rear guard stirred the cauldron. Despite being immensely outnumbered, the superior warriors had thus far blocked Kragan's milling throng from pursuing Rafel to the southeast. Having recovered from the shock of losing their earl, Coldain's men had turned and now fought their way forward in an attempt to link up with the part of Rafel's legion he had left behind.

Arn was not the only one who looked upon this scene and understood what was happening. The thousands of vorgs who had prevented the Talian conscripts from fleeing the battlefield now surged forward, killing the combat fodder who got in their way. The initial confusion of the thousands of enslaved recruits degenerated into utter bedlam, caught as they were between Kragan's hammer and Rafel's anvil.

Arn could not have asked for a better invitation. Chaos veiled an assassin as surely as lassitude. Striding down the hill, he slipped into the forest and turned north on a path that would swing him around the northern flank of Kragan's host.

Then he had only to await nightfall before taking his place within Kragan's horde.

—∽∾—

One moment Alan was killing his former countrymen, and the next he faced a multitude of battle-hardened vorgs. The number of his Forsworn who fought alongside him had dwindled to just over half their original number. And of those who remained standing, none were uninjured. Alan was unsure how much of the blood that drenched him came from his enemies and how much was his. Katrin, Bill, Quincy, and Kron were still among the living. If Alan had not been able to break through to link up with a brigade of his father's rear guard, neither he nor any of his people would still draw breath.

Once again he found himself under the command of Hanibal, whose leadership skill he could not deny. He had incorporated more than a thousand of Earl Coldain's surviving cavalry troopers, most of whom had lost their mounts, into his battle plan. The wielder Lektuvu never strayed far from Hanibal's side as he positioned himself to best observe the field of strife, directing her arcane ripostes to their best advantage.

What surprised Alan was the lack of wielders supporting the portion of Kragan's army he and his compatriots now confronted. Surely Carol had not killed them all. So where were they? Alan's ax struck another vorg to the ground as he deflected a spear thrust with his shield. Then the ax sang through the air to embed itself in the spear wielder's sternum. Alan yanked his weapon free as a trumpet issued a new command into the gathering gloom that foreshadowed sunset. Hanibal's front lines fell back through fresh reserve troops who closed ranks against the enemy.

For the last few hours, Hanibal had given ground, trading terrain to rest troops who were close to exhaustion. Alan knew the respite would not be a long one. Soon enough, he and the rest of his Forsworn would find themselves back at the front. In the meantime they would form a shield wall against archer attacks, bind each other's wounds, and quench their thirst from available waterskins.

Alan saw that the brigade's northern flank skirted the lake's south shore. Lightning crawled through the roiling clouds, drawing his gaze southward. The flashing radiance illuminated Lektuvu in her silver robe, hands extended toward a gap in Hanibal's defenses where the vorgs were attempting to bypass the brigade. Bolt after bolt interconnected in a lethal web that set that part of the forest ablaze. Lektuvu gestured again and wind roared off the lake, whipping the flames into an inferno that consumed all the vorgs who failed to retreat.

He made the rounds, checking the wounds of each of his warriors, clapping them on the shoulder and speaking words of encouragement.

Another of his company had fallen, leaving only seventy-one under his command. But none of the others gave him an accusing look. Why should they?

A horn sounded a different call to battle. This time there would be no exchange of positions on the front line. Hanibal had just ordered an all-out assault, a desperate move against a superior force. For this brigade there would be no steady fallback to the Endarian fortress in the lake. Tonight they would win their part of this battle or die.

10

A slow tremor built in Kim's hands as she attempted to heal the gaping forearm wound she had taken into her own body while healing one of Galad's archers. She had anticipated this. Despite the gloom as twilight surrendered to the night, she could see the devastation she had wrought on this meadow-bejeweled forest. If any plant was left alive along the path that Galad had opened in order to funnel the army back to the fortress, she could not sense it.

The miracle that Galad had accomplished on this day would shine through the annals of history. Her brother had channeled his miasmas with such complexity that Kragan's wielders had been unable to effectively weave their spells against the experienced mist warriors. Whenever the elementalists prepared their conjurations, his fighters would slip across a haze boundary through which no elemental spell could penetrate.

But neither Galad nor the half dozen other surviving time-shapers could shield the entire Endarian army. Those soldiers were inexperienced in traversing the time-mists, and they were unable to maneuver rapidly, bunched as they were for battle.

Galad noticed the blood seeping from her partially closed wound, concern filling his midnight eyes.

"What is wrong with your healing, Sister?"

"Look around us. There are no living plants from which I can channel the life energy."

Her brother's face hardened as he pointed to where his warriors had just moved to block an enemy advance.

"There are plenty of living targets to serve as a wellspring for your talent. Right now they are busy killing our people."

His sharp words recalled the memory of the teenage Endarian boy she had killed with forbidden life-shifting. The image of his battered and misshapen head as she had transferred a wild dog's wounds into his form seared her mind.

"The queen forbids it."

"The queen is not here. It is time for you to make your own decision. Will you let Endar fall, or will you help me prevent that catastrophe from happening?"

Overhead, lightning crawled across the sky, and Galad shifted the mists to engulf the vorg caster who had stood back from the combat, her arms extended toward the clouds. The electric glow disappeared into a different time domain.

A thick vorgish arrow struck Galad in the throat, a glancing blow that opened a spurting wound that he grabbed with his right hand in an attempt to slow the flow.

Kim froze as the archer nocked another arrow. Fury burned all indecision from her mind.

She opened a very different channel that connected her to Galad and the vorg simultaneously. The life transfer happened so swiftly that she felt only a moment's trauma as Galad's wound healed and opened in the enemy archer's throat. With a gurgling wail, the vorg fell, his arrow arcing away harmlessly into the gathering darkness.

Kim did not wait for Galad to rise. Rage powered her strides as she ran toward the combat. She stopped a dozen strides away from where hundreds of Endarians fought to prevent more vorgs from making their way out of the slowing pomaly mists. Opening her channel wide, she accepted churning rivers of pain as she healed friends by wounding foes.

Agony and wrath intertwined with horror in the shriek that rasped her throat. Even though each transference happened too quickly to form physical wounds on her body, the torture transported her to a world in which a horde of deep-spawn clawed her flesh with razor-sharp nails. The life essence that she channeled from one being to another gurgled within her. Along with the wounds she absorbed, her insides shriveled while she maintained the flow of energy into the target she was healing, leaving her parched with unbearable hunger and thirst. Her subsequent draining of life from her victim engorged her with such delicious euphoria that it left her lusting for more. The longing grew stronger each time she experienced the mixture of pleasure and pain.

Still, she did not falter. While Endarians still fell to killing blows that she could do nothing about, the mist warrior defensive lines, behind which she moved, firmed and held.

If she could endure until the utter blackness of the moonless night swallowed them, the mist warriors could break contact and flee through the time-mists back across the white bridge. She only hoped that her father's legion had secured the escape route.

—⁓—

Carol sat cross-legged near the arch that spanned the distance from the lakeshore to the Endarian fortress as thousands of Endarian soldiers crossed, many of them so grievously wounded that they had to be carried by their comrades. Her father had ordered her to concentrate her magic on countering enemy wielders rather than using attacks of her own. But to do that she needed to see the battlefield as he saw it. Since Rafel would be on the move among his troops, Carol could not remain at his side and muster the concentration her magical efforts would require. So she used his eyes instead.

She had startled him when she first touched his mind. The knowledge that she would need to ride along in his head, seeing and experiencing his thoughts and feelings, had caused the high lord considerable consternation before he agreed. She had been able to form the mental bond while within eyesight of her father. Once the link was established, she no longer needed to be within eyesight of the high lord to maintain it.

She diverted the lightning that snaked from the clouds into the horde of vorgs and brigands who fought to close the Endarian passage through Rafel's lines. Her skill controlling the beings from the elemental planes had grown to the point that she could sense the disturbance produced when other wielders summoned them. None of her enemies' minds could match her strength of will. Carol found it most efficient to just break their mental links with the elementals rather than drain herself with the effort of killing every wielder she encountered. She had no doubt that Kragan was holding off on a direct confrontation until she tired.

Several dozen of his spell casters had joined the fight. The two most powerful wore the magical amulets that Kragan had provided for them.

Since Vanduo had died fighting at Hanibal's side, only one of Rafel's other wielders remained alive. Her father had positioned him far forward so that he could help fight off those who sought to cut off the last Endarian units that had not yet passed through Rafel's lines.

Three worries nipped at the corners of her thoughts, trying to distract her from the critical tasks at hand. Arn, Kim, Alan. Although she knew that her husband was the killing machine the world had nicknamed Blade, he was wading into the heart of Kragan's army. An even bigger worry came from the knowledge that Alan had not yet made the passage of lines. Since she had dropped her mental link to her brother, she would have to see him to reestablish it. And Kim was missing as well.

Carol shook her head to dismiss such ruminations. Until the last soldiers had made their way back through Rafel's lines and he pulled his legion back within the fortress, she would continue to believe that her brother and half sister were alive.

As if in answer to her concern, her father's elation struck her. Hanibal and the remnants of his rear guard had just arrived. Alan and around five dozen of his Forsworn were among the survivors.

Carol felt tears of relief well up in her eyes, but that did not dim her vision. Her father stared outward and it was through those orbs that she watched the battlefield. Ripples in the elemental planes of air and fire pulled her attention back to her mission.

Maybe it was time to start killing Kragan's wielders after all.

—⚄—

Galad narrowed the channel of the rychly mist within which he led the thirty-seven of his mist warriors who had survived the desperate fight to prevent Kragan's throng from cutting off the Endarian army's escape route. He carried Kimber over his left shoulder, supported by his handless arm. That distraction made it harder to wield the mists, but he would allow no other to carry the sister who had suffered horribly so that this night's sacrifice would not be in vain. But the sight of his sister's face, just before she had collapsed, was stuck in his mind. If he had not known better, Galad would have sworn it was an expression of erotic rapture.

The brittle branches of the dead forest through which he moved reached out for him through the darkness, calling him to join them. And had it not been for Kimber, he already would have.

Sensing what lay beyond the fog that surrounded the path along which he led his comrades in arms, Galad maneuvered along the narrowing gap that Rafel had held open for the retreating force. But now that the bulk of the army had already made this passage through the high lord's lines, the opening was snapping closed. Minutes passed in the normal world while Galad's retreat through the rychly zone had taken more than an hour.

And then, through the hazed boundaries that surrounded his group, he saw that they had made it through the portal within Rafel's defenses. He slowed his stride and brought the remnants of his brigade to a halt before dispelling the rychly and surrounding pomaly mists that he channeled. All around them, Rafel's legion appeared startled at the sudden appearance of this battered band of Endarians. Galad was too wrung out to care. Then Rafel was at his side, tenderly taking Kimber into his own arms.

"Gaar!" he yelled. "We've done all that we can out here. Withdraw my legion into the fortress."

Then the high lord turned and strode toward the white bridge and fortress that were bathed in the eerie glow of the lightning that splintered the sky. Prince Galad and his limping band of exhausted warriors fell in right behind him.

Today he had watched the dismemberment of Endar's last brigade of mist warriors.

As he stepped from the southern shore onto the arching bridge, Galad lifted his eyes to the mighty time stone walls and the four towers that scraped the sky behind them. A question born of despair accompanied the sight.

Would tomorrow bring Endar's fall?

11

Endar Pass
YOR 415, Day 1 of Summer

Kragan stepped out of his tent atop the rocky knoll he had chosen for his privacy and a view of the battlefield. The morning sunlight glinted off the azure lake that surrounded the ivory fortress. Yesterday he had come very close to destroying the Endarian army. Only the master time-shaper and his mist warriors had prevented Kragan's horde from surrounding the bulk of the Endarian forces. Rafel had held open the breach through which the Endarians had escaped.

Commander Charna had ordered a halt to the attack after the enemy had retreated into their citadel. Such a hasty nighttime assault upon a well-prepared defensive bastion would have resulted in unnecessary losses with minimal gain. Instead Charna had set up camp, allowing the remaining tens of thousands of Kragan's vorgs and conscripted human soldiers to make their way through the tunnels to fill the fishbowl called Endar Pass.

All through the night, Kragan's wielders had hammered at the fortress within which Carol Rafel sheltered. The knowledge that her defenses had held despite the broad assortment of enchantments thrown against those ramparts did not surprise him. Neither had it surprised the primordial lord whose body Kragan shared. They merely wanted to deny her rest.

As he scanned the land south and east of the lake, a broad grin bared his fangs. The Endarian life-shifters had drained the formerly lush environment, leaving behind a dead zone that would remain lifeless for centuries. Kragan could not have done a better job himself, even if he could still connect to the source of his life-shifting powers on the far side of the Brinje Ocean.

The view was the reason he had ordered his cadre of magic wielders to clear the clouds from the skies, to give the Endarian defenders on those high walls and in their towers a perfect vista over the desolated land. Knowing his enemies as well as he did, Kragan had no difficulty visualizing the horror with which that vista smeared their souls. Their awareness that their own life-shifters had created a panorama of desolation made the picture all the sweeter.

Kragan opened his mental link to Charna.

"Order our wielders to renew their attacks. I think the Endarians and their friends have had enough sunshine for now."

Her growl carried equal hints of pleasure and anticipation. *"Certainly."*

"How many catapults are in place?"

"Only thirteen of our fifty are ready to launch," replied Charna. *"Most were toward the rear of our column and have just arrived. Do you wish me to begin the barrage with what we have?"*

"Gather our enemy's dead, cut off their heads, and hurl their bodies into those walls. Paint those white fortifications with the blood and offal of the Endarians and their human allies."

"And the heads?"

"Send them over the walls to bounce and roll through the courtyards and battlements."

Once again Kragan heard the elation that infected Charna's answer.

"Immediately, Lord Kragan."

He broke the link to his commander. Within moments clouds boiled into the sky. Wind, rain, hail, and arcing fireballs pelted the Endarian fortifications, only to be deflected from their intended targets. He did not doubt that Carol could also provide shielding from the detritus that the catapults would sling. No matter. Even Carol could not fight an army the size of his. And every additional action Kragan forced her to take would exact a toll.

With Kaleal's arcane power merged with his own, Kragan would sense her fatigue. When she was at her weakest, they would strike at her and she would counter. Only that unique combination of mind magics could serve up the entire world to him. Once again, the Scroll of Landrel would prove true.

Carol sat on a comfortable pallet within the tallest of the Endarian towers, legs crossed, staring through the south-facing window. She looked out upon the battlefield that spread out beyond the citadel's outer walls. She had not slept since the night before last, and the fatigue of fending off the unending magical attacks continued to drain her. Whereas she had accomplished a similar feat when she had defended Areana's Vale from the army of the protectors, this time Kim was not at her side funneling life energy.

Carol had done her best to push back all the worries that tried to hammer their way into the forefront of her thoughts. But the news of the trauma that had incapacitated Kim frightened her. The queen's reaction upon learning of the use of necrotic magic had been more disconcerting. Carol had seen a look of disgust transfix Elan's face as she stood over her daughter's unconscious form. The queen had merely stared and then turned away without even delivering a caring touch, leaving Rafel and Carol stunned in her wake. That picture remained in Carol's mind, again shaking her admiration of Endarian society.

This morning's sunrise had revealed a once-beautiful landscape turned to desolation. Kim and the other life-shifters had been responsible for that. But Queen Elan bore some of the blame, having refused to allow those few, like Kim, who were capable of transferring the life essence from their enemies to heal the wounds of Endar's defenders.

Kragan had called upon the air elemental Nematomas to usher in that sunlit view to drive a stake into the heart of every Endarian who saw the bleak wasteland that Kim and the other life-shifters had left behind. From the emotions that roiled throughout the ivory fortress in the lake, Carol knew that he had been wildly successful. The terrible loss increased the rift that had resulted in the attempted assassination of Elan. According to Kim, half of the Endarian High Council now blamed their ruler for the abomination beyond their walls. Even some of her ardent supporters were wavering.

With a renewed burst of will, she forced herself to center, casting aside the weariness causing her to lose focus. Carol blocked the weak attempts to break through her magical barriers. She forced herself to avoid trying to interdict physical objects launched at and over the fortifications, leaving it to the defenders to counter such attacks with ballista and catapult volleys of their own.

Kragan's game had been clear from the beginning. He feared confronting her on equal terms, so he needed her to exhaust herself defending against a multitude of lesser challengers. Knowing that, she could not afford to extend herself in areas where others could wage their own fight.

A sudden familiar tug on her consciousness pulled a sigh of relief from her mouth. Arn's presence blossomed in her mind. He had set Slaken aside, thereby revealing himself to her. Dangerous. If she could sense him, so could Kragan. Of course, she had been actively watching for him to set Slaken aside, something that Kragan would never expect him to do.

Keeping a part of her mind focused on maintaining her protections of the Endarian citadel, she sent her question to his mind.

"Where are you, my love?"

"Take a look for yourself," he answered her.

She intensified the mental link with her husband. The sight of Kragan's monstrous army from within was far more horrifying than the distant view from the tower in which she sat. Vorgs hammered their chests all around Arn as they howled a battle chant that built toward frenzy. Arn sat in the driver's seat of a supply wagon, wearing the shoddy leather armor of one of Kragan's human mercenaries. Arn cracked the reins, bringing the team to a walk that forced the vorgs to clear a path.

"Where is Slaken?" she asked.

"Sitting right here on the seat beside me. The vorgs unloaded the combat supplies, and I'm heading back to the supply train to pick up another load."

"But they won't know you."

Arn's mental laugh helped erase her worry. What did she know of an assassin's methods?

"Last night I killed a driver and took his wagon. Just before sunrise I spotted other empty wagons headed back to the rear and fell in behind them. Nobody cares who's hauling these supplies. Someone fills an empty wagon, tells you where to deliver it, and sends you on your way."

"What can I do to help you?"

"Show me where Kragan's headquarters is."

"I don't know its location," replied Carol.

Arn paused for a moment to look up at the sky.

"If you take control of one of the carrion birds, can you show me what it sees?" he asked. *"Every army has its patterns. I will recognize his head-quarters by the activity within and around it."*

"Even among all these teeming tens of thousands?"

"The differences will stand out to me."

Carol looked through Arn's eyes at the hundreds of vultures that circled beneath the murky clouds. She selected one of these and let her consciousness flow into the bird while maintaining a partial link to Arn.

From this viewpoint she could see almost the entire horde, and its true scale frightened her. What she had seen during yesterday's combat had been only a fraction of the host that had poured into the basin throughout the night. As she turned the vulture's eyes toward the southwest, she could feel Arn's surge of excitement.

"There," he thought. *"I want a closer look at the encampment along that ridgeline several leagues to the southwest. Can you fly us that way?"*

"I can do better than that."

Carol lensed the air as she had yesterday, turning it into a virtual far-glass. The bird's view magnified everything, making the distant ridge appear only a half league away.

To her untrained eye, the encampments there appeared much the same as others she had seen. But she felt Arn zero in on the westernmost of these.

"That's the one. Thank you, darling."

Carol felt the tension build within Arn as he framed his next request.

"I know how tired you are," he thought. *"But I need you to hold on until I set aside Slaken again. At that moment you will see Kragan through my eyes so you can attack him directly."*

"Remember, he wears a ward that I cannot penetrate," Carol replied, feeling her jaw tighten in frustration.

"Yes, but if the amulet prevents your mind magic from connecting to its wearer, it will also block Kragan from casting his mind magic on you. From the day when I saw that monstrous statue of you that he built beneath the city of Lagoth, I've known that he's determined to destroy you. He will remove the ward when he believes you're too tired to defeat him."

Carol shook her head, as if he could see her denial.

"Kragan will hurl his horde against these walls today. By the time you get close to him, I may be too exhausted to contend with the merger of his and Kaleal's minds."

"I don't need you to defeat Kragan," thought Arn, who failed to block his concern from Carol. *"I just need a distraction. Can you do that?"*

The vision that filled her mind took her breath away. For a moment she saw Arn step from the shadows and drop Slaken as Kragan spun toward him. If her response came a moment too late, her husband would die at the foul wielder's hand. She shoved the fear aside, knowing that Arn had experienced it too.

"I will be ready," she replied.

Carol severed her link with the vulture and allowed a gentle caress to pass from her mind into Arn's.

"Come back to me," she thought.

"Count on it."

Then she felt Arn reach for Slaken, and her link to her husband winked out, leaving Carol sitting in the white tower, hollow and alone.

—⁓—

Alan stood atop the mighty outer wall, flanked by Bill and Katrin. An Endarian life-shifter had healed the latter of the most serious of her wounds. Due to the drain associated with their lifesaving work, the healers rationed life energy, returning as many warriors as possible to battle readiness rather than restoring them to full health. Even so, the lawns, shrubberies, trees, and gardens within the fortress walls already resembled dead zones. The lovely, verdant setting had been transformed into a leafless wasteland, filled with brittle, lifeless limbs and branches, a graveyard radiating despair. Things that had once been vibrant plants had crunched beneath Alan's boots as he made his way to his current place of duty.

True to form, Commander Hanibal had placed Alan and his Forsworn atop the city wall, above the Endarian citadel's main gates in the position likely to be the center of the enemy assault. A fitting spot for the Chosen and his remaining followers.

Alan leaned through a crenel to peer down at the army that had massed on the south shore of the lake, a mere three hundred paces from these walls. What were they waiting for? The barrage of body parts and entrails that the vorgs had flung at and over the walls had ended, only to be followed by a cascade of rocks and boulders. The missiles could not damage the time stone battlements, but they could kill or maim the defenders. The Endarians answered the attacks with ballistae and catapults of their own.

"Look there," Kat said, placing a hand on Alan's arm, pointing.

Along the lakeshore, the crowd of vorgs parted, allowing a gray-robed she-vorg to step through the gap. The wielder passed one hand outward toward the lake, transforming its surface from water into an ice sheet that spread rapidly across to the rocky shore atop which the Endarian citadel rose. Carol's answer came from the tallest of the towers behind Alan. A fireball the size of a wagon shot down toward the wielder. But instead of striking the one who was Carol's target, it was deflected into the vorgs behind the robed one. Their screams failed to pull the grin from the she-vorg caster, who walked out onto the ice sheet, summoning a funnel cloud from the churning sky.

Alan's eyes swept the front ranks of Kragan's army, seeing dozens more wielders step out onto the lengthy shoreline to direct a torrent of destruction toward the white fortress.

"They're trying to kill your sister," Kat said.

Alan watched in awe as lightning, fireballs, hail, rain, and howling winds reached out toward him. Somehow, despite the number of wielders arrayed against her, Carol's defenses held, deflecting the raging magic. From his lofty perch, Alan saw a cyclone wreathe the fortress city only a few dozen paces outside the battlements. The bright light that had bathed his face in the morning retreated, leaving an eerie twilight that raised his hackles. He squinted, trying to see what lay beyond the downpour, but not even the dazzling flashes of lightning could illuminate anything beyond the wall cloud that had dropped down to curtain the lake.

The thunderclaps merged into a deafening crescendo that caused some of the soldiers who manned the wall to cover their ears with their hands. A sudden stillness froze the clouds in place, stopped the wind, and brought a silence that seemed even louder than the previous cacophony. For a handful of heartbeats, nothing happened. Alan tightened his grip on the haft of his ax, and the surviving dozens of his Forsworn hefted their weapons on either side of him.

Then, by the thousands, Kragan's army charged from the fog and across the hip-deep waters in the magic-free zone Carol had created just beyond the lake's near edge. All along the ramparts, ladders hit the walls, despite the thousands of arrows and stones the defenders launched down onto the vorgs, brigands, and the ten-foot-tall gray-skinned grun mercenaries who hauled the siege equipment into place.

"How?" asked Bill.

"Across the ice," said Alan. "Under cover of the storm."

A ladder hit the wall near Alan and lodged in two crenels. He looked down to see dozens of vorgs racing upward, set his shoulder against the tree trunk that formed one of the twin rails, and heaved as several of his soldiers rushed in to help him. A thick arrow grazed his left shoulder as he launched the ladder outward, sending it tumbling onto the enemy archers who had formed ranks to fire at the defenders atop the wall.

From the direction of the bridge, a massive battering ram rumbled toward the main gate, pushed by dozens of gruns shielded from arrows, stones, and oil by a deck of thick planks. A scream from Alan's left turned him toward trouble. An enormous vorg crested a ladder and swung his war hammer into a muscular Endarian with such force that it lifted the woman from the wall and splattered her corpse into the courtyard below. The thing's next blow split the skull of Colin Jalos, one of Alan's newest recruits. As the warrior stepped out onto the top of the wall, a dozen of his fellows scrambled onto the ramparts.

Alan's scream of wrath propelled his legs toward this new enemy. Every muscle in his body corded with hatred for Kragan and the tide he had unleashed in his sick desire to kill Alan's sister. If they were all to die here on this day, he would extract a toll in gore. If the Dread Lord summoned him and his Forsworn to the land of the dead, he would drag his foes into the dark alongside him.

Tossing aside his shield, he waded into his foes whirling the ax with both hands. Its crescent blade rent shield, armor, skin, and bone. He ducked under the whistling war hammer and swung his ax, only to have his wrist caught in a brawny grip. Instead of wrestling the ax hand free, Alan knocked aside the vorg's war hammer, sending it sliding along the escarpment. He grabbed the vorg's throat with his left hand and squeezed, lifting his assailant into the air. The warrior kicked out at him, but Kat's quick thrust spilled the vorg's guts down Alan's chest, bathing him in stench and offal.

Alan flung the dying body over the wall and onto those climbing a ladder toward the bulwark. The red haze of the battle rage that he had been trying so hard to control misted his vision and washed away fatigue. Great fountains of crimson splattered all those who fought alongside him and washed over the enemies who struggled to climb up onto the wall. And as he fought, the pulse that pounded Alan's temples drowned out the din of battle.

—⚬—

The minds of the dozens of wielders who had stepped forward along the lake added their power to the combined might of those against whom Carol already contested. The suddenness of this combined push against her magical barrier caused it to warp inward.

Carol summoned the reserves of power that she had been saving for her coming clash with Kragan and Kaleal's joined minds, dismissing the worry that scrabbled at the base of her brain. She could not allow this continuous assault to escape retaliation. These casters had shown themselves physically. Now Carol would exact retribution.

She centered, allowing her consciousness to soar into the void where those rancid minds shone among the tens of thousands of her enemies like signal fires in the night. One by one she linked to their psyches, snuffing out each wielder's connection to the denizens of the ethereal planes. Each opponent struggled to thrust her from his or her mind but succumbed to terror and death as Carol shredded the consciousness within.

From one to the next, she ripped through their ranks, failing to penetrate the wards of only four of Kragan's wielders. Despite her failure, she felt their fear as their compatriots crumpled to the sandy lakeshore all around them.

Her satisfaction at crushing the foes who sought to destroy her and everyone she loved faded to a new apprehension. The effort required to overwhelm a human mind was vastly greater than that required to control an elemental. Her rage had caused her to cross the line that prudence would have drawn.

She had fallen for Kragan's bait.

A lead cape of fatigue settled on her shoulders. As if she had called out to her husband, Arn touched the corner of her thoughts, her link to the man she loved forming in her mind of its own accord. He had once again set his blade aside. His voice whispered in her head.

"Stay with me, love. I need everything you can give right now."

The realization that Arn was asking for the distraction she had promised him leached hopelessness into her soul. Her pride had drained her such that she now had no hope of offering a suitable challenge to Kragan and Kaleal. The vision of Kaleal's muscular body standing atop a bare hilltop filled her sight.

Her memory of Arn had saved her then. Perhaps her lover would come through for her one more time. If he was to do so, she had to open herself to the devastation that the Kragan-Kaleal pairing could unleash. Carol clenched her fists so tightly that her nails dug into her palms, using the pain to gain the focus the summoning would require. She sent to Arn.

"Find cover, my love. I give you my all."

For the first time ever, she summoned a quartet of formidable elementals, one from each of the planes of fire, earth, water, and air. Through Arn she wrapped the supernatural beings in a grip that pulled wails of agony from the denizens of the astral planes. Then she hurled their magic at Kragan.

12

A mental shock wave rippled through the elemental planes as Carol shredded the minds of Kragan's wielders. Kragan experienced the cacophony of her mind magic as the rumble of a distant storm. For one individual to brandish so much force should have terrified him. Instead it brought a smile to his lips. His sense of the toll that her effort must be inflicting upon her was like the smell of victory.

In a gambit that was now about to net him the ultimate reward, Kragan had ordered every one of his sorcerers to reveal themselves, hurling all their combined might at Carol and those she protected. Kragan had known that their wills could not match that of the prophesied witch. And she had not been able to resist the lure.

Carol had just killed all but four of those Kragan had hurled against her.

Kaleal's throaty growl rumbled in Kragan's head.

"It is time."

"Yes," said Kragan.

In one swift motion, Kragan ripped the amulet free and tossed it aside.

—⚡—

Wearing the color-shifting Endarian uniform he had scavenged from a dead mist warrior, Arn watched Kragan from a desiccated stand of brush less than fifty paces away. Surrounded by an entire army and having melded himself with the primordial Lord of the Third Deep, Kragan believed he needed no protection.

Arn had set Slaken in the notch created by a crooked tree branch, allowing Carol to see Kragan through his eyes. But as her mind touched his, he found himself swept away in a roiling mass of deliriums that grappled with each other for dominance.

As if through frosted glass, he saw Carol seated cross-legged on a cushion inside a tower, her face a mask of concentration and horror. She stood up, walked to the open archway, spread her arms wide, and plummeted into the courtyard far below. Arn clenched his teeth to stifle the yell that tried to claw its way from his throat.

The scene shifted. Once again Carol stood inside the tower, her fingers balled into fists, her face a death mask of concentration. The air around her rippled, forming barely visible talons that clawed their way through the invisible shielding that protected her. Then her legs collapsed, dropping her to her knees and pulling a tortured moan from her lips. Her eyes widened, and to Arn, it seemed that she saw him watching her die. Then those ethereal nails ripped out her pretty throat.

One after another, a new vision replaced the last. In what seemed an endless procession, Arn watched Carol, Alan, Kim, Galad, Rafel, and Queen Elan die in a hundred different scenarios, finding himself helpless to alter the nightmares.

Arn felt himself pulled back into the present. Lightning branched through the clouds that swathed the day in rumbling twilight. Kragan stood out in the open, his body contorted as if he were lifting a great weight. The jaws in his feline face were clenched, his lips drawn back into a snarl, his slitted golden eyes locked on the distant ivory citadel as a mighty rumble built all around him. Great boulders flew through the air to strike at the wielder. Fire erupted around the primordial body, heat singeing Arn's eyebrows despite the boulders he hid behind. The wind howled, forming a funnel that whipped the flames into a whirling tower. Clouds released a focused torrent of rain into the fire that turned the water into superheated steam.

When the cataclysm subsided, Kragan was left standing in the center of a scorched black circle twenty paces wide, unharmed.

A realization dawned on Arn.

Landrel's prophecy was wrong. Carol could not kill Kragan.

That was just fine with Arn. Just as he had promised, Blade would exact his own vengeance.

—◆—

Across the league and a half that separated Kragan from his nemesis, he felt her psyche bind to his with a suddenness that surprised him. How had she responded so quickly to his presence? It was as if she already had eyes upon him.

With a roar he cast off the momentary dread as he and Kaleal met her assault. For several moments the potency of her magic threatened to break through the impenetrable shielding that he and Kaleal held in place. As stones battered that wall of solidified air, a firestorm whirled around it. The wind wailed as scorching steam tried to claw its way through Kragan's defenses.

Then Carol's exhaustion manifested itself. With a surge of satisfaction, Kragan crashed through her defenses and followed the mental link back to her body, forcing her to retreat into the shell of herself. Kaleal shifted their vision into the astral plane, letting the physical world fade into nothingness, the mighty fortifications atop which Carol stood evaporating around her. Carol floated in the vast emptiness, a beacon of light surrounded by a shimmering sphere that frayed at the edges.

"She is mine!" Kaleal said.

Kragan did not bother to argue. In mere moments Carol's will would fail. The thought filled him with a rush of passion, for victory was within his grasp. All he needed was for Carol to take the action that a veiled cipher within Landrel's Scroll foretold. Then the world would be his.

—⁓—

She had come so close but had failed to deliver the killing blow. Now Carol teetered on the verge of collapse as her defenses crumbled before Kragan and Kaleal's assault.

An odd itch tickled the recesses of her brain. Familiar, yet faint. The distraction carried a sense of urgency that threatened to disrupt her focus. There it was again, a sensation that she could not quite understand. It was not Arn. Her link with him had dissipated when she attacked Kragan.

No. This was a physical sensation that her centered mind should have shut off. Someone had placed a gentle hand on Carol's shoulder and then moved away so as not to break her concentration.

A subtle change crept upon her, a slithering coolness that drank of her exhaustion. It slowed the spread of her fatigue but was unable to erase the weariness. Carol felt the link with her half sister take effect, Kim's presence bringing a sense of relief that she was no longer alone. Yet she also felt terror, knowing that Kim risked the same terrible fate that Kaleal would soon inflict on Carol.

Kim's gentle words whispered in Carol's head.

"Fear not, my sister. We are not alone."

A new mental link snapped into place, chaining Carol, through Kim, to Galad, combining their three arcane talents—mind magic, life-shifting, and time-shaping—against Kragan and Kaleal's mystical onslaught. For the first time since her counterattack had failed, hope blossomed in Carol's soul.

Her enemies cranked their mental vise ever tighter despite the life energy that Kim funneled into Carol from enemies atop the wall beneath the tower. All she needed was a few moments of relief to restore her concentration. The conflagration of the conjoined minds of Kragan, Kaleal, Kim, and Carol whirled her through the void, and she was unable to reestablish her centered state.

Then she felt Galad join the fray, channeling the time-mists to surround her tower and expel Kragan and Kaleal from the psychic bond. Another shift stopped Galad from completing the mists as Kragan redirected his attack upon Kim's brother. The void within which Carol's light mingled with the others frayed at the edges, allowing tendrils of red to bleed into the black.

Carol focused her shielding so that it encased only Galad, Kim, and herself, leaving the fortress defenders to fend for themselves against Kragan's four surviving casters and the horde that battered at the citadel. Galad's time-mists failed to close completely, leaving a hole that left her locked in the grip of the Kragan-Kaleal mind link. Carol strengthened her own binding to Galad and Kim. As she did so, the mind storm created by the five interconnected psyches caused them to coalesce into one entity.

Using a variation of the technique she had long ago mastered within Misty Hollow, Carol stepped across the boundary into deep meditation. Normally she stood alone in a vast, black emptiness. But now Kim and Galad joined her on the astral plane, their hands linked to form an outward-facing circle. A globe of purest white enveloped them. But despite her best efforts, she could not quite complete the globe.

From the inky blackness that surrounded the trio, a red-veined black tendril wormed its way inward, splitting into three tentacles. Like snakes they reached out to wrap themselves around each of the siblings' heads. As they made contact with Carol-Kim-Galad, the bodies of the trio dissolved into churning mist, contaminating the uniform white glow. Inside the sphere, the whiteness boiled as tiny veins of red and black pulsed shadowed energy into their shared existence.

The Kragan-Carol-Kaleal-Kim-Galad mind churned, channeling Galad's rychly and pomaly mists in opposite directions and amplifying them a thousandfold. It felt as if an ice spear had plunged into the base of Carol's skull, and every ounce of her will was needed to prevent Galad's brain from overtaxing itself. In one momentous act, Carol directed the flow of Kim's healing into the part of her brother's mind that supported his mystical conduit.

With a start she sensed Kragan's sudden elation. A horrific realization shattered the meditation, sending a shudder through Carol's body and pulling a moan from her lips.

"No."

—⁂—

When Kragan felt Carol strengthen her mental link to the Endarian time-shaper, he wanted to roar with joy. This had been his true target all along.

All of the necessary elements were now locked into place. Kragan-Kaleal hurled a mental battering ram into the mix, implanting within Galad a vision of the time-mist barrier that surrounded the Endarian Continent. Kragan picked a particular place for Galad to target, fended off Carol's attempt to stop him, and forced the time-shaper to open a channel wide.

A shaft of accelerating mist shot out through the open archway as if launched from a ballista. On the opposite side of the room from where Carol sat, a counterbalancing pomaly time stone solidified.

Kragan fought off another of Carol's counterattacks and waited for the shaft formed of accelerating time-mist to reach its distant target.

Kaleal spoke inside Kragan's head.

"Her attacks grow stronger with each passing moment. We must break our link."

"Not yet," replied Kragan, despite his growing sense of dread. How could Landrel's prophesied witch's mind magic be so potent after all the sorcery she had expended?

Kaleal's roar of fear-laced rage filled Kragan's head. A white-hot poker seemed to have found its way into Kragan's skull, yet he refused to break the psychic connection to the young woman.

When the time-shaft struck the mist barrier that surrounded the Endarian Continent, the sudden restoration of Kragan's link to the source of his life magic knocked him to his knees and severed his bond to Rafel's daughter. So many years had passed since such power had filled him that he had forgotten the ecstasy that accompanied the rush.

Kragan had accomplished what the master Endarian time-shapers who had sacrificed themselves outside of Lagoth believed impossible. He had punched a hole through the distant time-mist barrier and, in so doing, made himself whole once more.

With a low growl of satisfaction, Kragan rose to his full height just as a flash of movement pulled his head to the right. The hurled dagger came to a stop an arm's length from his throat, caught in the grip of the air elemental he had summoned. Kragan thrust the weapon back at his attacker, but the elemental failed to reach its target, banished back to its mystical plane by powerful wards. Kragan recognized the foe who advanced toward him, despite his camouflaged uniform and hood.

"Blade!"

The word rumbled from his throat like a curse as Kragan's claws unsheathed themselves. He needed no magic to kill this little man.

Kragan leapt forward, his right hand whistling through the air on an arc that would split the assassin from throat to groin. It wasn't the speed with which Blade moved that shocked him. What stunned Kragan was the ease with which the man avoided his blow, shifting his body to the left as if he had seen this strike coming before it began. Blade's counterstrike opened a gash from the wielder's right elbow to his wrist, splattering acrid blood into Kragan's face.

With a thought, Kragan attempted to liquefy the earth under his opponent's feet, but his magic failed to affect the earth near the bearer of the runed knife. No matter how hard Kragan tasked the earth elemental Dalg, the being's attempts to approach Blade proved futile. Fury sharpened his vision as Kaleal forced his way to the forefront. Kragan did not resist. He would let the primordial lord who had wielded this body for an eternity control the fight.

Again and again, Kaleal sought to close with Blade. Kaleal bloodied the man, but the assassin managed to avoid a fatal or disabling wound. When Blade stumbled, Kragan felt the thrill that launched Kaleal into the man's body, fangs bared to rip out his throat. To Kragan's horror he felt the bite of the black blade as the assassin rammed it between Kaleal's gaping jaws, sending half of the foot-long knife jutting out the back of the body that Kragan shared.

The oddest sensation accompanied the realization that his spinal cord had just been severed. Having lost all feeling below the neck, Kragan felt his head hit the ground as if it had detached. He tried to smile up at the man who had just delivered the killing blow, tried to say that this was only the beginning. Instead Kragan felt his life essence sucked from this body like smoke on the wind.

—◊—

Kaleal watched the world of mortals dissolve around him, leaving him standing in the throne room where Landrel's spell had trapped him for thousands of years. Without a body and mind to anchor him in what men regarded as reality, he had been returned to his prison.

The wail that roared from his throat pulled streams of dust from the thick rafters and echoed from the walls. Once again the man called Blade had been his undoing.

—〜〜—

Arn pulled Slaken from between Kragan's jaws as the once-mighty body collapsed in a limp pile at his feet. For a moment it seemed that Kragan's eyes looked up at him before acquiring the glassy blankness with which Arn was well familiar. What happened next caused him to take an involuntary step backward.

The skin shriveled and collapsed until it formed a thin shroud over ancient bones. Within moments all that remained was a dessicated corpse. Even the rich blood on Slaken's blade turned into fine dust that the breeze carried away.

A sudden change rippled across the battlefield, raising the fine hairs on the back of Arn's neck. He shifted his gaze to the nearest of the vorg encampments, just a few hundred paces from where their master's lifeless body now sprawled. It was as if Kragan's powerful presence had bolstered the will of this entire horde. When Arn had slain the wielder, he had cut the cord that had funneled the desire to fight into tens of thousands of vorgs, brigands, and gruns.

The wall clouds that had encircled the Endarian fortress parted, blown away on a fresh gale out of the northeast. Fireballs and lightning rained down upon the stunned vorgs, unchallenged by whatever magic wielders still accompanied them. Arn felt a cold smile form on his face, knowing that he had unleashed the full power of Carol's wrath upon enemies who no longer had a protector capable of contesting her might.

The units closest to the white citadel stampeded toward Arn. Despite the efforts of their commanders to restore order, the contagion spread outward, causing an ever-increasing mass to desert the battlefield. Arn knew they were fleeing toward the exits from this basin, but he did not linger to watch. Sheathing Slaken, he pulled his color-shifting hood more tightly around his head and ran through the dead forest, headed for the wooded ridge a quarter league to the south of Kragan's overlook. As much as he hungered to extract his vengeance from Charna, it would not do to be caught out in the open when the roiling horde retreated through the area.

—⚏—

A searing needle of pain speared through the back of Charna's throat and dropped her to one knee, causing her guards to rush to her side. She barely saw them, so wrapped was she in the vision. Her eyes looked up past a bloody knife into Blade's merciless eyes as he stood over her, knowing that this was Kragan's sight, not hers.

Then she seemed to dissolve, snatched out of that primordial body and hurled across the land to the northwestern coast and then over the sea. She passed through a yawning gap in the mist barrier that had wreathed the Endarian Continent for more than four centuries. She raced across the white-capped waves and over a distant landmass of which Kragan had told her. The Continent of Sadamad. An irresistible force pulled her consciousness down through a forested hillside and into darkness.

Agony woke her from the trance, the pain fading as swiftly as it had assaulted her. She shoved aside the hands of her guards and staggered back to her feet, sweat dripping from her brow despite the freezing wind that howled down from the glacier-capped peaks in the northeast.

She had seen Kragan's death, yet she still felt his presence. Distant, but still out there. She found herself staring to the northwest, the direction in which her strange vision had carried her. Sadamad.

The change that rushed over the battlefield summoned her back to reality. In a handful of heartbeats the tide of battle had turned on itself. The typhoon of magic that had assaulted the white citadel had wilted before the fury of Rafel's witch. She swept the ladders and siege engines away, the howling wind heaving them onto the frozen lake, even as the ice transformed back into water. Thousands of Charna's warriors sank beneath the waves, pulled down by the weight of their own armor.

The fortress's mighty gates opened, belching forth High Lord Rafel's legion. The disciplined human troops struck the startled vorgs that blocked the bridge, adding to their panic as they fought among themselves to flee the onslaught. Supported by thousands of Endarian archers, Rafel carved his way through Charna's army, searching for its beating heart.

Charna yelled commands to her flag-bearers, and they relayed her orders to deploy her reserves. She had seen what happened when an army fled the battlefield. If she didn't stop this right now, the panic would become a rout. It had taken more than a full day and night to funnel the throng of soldiers through the tunnels and into the basin. They would jam up trying to escape, and few would survive.

Hefting her war hammer, Charna strode forward to take command of her elite combat reserve. Her counterattack would put steel into the spines of this horde. Despite this disaster, she would see Rafel's head on a pike before this day's end. Even his witch of a daughter could not prevail against this mighty throng. Charna would not allow it.

—⁓—

High Lord Rafel, with Battle Master Gaar at his side, led his infantry forward at a double-quick march. His lungs burned, his veins throbbed, and a handbreadth gash on his left side wept blood down his pant leg. His booming laugh as he and his troops forced their way forward through the enemy ranks bolstered their spirits. His legion's efforts on this day had turned the tide of battle, and victory was at hand. With bold action, he would seize it.

By the gods, he felt young again.

His arms wielded shield and sword in a dance he had practiced since long before he commanded the army of Tal during the Vorg War more than three decades ago. On this day he would win this battle for Queen Elan, and for Kim. Then he would cut Kragan's head from his shoulders and mount it atop a pike.

Rafel battered a vorg with his shield, causing her to trip on a rock and topple backward. As she snarled up at Rafel and attempted to rise, the high lord thrust the tip of his sword between the warrior's jaws and out the back of her neck.

A deep bellow pulled his head up in time for him to see three of the ten-foot-tall gray-skinned gruns bounding toward the spot where he and Gaar fought alongside Rafel's personal guards. The first of these batted aside two of the guardsmen and then struck at Rafel with a mace as big as the high lord's body. He dived to his right as the ground shook with the club's impact, coming out of the roll with a swing that severed the tendon behind the grun's ankle and dropped it on its face. Gaar's battle-ax put an end to its attempt to rise.

Rafel roared his defiance and charged the closest of the two remaining gruns, just to have the monster block his whistling sword with a forearm. The blade anchored itself in thick bone. The grun twisted its arm, tearing the sword from Rafel's grip. Knowing it would not save him, the high lord braced his shield to block the mace that crashed into his body. The fierce impact broke his left arm and caved in his ribs.

Rafel's last sensation amidst the blossoming fountain of pain and blood was that of flying.

He never felt his body hit the ground.

—◊◊◊—

On foot, Alan fought his way into the mass of fleeing vorgs with Quincy, Bill, Katrin, and Kron protecting his flanks. The four dozen who were the remnants of his Forsworn formed the tip of the spear that marked Rafel's counterattack across the bloody arch of the bridge that connected the Endarian citadel to the southwestern shore. A buzzing filled the air as waves of arrows passed over their heads from atop the high walls.

Rafel and Gaar followed behind Alan's company, leading the rest of the legion across the span. Alan's ax felled vorgs and brigands with each swing. This wasn't combat. It was butchery. But no hint of pity worked its way into his thundering heart. When they reached the shore, Alan led his followers on a charge that created an opening for Rafel's cavalry to further stampede their enemies.

Behind the hundreds of horse soldiers came Rafel and Battle Master Gaar, leading the rest of the legion forward to massacre their fleeing foes. Alan led his group into this pursuit on his father's right flank as they fought their way along the southwestern shore of the lake.

A new current stirred the maelstrom, slowing Rafel's advance. To Alan's left front, a score of gruns smashed their way through the line of cavalry, their leathery gray skins covered in gore. And behind them hundreds of elite vorg warriors fought to turn the tide of the battle.

"The high lord!" Katrin's voice cut through the din, drawing Alan's attention to where she pointed.

A handful of grun mercenaries had battered their way through Rafel's infantry to engage Rafel's personal guards. A howl of fury issued from Alan's lips as he saw a great mace strike his father's shield, smashing it into Rafel, sending him to the ground.

Alan turned toward the fray, his ax ripping through those who sought to block his path. The scene that confronted him froze his heart. Two gruns remained standing over the broken bodies of Rafel and his guards.

Alan's yell turned one of them to meet his rush. The ten-foot monster swung its weighty mace, only to have its arm severed at the elbow. Alan whirled into a strike that removed the gray head and toppled the body atop that of Gaar just as Kat hamstringed the other grun. Kron's hammer caved in the side of its head as it fell.

A glance at his father's body confirmed Alan's fears. The mace had caved in the high lord's chest, leaving shattered ribs jutting out through the skin. Gaar had died fighting alongside him.

As much as Alan wanted to yield to grief, with victory hanging in the balance, now was not the time.

He climbed atop a boulder, held his ax high, and yelled, his voice carrying above the din for all to hear.

"Vengeance!"

When he leapt down and ran toward the fiercest fighting, his Forsworn at his heels, the stunned soldiers who had witnessed their high lord's fall echoed Alan's cry and followed.

—※—

Arn stripped out of the Endarian uniform and tugged on the ragged leather armor of the brigand whose throat he had just cut. It was time to take advantage of the chaos that had descended upon this battleground. He had worn more uncomfortable helmets, but this one ranked high on the list, a brass seam pinching the scar where his left ear had been sliced to a point all those months gone by. The nose strip was a bit too wide, causing a partial loss of vision. Despite these drawbacks, the way the armor masked his features satisfied him.

He stepped from the copse of dead trees, his long stride carrying him toward the place where the central battle raged, ignoring the vorg and human deserters who streamed past him in their haste to reach Endar Pass's southwestern exit. Rafel and the Endarians had pursued the fleeing vorgs but had encountered heavy resistance. To Arn that meant one thing: Commander Charna had rallied her elite troops for a desperate fight. She would be there, directing her forces.

The memory of his mother's screams as five-year-old Arn Tomas Ericson peered out through the crack in the wood box filled his head. His right hand settled on Slaken's haft, leaching a fire from the runed handle, fanning his thirst for retribution. The thought that one of Rafel's soldiers or Carol would kill Charna before Arn could reach her sped him forward.

The greatest risk he now faced was from Rafel's soldiers. Even though he was behind Charna's battle group, the combatants were interspersed along a ragged front. He wanted to get close enough to her to take advantage of the opportunity that would present itself when the pandemonium reached its peak.

Cresting a small rise, Arn caught sight of the group of signal flags that were never far from the army's commander. Charna was much closer to the front lines than he would have expected. Perhaps that indicated that her counterattack had failed to halt Rafel's assault. An inward bulge had developed along Charna's northern flank, threatening to break through and encircle her. As Arn studied it, he spotted Alan leading a fierce assault by several hundred of Rafel's soldiers.

Charna recognized the danger and moved away from the front lines, accompanied by a half dozen of her personal guards. Suddenly the she-vorg collapsed, writhing on the ground as she clutched her head. Charna's guards left her where she lay and fled with the other retreating vorgs.

Dread bloomed in Arn's mind. Carol had found the commander.

Stepping behind a tree, Arn jammed Slaken's tip into the decaying bark of a dead pine and released his grip on the knife, opening his mind to his wife, focused on one desperate request.

"Carol, stop!"

Arn's words halted Carol's assault on the commander's mind an instant before her mental attack would have destroyed Charna.

"Why?"

"That's the one who murdered my parents. She's mine."

136

Arn felt her fury at the revelation that this was the vorg of whom Arn had told her.

"I will keep her down until you get to her. Be quick."

Arn grabbed Slaken, severing his connection to his wife's thoughts, and ran toward the withered thicket into which Charna had fallen. Having seen their leader drop, the force she had led had lost all will to fight. They fled the battlefield in a wild panic, many dropping their weapons to run faster.

Arn tossed aside his helmet, grabbed the she-vorg, and flipped her onto her back, his knife at her throat. He felt Charna stiffen as Carol released her mental grip. His name hissed from her lips.

"Blade."

Arn shifted his knife, ever so slightly, drawing a thin trickle of blood from her throat. To have the one who had butchered his parents in his grasp almost made him yield to temptation and slash her neck from ear to ear.

"As a child, I watched you kill my mother in our cottage outside Hannington."

She flinched, and his knife opened another small wound beneath her chin. He watched the muscles in those jutting jaws shift beneath her skin, and the sight triggered the memory of her tearing his mother's throat out. Soon he would return the favor.

"Right now, you're going to tell me the name of the wielder who bound her to the wall for you."

"Why would I do that?" Charna rasped. "You'll kill me anyway."

"There are a lot of different ways to die. You get to choose the quick way, or I get to use my imagination. Either way, you'll tell me what I need to know."

Her eyes widened at the imagery his words painted in her mind's eye.

"I will make a deal with you," said Charna. "If you let me live, I will guide you to him. You will never find him on your own."

"Give me his name."

"Kragan."

The revelation both stunned and thrilled Arn. With a move of his hand, his vengeance would be complete. But he would not kill her before telling her of Kragan's fate. Arn grinned, although his expression held no humor.

"Kragan is dead. I killed him. Killing you will complete the oath I made as I stood over my mother's and father's graves."

Charna's mouth twisted into a grin as cold as Arn's.

"Kragan is a body hopper, a master of the third branch of life magic. He has worn hundreds of forms during the millennia of his life. I have watched the ritual where he stole another's body. If his current form is killed, his life essence returns to his original corpse, reinvigorating the body. So long as his original form exists, Kragan is immortal. He will steal a new body and then reinter his own corpse so that no one can find and destroy it."

Arn felt a chill hand grip his heart. He knew a lie when he heard it, and Charna's words had the certainty of truth. Again he felt the temptation to gut this contemptible being and trust his intuition to guide him to Kragan. But how would he recognize his enemy?

"Do you know where his corpse lies?" Arn asked.

"No," said Charna, "but he and I are bonded. I can sense Kragan's presence. And that sense can guide me to him."

Truth. That was all that Arn heard from her.

"You know that even if you take me to Kragan, I will kill you after I have dealt with him."

"Perhaps. Maybe he will kill you this time. I prefer those chances."

Arn's jaw tightened until he could hear his teeth grind. Was he really going to let this murderer continue to live, after all these years that he had sought vengeance? With a scowl, he rose to stand over her.

For a moment he was five years old again, feeling his mother stuff him into the wood box and close the lid, listening to her screams as the commander tortured her before ripping her throat out. The memory was so vivid that his heart raced, making him light-headed. He almost succumbed to the urge to take his time killing Charna. But he wanted Kragan even more.

"Lie to me and our deal is off. Do you vow on your life to guide me to Kragan?"

Charna stared up at him, unwilling to draw the deadly response he longed to make.

"I so vow."

"Stand up. Place both hands behind your head. Do not take them down."

Charna climbed to her feet, her unsteadiness a testament to the toll that Carol's mind lashing had taken on her. Arn stepped behind her, patting her down for weapons. Aside from the war hammer that lay on the ground two paces away, she carried just a belt knife. This he tossed aside.

Then, as afternoon surrendered to evening, Arn escorted his prisoner back through Rafel's forces and into the Endarian fortress.

PART III

The thaumaturge shall not wait. Newly arisen, he deciphers my secrets. Thus in great haste will he set forth, lest his nemesis unravel the same truths and gather the trident fragments to herself.

—From the *Scroll of Landrel*

13

Kalnai Mountains, Continent of Sadamad
YOR 415, Day 1 of Summer

With a rustling like dried autumn leaves stirred by a breeze, the mummified skin that draped the old bones knitted itself back together. Dead cells plumped and expanded, the life energy causing them to divide. Muscle, ligaments, and tendons attached themselves to the skeleton as blood flowed into freshly formed veins and arteries. The brain that grew to fill the skull pulsed as Kragan's consciousness struggled awake.

Agony pulled a groan from vocal cords that cracked and healed. Although he had experienced this forced rebirth before, the last occurrence had been more than three thousand years ago. The knowledge was scant comfort to him.

He wanted to shriek but dared not. Best to lie as still as possible inside this ancient sarcophagus until the rejuvenation process terminated.

When he finally moved, Kragan opened his eyes to utter blackness. With a groan he lifted his hands, pressing them into the magically preserved wood of the casket lid, and lifted. When the thing failed to budge, panic sucked the saliva from his mouth. Had the tomb within which this coffin rested collapsed atop it?

Then Kragan remembered. No earthen barrier could contain him. But the dull throbbing in his head dissuaded him from attempting to summon such powerful elemental magic. He shoved harder and was rewarded with creaking movement. The heavy lid slid aside and then tumbled to the stone floor with a crash that echoed in the chamber.

While a potent spell might be a stretch for him at the moment, he had no difficulty lighting the tomb. It was not a large space, merely a natural cave that he had fashioned into a tomb with his art. Except for one that clung to the stone wall by a thread of metal, the sconces that had once held torches had rotted and fallen to the ground.

Kragan climbed out of the casket to stand erect. A mirror fashioned of gold summoned him forward, although he moved with some reluctance, knowing what he would see within its reflective surface. There, staring out at him from the dusty surface as if through a fog, stood a being whose head would have been waist high to Kaleal. On this diminutive naked body, the feet, hands, and head looked abnormally large. His wild amber hair reached almost to his shoulders.

He saw his lips curl as his mind retreated into memories of the moment when he had realized that he and the rest of the Zvejys people were not like other humans on Sadamad. They had adapted to the swamps that formed their homeland, and he had grown up in a society of fishermen. They were quick of mind and dexterous of hand, their large feet and slight bodies allowing them to cross the swampland that would slurp the larger folk into the depths.

The Zvejys fishing village of Klampyne occupied the northeastern gullet of Whale's Mouth Bay, surrounded on three sides by the extensive Balu Swamp. The thick marshes protected the Zvejys from the nomadic marauders who roamed the southwestern tip of the Kalnai Mountains.

One day Kragan's father and uncle had invited him to accompany them on their boat to transport their catch to the port city of Varjupaik, where a merchant ship was being loaded with fish. It was there that, for the first time, Kragan watched Uncle Zumalt work his life magic, preserving the catch from decay until the merchant seamen could deliver it to a distant seaport. The sorcery had fascinated Kragan. But it was another event that had changed his world.

A young woman sailor had drawn Kragan's eye, inspiring in him feelings he had never known. She was statuesque, her beautiful face and flashing blue eyes framed by short golden locks. But her reaction when Kragan had the temerity to ask her name had changed that vision of beauty into one of ugliness. She had looked down at him, laughed, and pointed. Her hilarity had spread to her shipmates, some of whom doubled over with mirth.

For several moments Kragan had stood frozen to the planking, seeing himself as they did for the first time. An undersize swamp-man had thought himself worthy of conversation with a normal woman. Pathetic.

When the three Zvejys kinsmen had returned home, Kragan had asked his uncle to train him in magic. Despite Zumalt's protest that the talent was extremely rare, Kragan had talked his uncle into testing him.

Zumalt had been stunned to find within the young man an ability well beyond his own. During the years that followed, Kragan had studied the wielding of life magic with an all-consuming obsession. Buried deep within his uncle's books, he learned of forbidden rituals outside the abilities of all but the fabled wielders of old.

Uncle Zumalt had been Kragan's first kill. He hadn't wanted to slay the man who had shown him such kindness, but the allure of the artifact that amplified Zumalt's life magic had wormed its way into his dreams. After his uncle had shown the object to Kragan and told him how it affected his ability, the mummified finger had become Kragan's all-consuming obsession.

The price of stealing a body was a life. Kragan had always thought that odd, since the price of reanimating a corpse was also a life, a transaction that seemed to be in better balance. But body hopping involved an additional cost that left behind a corpse. In this case it had been Kragan's. The one he had hidden in this very cave.

Now he wore this despised form once again. All because of Blade. Curses hissed from Kragan's lips.

He turned away from the mirror and walked to a stone mantel atop which an obsidian box rested. He summoned a minor air elemental, and its magic lifted the lid. The spring-loaded needle darted from its recessed home with a harmless snap that sent red flakes of dried poison onto the shelf.

The mummified thumb within had been Zumalt's most prized possession. Kragan did not know how his uncle had come by one of the artifacts that had composed Landrel's legendary trident of magic amplification. It was a secret that the wielder had taken with his soul to the land of the dead. Kragan had performed the ritual that had bound him to the object. No other could use the arcane object while Kragan lived.

In an age long gone, Landrel had taken a thumb, index, and middle finger from each of three long-dead masters of the magical forms—one master each of time, life, and mind. He had molded the fingers into his trident. That thought knotted Kragan's gut. In Endar he had almost retrieved the second of the nine fingers that would be required to reassemble the weapon he craved.

His hand subconsciously rubbed the hole in the side of his head that was all that remained of the ear he had removed so long ago. He became aware of a tingle in his mind. His she-vorg commander and friend was still alive, as was his arcane connection to her. As he focused on that link, a new vision blossomed in his mind.

Charna paced within a white-walled prison cell. He strengthened his connection to her.

"Why have the Endarians captured you?"

The she-vorg halted, then answered him with her own thoughts.

"When you fell, the Rafel witch killed your wielders and set upon your host, scaring the fight out of the warriors. Our horde fled back toward the tunnels, and I tried to stop them. I failed."

"That is not what I meant. Why have the Endarians left you alive?"

"Remember the peasant woodsman and his wife that we killed on a hunt outside Hannington?"

Kragan paused, savoring the memory. "Yes."

"Their young son watched us kill them. He has grown up to become Blade."

A lightning bolt of shock crackled through Kragan as Charna continued.

"Blade forced me to tell him that you were the wielder who was with me that night. I told him that you yet lived and promised to guide him to you. The fact that I remain alive means he believed me."

A warm glow replaced his surprise. If Blade came for him, Carol would come with him. Here, near the source of his life magic, Kragan would end them both. Then, wearing Carol's body, he would return to Endar in triumph.

"Bring them to me."

Kragan severed the link and reached for the earth elemental with which he would create an exit from this tomb. It seemed that he was to have another chance to deal with Carol and her pet assassin.

But first it was time to take on a new form so that he could return his true body to its secret tomb.

14

The constriction in Arn's throat threatened to cut off his breath as he blinked away the wetness that filled his eyes. The bodies of High Lord Rafel, John, Battle Master Gaar, Earl Coldain, Garret Coldain, and Coldain's twin girls had been collected from the battlefield to lie in state in the Endarian throne room. They now lay on the floor atop the individual tapestries that would soon become their death shrouds. They were arranged with their heads closest to the throne, feet toward the massive double doors that had been closed for the private viewing.

Carol knelt beside her father's broken body, head bowed, tears dripping from her nose and chin to splash upon his rugged face. Kim knelt beside John, holding both his hands in her own as she wept for her husband and best friend.

Arn, bracketed by Alan and Galad, stood to the left side of Rafel's body, facing along the row of honored dead, giving the two sisters space for their grief. For Arn to lose his adopted father at the moment that victory had been within the high lord's grasp seemed a cruel turn of fate. Rafel had saved a disturbed twelve-year-old Arn from the king's gallows. The leader of Tal had seen to Arn's training and brought him into the Rafel home, replacing the family he had lost at the age of five.

His gaze shifted to his friend John. Of the four who had bonded during those months of hard travel and combat as they journeyed to Endar Pass, just Arn and Kim remained.

—๛—

Carol's breath came in ragged gasps as she knelt beside her father. The previous night, when she had first learned of his death, she had been shaken but too exhausted to give proper vent to her grief. With this morning's sunlight slanting through the throne room's high windows, she half expected the man to sit up and complain that nobody had woken him before dawn. For the high lord, there would be no more awakenings in this world. The same was true for Earl Coldain and his son, whose bodies had been found together on the battlefield just a few hundred paces from Coldain's murdered daughters. And Kim would never hold John in her arms again.

Her thoughts turned to Ty, the bare-chested Kanjari warrior who had given his life to save Carol's. If he truly was the Dread Lord, ruler of the land of the dead, then last night he had been standing at the gates to welcome her father and the rest of these fallen into his realm.

Carol took a deep breath and held it for several heartbeats, forcing her sobbing to subside. When she exhaled, she took another. Then she wiped her face and climbed to her feet. Despite the plethora of tragedies that Kragan had inflicted upon her people and the Endarians, she would allow herself no period of mourning. There was too much work to be done, lest disease spread, compounding their difficulties. And with her father dead, that left her in charge of the people of Tal.

She placed a gentle hand on Kim's shoulder. Then she turned to find herself gathered into Arn's strong arms. He said nothing, made no soothing sounds, merely allowed Carol to press her face into his neck as her body shook with sobs that she had thought stifled. For endless moments she remained there, unashamed in her grief.

When she finally pushed back, she saw that tears streaked Arn's face, cutting twin paths down his ruddy cheeks. The sight granted her some comfort, just enough to allow her to collect herself.

She shifted toward the throne, gesturing for Arn and the others to follow. Carol stopped two paces in front of Queen Elan, bowed her head, then straightened to stare into the monarch's obsidian eyes.

"Queen Elan," she said, "I request a meeting with you and the rest of your High Council, that we may discuss our strategy going forward."

The queen's grim mask remained in place as she spoke.

"For what purpose? We have won this battle at great cost. Only a small fraction of Kragan's horde has escaped from Endar. All the rest lie dead on the killing field, being piled for incineration."

"All but our prisoner, Kragan's commander," Carol said. "She has told us that Kragan's essence escaped to rise again in a secret tomb on the distant Continent of Sadamad. I have looked into her mind and seen the truth in what she speaks."

Elan looked from Carol to Kim and then to Galad, who stood to the side, unconsciously rubbing the stump of his left wrist. Seeing him nod his approval, the queen signaled to one of her guards.

The woman approached the throne and knelt, head bowed so that her waist-length black hair touched the floor.

"Your orders, my queen?"

"Summon the High Council to my throne room. Tell them to make haste."

"As you command."

The woman rose and strode from the room.

Over the next several minutes the members of the High Council assembled alongside Carol, Arn, Kim, Galad, and Hanibal before the throne. Carol discerned, since Elan would be the only one seated, that she meant for this discussion to be as short as possible.

High Councillor Failon, the most respected of Endar's historians, was the first to be called forward by the queen. He strode up beside the throne and turned to address the assemblage. Despite his age, Failon's voice held all the vigor of youth.

"My queen, fellow councillors, and human allies. It pains me to bring further ill tidings to those who have already suffered so much."

A chill crept into the marrow of Carol's bones.

"The events of these last few days and the information provided by the prisoner, Charna, have caused me to reexamine a significant passage within the Scroll of Landrel. What I and the other scholars had interpreted as a prediction that Kragan would flee from Endar Pass at the head of his defeated army instead confirms his soul's return to his corpse on Sadamad."

The old Endarian's expression grew more serious, his brows almost knitting themselves together.

"Our reexamination of this section of the prophecy also revealed another of the ciphers hidden within the text. We already knew that Landrel foretold his own death at Kragan's hands. What we have now discovered is that Landrel made two copies of his scroll. One he hid within a time stone. The peasant who discovered that stone triggered its dissolution, revealing the scroll within. That scroll was destined to be given to High Lord Rafel and delivered to Endar at the height of the Vorg War.

"But it is the other copy that now concerns us. It was in Landrel's possession when Kragan murdered him. As Blade informed us, Kragan created a giant statue of Carol beneath his city of Lagoth. The she-vorg says that Kragan fashioned more than one such likeness. It now seems clear that Kragan took that image from the copy of the Scroll of Landrel."

Carol spoke up. "What if he did? Even if Kragan made a magical return to Sadamad, he could not have taken the scroll along for the journey."

Failon turned his hard gaze upon Carol.

"Kragan was obsessed with the contents of Landrel's prophecy. A mind such as his would have committed the entire thing to memory many centuries ago. If he so desires, he can re-create it."

"Why would he?" Carol said. "Having studied it for all those years, he knows the prophecy better than anyone."

"And that is where the latest cipher comes into play," said Failon. "Landrel intended that only the climactic events that are now unfolding will reveal his hidden messages. The ancient master has reached out through time itself to manipulate all of us. Only a master of time-sight, the third branch of time magic, could accomplish such a feat. Even Kragan is subject to that manipulation."

Arn interjected. "Nobody can control the future."

"Perhaps," said Failon, "but Landrel is trying."

Carol swallowed hard. "What do you mean he is trying?"

"Every action we take changes the future. We lack the talent to see how. Three magics branch thrice. Landrel was master of all nine. But the rare far-sight ability was his supreme talent.

"Landrel could see all the paths to the futures that spread out before him. And he understood that inflection points occur where multiple paths cross each other. It now appears that he planted seeds in some of these junctions. Landrel is using the two scrolls to nudge us into the future he desires to bring about."

Carol took a step closer to the ancient Endarian scholar, sensing the answer to the question she had to ask. "And the other seeds?"

Failon pointed to the lone pedestal that rose from near the room's western wall and the white block that rested atop it.

"Within that time stone rests one of the nine desiccated fingers from which Landrel created his trident of magic amplification. Each form of magic—life, time, and mind—has three separate branches. This is one of three fingers attuned to life magic. I believe that Landrel scattered those nine artifacts around the world so that they would be discovered by whom he wants to find them. Even now he is manipulating us."

"But for what purpose?" Carol asked.

Failon ran a bony hand through his gray-streaked hair, causing it to shift on his shoulders.

"We had hoped to discover that and other answers within the Scroll of Landrel."

He reached inside his gray robe and removed not one scroll, but two.

"Our warriors discovered Kragan's copy among the belongings within his camp. Our scroll and this document are not identical."

The pronouncement sent a muttering undercurrent through the assemblage and pulled a gasp from Carol's lips. On the throne, Elan showed no sign of surprise, a lack of reaction that told Carol that the queen had already known. Landrel had created two different versions of his prophecy. And if Failon's assertions of Landrel's clairvoyant talent were accurate, the ancient wielder had arranged for Kragan to deliver his copy into the hands of the Endarians who already possessed its counterpart.

Failon continued, his concern painting a frown on his face.

"From the distant past, Landrel sends us a message about the future he intends to make happen."

"Isn't that a good thing?" Carol asked, feeling Arn step to her side as if he sensed an impending threat.

The muttering among the councillors died out, all eyes drawn to Failon, who took a deep breath and straightened.

"Landrel was many things, both great and terrible. He betrayed Endar and spawned the vorg, something he should have foreseen. His actions have led to the deaths of hundreds of thousands of his own people at the hands of those creatures, including those who sacrificed themselves on this battlefield. Whatever he is attempting with this latest gambit will exact a similar price. We cannot be sure whether he intends to provide a road map to our salvation or our destruction."

When Queen Elan spoke, all eyes shifted to her.

"Now we face a dilemma. The ciphers our scholars have unraveled within our version of the scroll indicate that Kragan will try to recover the remaining artifacts of amplification. Landrel has stated that his children hid six of these on the Continent of Sadamad."

The queen locked her gaze on Carol's and continued.

"Carol, both you and Arn have stated that the she-vorg speaks the truth. If Kragan has arisen in his homeland, he will use the clues within Landrel's Scroll to find those powerful fragments of Landrel's Trident. Each one he gathers will increase his power, until he may become unstoppable. Then he will return to claim the fragment contained within the time stone here in this chamber."

Carol's eyes followed the queen's pointing hand to the time stone atop its pedestal.

"Then we have to stop him," said Carol, surprising herself with the firmness in her voice. "We will make Charna complete her bargain with Arn and lead us to Kragan."

"Given our losses," said the queen, "I cannot spare a large force to accompany you across the sea. Nor could we transport such an army if I had it to send."

"And," said Hanibal, "we cannot leave Areana's Vale poorly defended for the length of time that such a dubious expedition would require."

Carol saw Alan turn on the commander.

"It is not your place to make that decision," Alan said, grabbing the commander's neck in his powerful right hand and pulling him in until they stood nose to nose. "My father declared that Carol would take his place should he fall. She is now high lorness and leader of our legion. It will go where she commands."

"Enough," said Carol, her voice calm but commanding. "I have no intention of taking a large contingent to hunt down Kragan. An elite unit of volunteers will better suit my needs. What do you say, Brother?

Will you volunteer yourself and the remnants of your Forsworn to accompany Arn and me on our journey across the ocean?"

Alan shoved the red-faced and sputtering Hanibal away and turned toward her, the muscles in his jaws working to bite down his anger. But as Alan looked at Carol, his hard gaze softened.

"You could not keep me back," he said. "Just as I could not stop my Forsworn from accompanying me."

"I, too, will go with you," said Kim, anger and anguish marring her features. "I have a blood-debt to settle with Kragan."

"You will have need of my talents," said Galad.

Carol nodded in acknowledgment, then turned to Commander Hanibal, knowing that the order she was about to give would infuriate her brother.

"Commander," she said, "as soon as we are done helping dispose of the dead within this basin, you will march our legion back to Areana's Vale and take charge there. You are to lead and safeguard our people until my return. Do you swear to uphold this duty?"

Hanibal dropped to one knee and bowed his head. "Until death, High Lorness."

Ignoring Alan's hiss, Carol stepped forward and placed the palm of her right hand atop Hanibal's head.

"Then I hereby name you lord protector and regent of Areana's Vale. Let it be so witnessed."

When she removed her hand, Hanibal rose to his feet, turning to face the queen.

"By your leave, Majesty," he said, "I will return to my troops and set them to their task."

Elan nodded. Then, with a slight bow, Hanibal turned and walked out of the room.

Carol glanced at her father lying beside his battle master, unable to shake the feeling that she had just made an epic mistake. But when she turned to depart, she saw Kim confront Alan.

"I must ask you one thing," Kim said to him, her eyes full of accusation. "Can you assure me that your curse did not get my husband killed?"

Carol felt the wind sucked from her lungs, leaving her stunned and speechless.

Alan met Kim's gaze, the lines in his face adding years to his appearance.

"I'm sorry," he said, "but I cannot."

Then Alan turned and walked out of the throne room.

15

Endar Pass
YOR 415, Day 4 of Summer

Carol awoke from Arn's chaotic dream with a start that failed to wake
him. The nightmare was one of many that sometimes entered her mind
as she slept beside her husband. She could share his thoughts only when
he set Slaken aside. Normally that mental link required effort. But when
they drifted off to sleep, their naked bodies cuddled together, the dream
link often formed of its own accord.

Just as had happened within the distant ravine they had named
Misty Hollow, tonight's nightmare had replayed itself repeatedly, each
time a different vision of what might lie ahead of them. Although she
failed to remember what had so disturbed her, her eyes were drawn to
the black knife sitting on the small table on Arn's side of the bed. The
moonbeam that speared through the window of their palace bedroom
seemed to crawl along the runes carved into the ensorcelled haft, mes-
merizing her.

Perhaps yesterday's memory of her father resting atop the funeral
pyre as the flames consumed his body was what so disturbed her. She
examined that thought, rolling it around until her mind gave the lie

to it. Something that she could not quite remember from Arn's dreams filled her with dread that she would lose this man she loved. As she stared at his knife, Carol was torn by the desire to destroy the thing before Arn awoke.

She knew the urge was irrational. Slaken had kept Arn safe from the magic of Kragan and his wielders. Still, she could not shake the feeling that, given the choice between her and that wicked blade, Arn's thirst for vengeance would make him choose the knife.

Carol angrily thrust the thought from her head. Why was she reacting to this weapon as if it were her rival?

A shrouded memory crowded into her spinning thoughts. The choice between Carol and Slaken had been the centerpiece of Arn's dreams.

Carol rose, slipped into an Endarian robe, and stepped out onto the southern balcony. A rosy pink glow painted the southeastern sky, providing a stunning backdrop for the glacier-capped peaks. That view provided a stark contrast to the dead forest that lay beyond the lake. Her gaze shifted to the courtyards and gardens down below her tower, her gut clenching at the sight of what had once been places of beauty and were now filled with brittle remnants of flowers, plants, and trees. The smaller plants reminded Carol of the windblown weeds she had seen while traveling north along the Mogev, mere shells of their living selves. The trees, shorn of all needles, reached their skeletal branches in fruitless supplication to the gods.

When she had first gotten here, Carol had thought she might never want to leave. Now she could not wait to depart. And today their trek would commence.

A touch on her waist made her jump, an audible gasp escaping her throat.

"I'm sorry," Arn said. "I didn't mean to frighten you."

Working to still her pounding heart, Carol turned toward Arn, who stood wearing a black Endarian robe in contrast to her white one.

"I thought you were still sleeping," she said.

Arn walked forward to lean upon the ivory balcony railing.

"Bad dreams woke me," he said.

"I think I shared them."

Arn turned and took her in his arms.

"Again? You just seem to catch the bad dreams."

"Or maybe they are the only ones that I remember," said Carol. "I can barely recall these."

"Good." He looked at the sky, releasing her from his arms. "We'd better get ready. It's almost sunrise."

Carol dressed, putting on her riding clothes and boots. They had bagged everything else yesterday and left those bundles at the barracks where Alan and his Forsworn were staying. By the time she and Arn reached the courtyard, Alan and his company were already mounted, as were Kim and Galad. A packtrain consisting of more than a dozen horses stood ready to go.

Ax and Storm were already saddled and being held by two young Endarian grooms. Storm pawed the ground at Carol's approach, as if to say, "Where in the deep have you been?"

As Carol and Arn swung up into their saddles, Queen Elan, in an emerald gown, approached the company. She carried a bound document in her right hand, one that Carol recognized as the original Scroll of Landrel that had been in the hands of Endarian scholars for more than three decades. Elan handed it to Kim, surprising Carol with the affection in her face. Apparently the avalanche of tragedy had released the anger that had hardened the queen's heart toward her daughter.

"You will have need of this on your journey," said Elan, taking Kim's hand in hers and staring into her daughter's eyes. "Study it well. I hope that it will reveal its mysteries to you."

"Thank you, Mother," said Kim. "I will pray that it helps us deliver justice to Kragan."

The queen strode to Galad.

"Speed your group while the land is beneath your feet. Once at sea, the time-mists will be of little value."

A puzzled look wrinkled Galad's forehead.

"I can summon the mists over land or water," he said.

"Yes," said Elan. "But the ships' crews cannot navigate without a clear view of the heavens. Even with your ability to see through the mists, you can only see the sun, moon, and stars as smears across the gray sky, no clearer than looking at the spokes of a rapidly spinning wagon wheel."

"Ah. I understand."

The queen patted her son's damaged forearm. "Be safe."

Then Elan made her way to Carol.

"Be careful of the she-vorg," she said, nodding toward the horse with Charna shackled to the saddle. "That one is not to be trusted."

"I do not trust Charna," said Carol. "She will do as she has agreed or Arn will kill her. Sooner or later, he will take his vengeance on her."

Elan shifted her gaze to Arn. "May your next killing blow bring Kragan to a proper end."

The queen did not stay to watch them depart. Instead she returned to the palace without another glance in their direction.

And then Galad's time-mists enfolded them. Thus did Carol's company make their way across the bridge, around the lake, and into the Endarian lands to the northwest, Carol's heart filled with determination to avenge her father, knowing that she would do so or die.

16

Varjupaik, Continent of Sadamad
YOR 415, Early Summer

Kragan strode the bustling city streets of the southwestern port city of Varjupaik wearing the stolen body of the first mate he had replaced. Kragan had returned his own misshapen corpse to its tomb in the southernmost tip of the Kalnai Mountains, and not just because that form disgusted him. He would not risk the destruction of his true body.

His loose-fitting purple blouse was tucked into tight black trousers that disappeared inside the tops of the crimson boots that completed the uniform of Varjupaik's merchant sailors. Kragan's hand moved to his chest to stroke the silky shirt's fabric, feeling the shriveled thumb that hung from his neck on a slender chain.

Having long ago memorized Landrel's Scroll, Kragan had spent several days re-creating it. The act of writing the words had triggered the breakthrough. As he scrawled the letters on page after bound page, Landrel's cipher had leapt from the document. The discovery that had propelled him to make the shipboard journey around the southwestern whale head–shaped peninsula to Varjupaik lent urgency to his stride.

Kragan now knew where Landrel had directed his offspring to hide the six trident fragments he had sent to the Continent of Sadamad. Long ago, Kragan had secreted one of these within his hidden tomb. Landrel's offspring had dispersed five more fingers to the merchant city-states of Varjupaik, Rukkumine, Jogi, Paradiis, and Vurtsid. Hidden in plain sight, they rested inside the temples of the sea goddess, Dieve, each one locked within a time stone of Landrel's creation.

The cipher that wound its way through the prophecy had also revealed the reason for Kragan's haste. Time stones, just like the other time-mists, had a finite lifetime before they dissipated. Even Landrel's magic had its limit. And one by one, the moment when they would release their hold on the finger bones trapped within was racing toward Kragan.

Centuries ago, Uncle Zumalt had found the fragment that Kragan now wore. So Landrel had made a mistake in creating the time stone that had encased it. A new thought struck Kragan. What if the Endarian wielder had intended for Zumalt to discover the artifact, had wanted it to make its way into Kragan's possession?

Was Landrel attempting to manipulate Kragan even now?

Kragan gritted his teeth. The complexity of such far-sight went beyond the realm of possibilities.

Making his way through a crowd of colorfully garbed people gathered in the central square, he turned toward the ivory-domed edifice on a rise that gave it a clear view of the sea. In less than three hours, Dieve's temple would fill with worshippers, anxious to send the evening prayers to their goddess. And the city's merchant queen would be among them. Kragan would be in and out of the sanctuary long before then. He had a midnight funeral to attend.

Kragan ascended the twelve wide steps that led to the shrine's blue-green arched entryway. The towering double doors stood open, and he walked through them into a room that spanned thirty paces from front to back and from side to side. Inlaid seascapes covered the walls, while the floor, tiled with aquamarine, caught and twisted the light from the dozens of candles that lined the cloudy dais in the chamber's center. The ancient rectangular platform had stood here for thousands of years, constructed of Endarian time stone blocks by one of Landrel's sons as a shrine to Dieve.

He strode past three blue-robed monks to kneel before the altar, his head bowed in the traditional prayer position. When he rose, his eyes shifted to the milky-white cornerstone on the right side of the platform's base, noting that it was several shades darker than the other time stones. Kragan felt himself suck in an involuntary breath. To be this close to another skeletal fragment from Landrel's Trident filled him with an almost irresistible urge to kill these superstitious old fools and summon the magic necessary to remove the time stone from the altar. But this was not the right moment. That would come four hours before dawn.

Now that he had seen the oddly shaded cornerstone, Kragan rose to his feet, turned, and made his way past the scant worshippers and back the way he had come. If he was to achieve the focus required to channel the necrotic life magic for tonight's summoning, he needed several hours of undisturbed meditation. Even so prepared, Kragan knew that he could not wield that much power without the age-old finger bones touching his skin.

He turned into a narrow alley that led to an abandoned, ramshackle building. When he reached it, he stepped across the bricks that had tumbled to the ground and entered through the hole they had left in the wall. Dust motes danced through three narrow sunbeams that speared down through the roof. The stairway to the basement had collapsed, leaving a dark hole in the floor near the back wall.

When Kragan reached the edge of the pit, he formed a mental link to Ohk, commanding the air elemental to create the invisible stairs that would give him a path downward. Summoning a magical globe of light, he followed the steps through the hole.

—⚊—

The graveyard of the royal merchant guards was shrouded in fog that filtered the midnight moonlight, making it appear that wraiths flowed among the monuments to fallen heroes. As Kragan, wearing the blue robe and hood of a monk, strode between the stone images of warriors and their instruments of battle, he could feel the bones that had been entombed beneath the ground over the last several thousand years. In a strange way, this place felt like home.

Tonight some of these titans of combat would struggle from the grave to clash once again. The price was a life for a life. He was so filled with stored-up power that only the mummified talisman made containing that energy possible.

He heard voices before he saw the crowd gathered around a newly reopened burial chamber guarded by the twelve-foot-tall statue of a warrior, both stone hands resting on the marble haft of a battle-ax. The ceremony was already in progress. Tonight's funeral was for Veronis, a captain of the royal guardians of the merchant queen, who had fallen shielding her body with his own, victim of an assassin's poison dart. Despite the onset of death, Veronis had broken the assassin's neck before perishing atop the man's corpse.

A full contingent of one hundred of his fellow guardsmen had assembled to honor Veronis's passage into the land of the dead. A weathered commander of the guard recited the eulogy in a voice that resonated within the graveyard.

Shrouded within a miasma by the air elemental Nematomas, Kragan moved to within a half dozen paces of the rearmost rank of mourners. Then, with a low moan, he released two hundred tendrils of necrotic life energy, funneled through the artifact of amplification. Half of these smoky strands crawled into the ground. The rest of the murky tentacles spread out to each member of the assemblage, entering their bodies through nose and mouth.

The formation of guardsmen became a writhing mass as they dropped where they stood, their mouths open in shrieks that failed to crawl from their throats. Kragan felt their life essences flood through him, the intensity almost bringing the wielder to his knees. Far from instantaneous, each guardsman's death happened slowly, the speed depending on the state of decay of the corpse being reanimated with his vivacity.

Veronis was the first to crawl from his grave to lie gasping among his dying comrades. Kragan had to assist the others to the surface as they revived, using the earth elemental Dalg to peel back the earth and stone that covered them. The effort required to control Dalg while channeling this amount of life energy caused Kragan to cling to a stone monument to keep from falling.

When he finally straightened, Kragan watched as the hundred freshly raised warriors walked forward to kneel before him, their muscular bodies naked but unashamed. His mental link to each of their minds was strong. Each of these restored warriors understood that, despite what they might want to do in this new life, they were bound by Kragan's will. That knowledge angered them. Kragan cared not.

With a thought he set them to stripping the uniforms and weapons of the dead royal guardsmen so that they might clothe themselves. All except for Veronis, who had been interred in his livery with his sword clutched to his chest.

"Veronis," said Kragan, summoning the captain to him.

"Yes, my lord?"

"I place you in command of this company. Take them to the palace of your merchant queen. Slay the night shift, but let no harm come to her. Keep the queen in custody and await my return. I will rejoin you well before dawn."

The muscles on both sides of the captain's face clenched and twitched. But he bowed his head in acknowledgment. "As you command."

Kragan turned away, managing to avoid stumbling in exhaustion. Now was not the time for rest. He had much work yet to do before the night ended.

—⟊—

A blood-clotting wail pulled Queen Lielisks out of a dreamworld where she walked barefoot through blossoming red cerini plants, calmed by their wondrous scent. A flash flood of irrational terror washed away that sense of tranquility, pulling her upright in the bed. The clash of steel, the shouts of alarm, and the cries of the dying echoed through her hallway. The double doors crashed inward as two of her trusted night guards burst into the room. One rushed to her bedside, sword in hand, while the larger man turned back to face down the hallway.

"Majesty," said the breathless Serzantas, "we must get you to safety. Quickly."

Lielisks threw off her covers, mindless of the scandalous way her nightgown slid up her thighs as she swung her long legs over the side of the bed. Without bothering to put on her slippers, she rushed to the door at Serzantas's left side.

By far the bigger of the two royal guardsmen, Milizinas threw himself at the man who had just fought his way through a half dozen of the queen's guardians. Of all her royal guards, he had been the second-best fighter, inferior only to her dead hero, Captain Veronis. Although the attacker was blocked from the queen's view by her protectors, her heart leapt with hope as Milizinas's sword whistled through the air. Sparks danced as metal clashed against metal.

To Lielisks's horror, the enemy pushed Milizinas backward with a rage-filled bellow. The royal guardsman redoubled his efforts, hacking and parrying with lightning-quick moves. But fast as he was, his opponent was quicker. And each blow her protector blocked staggered him.

By the goddess, why were no reinforcements coming to her aid? The cacophony of combat from elsewhere in the palace answered her question. It sounded as though hundreds battled within, their screams and yells almost drowning out the din of clashing weapons.

Milizinas staggered back into Serzantas, splashing Lielisks with his blood. Arterial spray from the large man's missing right shoulder doused her face and hair. Then his eyes rolled up and he collapsed at her feet. A man in the uniform of a royal guardsman stepped into the room, his ax dripping gore. It was a face such as Lielisks had never seen. Long raven hair and beard and bone-thick eyebrows gave him the look of a wild thing from legend.

Serzantas leapt forward, thrusting with his sword. The intruder deflected the stroke with a quick movement of his ax and grabbed Serzantas by the forearm of his sword hand. The wild man gave the arm a vicious twist, and the merchant queen heard a loud snap followed by the clatter of steel on stone as her guardsman's sword bounced across the floor.

The bearded man did not swing his ax. He chopped down with it, splitting Serzantas's skull from crown to chin.

Lielisks found that she had backed up against her bed without realizing that she had moved. Now this bear of a man advanced toward her. A stern command rang out, bringing the giant to a halt a mere two paces in front of her. She saw Captain Veronis enter the room behind him. Relief flooded the queen at the sight of her hero.

Horror immediately pushed away that brief emotional respite. Veronis was dead. She had held his convulsing body as he died in her arms.

Now he stepped up to her, his ice-gray eyes shining with moisture. But within those orbs that she had once thought so beautiful, she saw a merciless resolve that froze her heart. This man, or whatever he had become, had returned from the land of the dead for her. And he had brought an army of his brethren with him.

For the first time that evening, Lielisks screamed. It was not to be the last.

—ᴍ—

As Kragan had expected, the guardsmen outside the temple answered the calls of the palace horns, summoned to protect the queen. With almost all the city-state's soldiers asleep, only the night watch was able to respond to the unexpected palace assault. The monks would awaken and make haste to bring their magic to bear against the invaders, but they would not expect Kragan to be waiting in ambush for them.

When the doors opened, they flooded out in a tight group of twenty-three. Kragan gave them no time to disperse. Just two survived the fireball that Kragan sent exploding into their midst. Shafts of magical light streaked from the outstretched palms of one of the survivors, but Kragan deflected these missiles with a thought. He pulled forth lightning from the heavens, only to have it scatter from the shimmering shield erected by the first monk's partner.

Not for the first time since he had been reborn, Kragan missed the power his merger with Kaleal had granted him. Although the artifact he wore around his neck amplified his natural talent for necrotic life magic, it would require different finger bones to enhance his mind magic. The loss of his connection to the primordial had weakened him, but that did not mean he was feeble. Kragan shifted his concentration, liquefying the ground beneath a portion of the temple's front wall. With a grinding howl, the stones separated and crashed down onto the two monks, burying them in rubble and leaving a gaping hole where the great doors had stood.

Kragan walked into the pall of dust, maintaining a bubble of clean air around him as he climbed over the heap to enter the shrine. Calling forth floating globes of light, he lit the altar despite the powdery cloud that had snuffed out the candles. He knelt before the cornerstone and studied the construction.

If this entire pedestal had been formed from a single piece of time stone, what he was about to do would not have been possible. But this dais had been created by cementing individual time stone blocks together. The fact that the cornerstone was a different shade of white than its brothers showed that the moment it would dissolve was approaching.

The thought that Landrel had foreseen this very moment disconcerted him. Not only had Landrel foreseen it, he had meant for the time stone to give up its secret after Kragan took possession of it.

With a minor burst of magic, Kragan removed the mortar that held the cornerstone in place and pulled it free. He picked it up, surprised at how light it was in his hands. The brick measured two hands in length and a single hand in height and depth, yet hefted like a stone he could skip across a pond. To think that this block was a congelation of time that would soon dissipate into mist boggled the mind.

Kragan rose to his feet, turned, and hurried from the damaged room, unmindful of the gathering crowd of citizens whom the noise had roused from their beds. To their sleepy eyes, he would be just a merchant marine who had come to investigate the catastrophic collapse of their holy place.

His long strides carried him around a corner and up the broad avenue that led toward the distant palace. As he drew closer, sounds of combat drifted to Kragan on the night's breeze. Lensing the air, he pulled the view of the dimly lit palace into sharp focus. The sight put a smile on his lips.

There were no flames. No convergence of the army or city guards. As he had anticipated, just the night watch had responded to the reports of disruption at the home of the city-state's mistress. If they had crawled from their bunks at all, the merchant marines would rush to augment the force that manned the city's outer wall to fend off an invading force.

The queen's royal guards were quite capable of defending the palace. Unless, of course, the bulk of that guard had been sacrificed to raise a host of dead heroes.

By the time Kragan reached the palace gates, all sounds of combat had stilled. Captain Veronis strode out to meet him.

"The palace is secure, Lord Kragan. The queen is in our custody."

"Take me to her."

With a signal to the new guardsmen, Veronis turned toward the palace. Kragan heard the clank of steel on steel as the massive gates closed behind him.

The merchant queen lay atop her bed, her hands and feet chained to the bedposts. A purple cloth gagged her mouth.

"Leave me and close the door. Let no one enter."

"Yes, lord."

Kragan stepped to the bedside and peered down at Queen Lielisks. Her long blonde hair clung to her damp neck, pasted there by blood and tears. Her cobalt eyes widened as Kragan sat down beside her.

He removed his boots, socks, and shirt. Moving slowly, Kragan crawled atop her, stretching out so that his fingers intertwined with hers, his bare feet caressing hers. Her body heaved, but Kragan bound her to the bed with tendrils of red magic. Then, ever so slowly, he pressed the right side of his face and neck to hers, feeling the mummified thumb press into the flesh of his chest as he wielded the life enchantment.

Torment rocked Kragan as veins and arteries crawled out through his skin to burrow into Lielisks's.

17

Uostas, Northwestern Endar
YOR 415, Early Summer

Arn blinked as Galad's time-mists dispersed from around the traveling party, his eyes adjusting to the sudden brightness. Mere moments earlier he had walked beneath a mist-shrouded sky, but now the sun shone brightly. For more than a month, the time-shaper had escorted the company through the mists toward the Endarian seaport of Uostas.

Arn still had trouble grasping how differently time passed outside this rychly mist. In the real world their journey had taken just a handful of days. But for Arn and the rest of the travelers, the trip had taken the same number of weeks that journeying such a distance normally required. As they had traversed the lands of northwestern Endar, Arn had studiously observed how Galad wielded the fogs.

It was not just a matter of summoning an equal quantity of rychly and pomaly mists while they traveled. Galad created gentle gradients in the layers of mist to allow Carol's company to pass from one stratum into another until they reached a zone where time passed the fastest. Those who moved through these boundaries felt the pressure that resisted their passage. Once they were inside a new time zone, that area appeared clear, surrounded by the now hazed-over zones where time progressed at different speeds.

Galad was forced to take the group back into the real world several times each day so he could study the distant terrain to get his bearings. Otherwise the maximum distance that any of them could see was the area within the time zone Galad had created. Being within a mist meant you couldn't look out upon the world where time passed at its normal rate. Even Galad could not get a clear view of the sun, moon, or stars, just the oddly shaped bubble within which you moved. And within those mists, Charna also lost her sense of direction relative to Kragan.

It made Arn's head hurt to think about those complications. No wonder mist warriors were in such short supply.

As his pupils adjusted so that he no longer needed to squint, Arn looked down from the crest of a hill toward the port city of Uostas. The buildings clustered around the sheltered harbor were the most colorful he had seen. All had steeply pitched roofs painted red, green, blue, or yellow. Most of the houses were otherwise painted white, although some had been left the natural color of the wood of which they were constructed.

Hundreds of fishing boats were tied to piers or anchored farther out in the harbor. The largest of these were ships that had tall masts and looked capable of long journeys around the coastline of the Endarian Continent. Centuries ago, similar ships had set out across the Brinje Ocean, chasing the trade routes to and from the Continent of Sadamad. Prince Galad and Princess Kimber intended to hire two of these ships to carry them and their dozens of human companions to that far-off land.

Kim had retreated behind a somber mask since John's death. Arn also missed his friend, but the loss of Kim's laughter and gentle gestures pained him. The princess now used her focus on the mission to push her grief into the background. Only twice on this journey had that facade cracked such that Arn heard her sobbing in the night.

Alan called a halt and accompanied Galad and Kim over to Carol.

"I think it wise that the group remain here while I arrange for our passage," said Galad. "Once I have informed the village master that I am escorting a company of heavily armed humans on a mission for my mother, you can expect a warm reception."

"What of me?" Kim asked.

"I need you to stay here in the event that some party seeks to challenge the group's intentions while I am gone."

Arn detected a hint of irritation in Kim's manner, but she accepted her brother's logic and did not argue.

Standing beside his wife, Arn slipped his hand into hers as they stood watching the silver-capped waves break along the shore. The sight reminded him of the time he had visited Earl Coldain's keep in southeastern Tal, the first time he had seen the ocean. The thought that they would soon board ships to cross this one in pursuit of the wielder who had butchered his parents sucked the warm feeling from his chest.

The sense that he was being watched caused him to shift his gaze to the spot where Charna stood between a pair of armed guards, manacled hand and foot. As the she-vorg stared at Arn, a sneer curled her lips, revealing the long canines that had torn out his mother's throat. It took all his will to keep from releasing Carol's hand and cutting Charna's head from her shoulders.

He took a slow breath and shifted his attention back to the roiling seascape. First he would end Kragan. The vorg's time would come.

—◊◊◊—

Carol saw Galad return just as the afternoon sun sank into the sea. A lanky Endarian woman, wearing a gray uniform unlike that of any of the members of the Endarian military whom Carol had observed, accompanied the prince, along with a group of men carrying bulging packs. A silver clasp attached to the woman's collar seemed to be an insignia of rank, which Galad confirmed with his introduction.

"Lorness Carol," he said, "allow me to introduce Mistress Jura, the village master of the seaport of Uostas. Given short notice, she has secured the two ships that we require for our journey, although it will be three days until they are stocked for the voyage and ready to sail."

"Wonderful news," said Carol. "Thank you, Mistress."

Jura pointed at the sunset. "We have only seen that sight for the last few days. Before then, the mists shrouded the western horizon. Prince Galad has told me and the city elders how a portion of the barrier has been dispelled, leaving an opening to the wider ocean beyond. We are excited to support your expedition to the ports of our historic trading partners on Sadamad."

"I wish our journey had such a hopeful purpose. We hunt the enemy who overran Tal and almost destroyed your Endarian capital. I fear that his ambitions in that regard have not diminished."

"I regret that I am unable to house your entire company," said Jura, "but I can secure accommodations for the key leaders of your group and their spouses."

"Most kind," said Carol, "but I will make camp with our soldiers until the ships are ready to board."

Jura signaled to the leader of the Endarian pack bearers, and they set their burdens on the ground.

"At least we can make sure you eat and drink well at this camp," Jura said. "I caution you to go slow with the drink. It is a local brew named after a predatory fish we call ryklys. It is known for its bite."

The company camped that night beside a burbling stream, grateful for the hearty rations and potent drink that Mistress Jura had delivered. Since they would camp here for three nights, the group erected slanted shelters from the waterproof blankets that the queen had provided for each traveler.

A boisterous bout of singing around the campfires attested to the truth of Jura's warning. Carol had little doubt that some of Alan's company would pay a price for tonight's merriment come dawn. But the bawdy banter lifted her spirits and even managed to dispel the dark mood that had settled upon Arn.

When she and Arn finally retreated to the tent they had erected from two of the marvelously light Endarian coverings, they slipped out of their clothes and into each other's arms. Tonight, as Arn set Slaken aside, Carol felt a strangeness slip over her.

A bird's-eye view of the scattered tents, campfires, and revelers sprang into motion in her mind. The soldiers came and went as the stars moved through the sky in accelerated motion. She watched Alan walk away from his company to seat himself on a ledge, staring westward across the sea. And as was their habit, Katrin and Bill shadowed him.

In a flash the night passed before her eyes. The camp slept and then crawled awake with the dawn. She saw herself exit her tent in her riding garb, followed by Arn, with Slaken and his other four knives sheathed at his thighs and inside his boots. She watched herself glance up at the sky where a lone vulture circled beneath gathering storm clouds.

Beside her Arn shook his head, and the vision faded. She found herself staring into her husband's deep-brown eyes, his face cradled between her palms.

"You saw that," he said.

His words were not a question, but she nodded as if they had been.

"The dreams keep getting worse," he said. "They invade my mind whenever I set Slaken aside. Not just in my sleep anymore."

His words put a tightness in her chest that almost robbed her of words. She swallowed, took his two hands in her own, and responded.

"But just now, you shook the vision off. You controlled it."

Arn propped himself up on an elbow, his intensity palpable.

"This time," he said. "I fear that I may not be able to for much longer. It makes me think that I should keep Slaken with me at all times, lest my madness infect you."

Anger, born of dread, boiled up inside her.

"Madness! Don't you dare speak to me about madness. You are the one who saved me from that state of mind in Misty Hollow."

"Yes, but I did so wearing Slaken."

"Not the last time. You made yourself a beacon to guide me back to my body."

"And for a few moments, Kaleal possessed me. You told me you felt something rip in my mind when you dispelled the primordial lord. What was it you called the damage? 'Such a tiny thing.' I'm afraid it's getting bigger."

18

Kragan, wearing the aquamarine royal gown that clung to this new body's curves, strode into the queen's audience chamber through a side door, escorted by several of her new guardsmen. She slid onto the red velvet–cushioned seat of the solid gold throne, letting her fingers caress the mystic remnant of Landrel's Trident that rested at her bosom.

"Bring them in," she said, motioning to two guardsmen. They opened the two twelve-foot-high doors and walked from the room. The rasping of feet and the rattling of chains preceded their return, leading the manacled leader of Varjupaik's senate and seven of his fellow senators, still wearing the bedclothes in which they had been captured.

When the gray-haired Senator Tarybos saw his queen, his amber eyes widened in shock. Fury wiped that look from his face.

"What is the meaning of this outrage?"

The curved dagger that a once-dead guard raised to touch his throat silenced him. Strong hands pushed the senators, male and female, to their knees before the queen.

Kragan let a smile curl her delicate lips.

"As if you don't know," she said, letting venom drip into her voice.

She signaled with her left hand, and a black-bearded behemoth dragged a dead man into the room by his foot, depositing the corpse between the queen and the senators. Kragan pointed down at the sailor she had seen in the mirror just yesterday morning.

"This is the man who led the attempted coup that Captain Veronis just thwarted."

"Impossible," said Tarybos. "Veronis is dead."

"Captain," Kragan said, "step forward."

Veronis walked from behind several guards to stand over the corpse, his eyes locked on Tarybos.

"As you can see," said Kragan, "my heroic captain is very much alive."

She leaned forward, her eyes narrowing.

"Veronis uncovered the foul plot to overthrow me using my own guardsmen. Together we have thwarted your Rukkumine-backed ambitions. We faked Veronis's death and arranged for his midnight funeral, where my mercenaries slaughtered most of the traitors. Then they returned to these halls to cleanse this building of the infection you spread among your fellow senators and my royal guard."

"Lies!" Tarybos yelled, earning himself a backhand that sent him sprawling.

"At noon today," said Kragan, "you will make a public confession in the central square, admitting that you and your colleagues conspired with the merchant king of Rukkumine, seeking to overthrow me."

Tarybos spit. "I will never confess to something I did not do."

Kragan rose from the royal throne and walked forward to stand over the senator.

"Oh, my dear Tarybos. I very much think you will."

Below her, the senator howled as one after another of his fingers bent backward and snapped. When she stopped, Tarybos stared up at her, his face a mask of horror.

"What foul enchantment is this?" he asked. "You have embraced witchcraft!"

Kragan smiled as she leaned down to take one of Tarybos's injured hands in a delicate one of her own.

"Senator, you have no idea."

Then, with a wrenching squeeze, she ground the broken bones together.

—◊—

Queen Kragan sat on an azure throne atop a dais in the city coliseum, having climbed the ten steps that led up the pyramid-shaped structure. The tens of thousands of citizens who had assembled to observe the execution had just finished pelting the eight senators who knelt at the base of the dais, hands chained to ankles, with eggs and rotten fruit. But when Kragan stood, the babble subsided.

Although the acoustics in this amphitheater were exceptional, Kragan added a bit of magical amplification to ensure her gentle voice reached all ears.

"Citizens of Varjupaik, you have heard these senators confess their involvement in last night's attempted coup. This was a plot paid for and perpetrated at the direction of Godus, the rogue merchant king of the city-state of Rukkumine."

Loud boos echoed from the stadium walls as many in the crowd stood to shake their fists in outrage. Kragan lifted her hand and the cacophony stilled.

"Headsman," she commanded, "do your duty."

A muscular man dressed all in black and wearing a midnight hood stepped up to the kneeling form of Tarybos, the senator first in line from the queen's right. The executioner jabbed the tip of his curved sword into Tarybos's back, causing the man to arch his spine. In a swift motion, the sword whispered through an arc that sent the senator's head rolling across the coliseum's dirt floor. The body did not fall over but merely slumped forward, the result of the way it was bound.

A low moan of dread issued from the throats of the other senators. The sound thinned as the headsman made his way along the line, adding one head after another to the collection in the red mud. When he reached the last of the condemned, the man's howl of terror degenerated into a high-pitched keening noise that came to a sudden end.

For several moments silence hung over the arena. Then the populace erupted in wild cheers.

Once more, Kragan gestured, quashing the uproar.

"Witness the way traitors die. As your merchant queen, I have vowed to make Varjupaik the wealthiest city-state in all of Sadamad. Fear of our success has prompted one of my rivals to instigate this treachery.

"Rukkumine has damaged our goddess's temple. This I will not tolerate. We will exact retribution upon King Godus and his people. Today we begin the task of readying our merchant fleet for combat. Citizens of Varjupaik, prepare yourselves for battle."

As Kragan descended the steps, an angry murmur rippled through the assemblage. The sound warmed her ancient soul. She had planted the first seeds of war against their traditional rivals. Now she just needed to fertilize them.

—m—

Kragan walked into the queen's chambers and heard the guards pull the doors shut to allow her privacy. They would not open the portal again until she called for them.

A glance at the corner bookshelf brought Kragan to a sudden halt. The Landrel time stone was gone. Sudden anger transformed into fury that someone had gotten past the guards to defile her lair by stealing something she had put so much effort into acquiring. But as she started to call out, something else attracted her eye. In the shadows at the very back of the shelf, a small object had almost disappeared into a knothole in the wood.

Kragan walked forward. Conjuring a light, she leaned close to the shelf, her heart pounding.

There it was, a mummified index finger, with traces of parchment-like skin clinging to the bones. The time stone had not been stolen but had reached the end of its allotted lifetime and dissolved into smoke, sending its content tumbling onto the shelf.

She reached forward, carefully lifting the ancient thing from the crack into which it had almost disappeared, cradling it in her right palm. With her left hand she lifted the chain from which the desiccated thumb dangled against her chest.

Kragan turned to the queen's study table, seated herself, and placed the ancient fingers side by side on the flat surface. In this position they looked like part of a dead hand that had broken through the wood as they clawed their way free. The size matched. They were both from a woman's hand . . . the same hand.

By sheer luck, Kragan had come into the possession of two of the three fingers from the ancient master of life magic. Her name had been Dziviba, and she was said to have once commanded a vast army of the dead. With only the ancient thumb to amplify his channeling, last night Kragan had raised a hundred warriors from their graves. What wonders could she work with two of the digits that had once conducted so much power?

As she studied the thumb and index finger, her thoughts turned to the three ancient masters from whose decaying corpses Landrel had cut the thumb, index, and middle fingers. Kragan had noticed at a young age how the pinky and ring fingers of his dominant hand automatically curled during casting, leaving the other three fingers extended.

Although Kragan did not know why this maximized the channel, she supposed it had to do with the way the brain favored the dominant hand in all wielders of magic.

Summoning a minor fire elemental, Kragan set to work binding the second precious finger to her neck chain.

When she had retired to the queen's chambers, Kragan had intended to restore her temperamental mind link with Charna so that she might check on her pursuers' progress. That link had failed so often that it had become clear that whenever Charna and her companions were swathed within the Endarian prince's time-mists, those arcane fogs severed the connection. But now that Kragan had two of Dziviba's three magical fingers resting on the table in front of her, she forgot about the mind link she had intended to activate.

Thus did she miss the sight of Carol's company as they sailed through the gaping hole in the time-mist barrier that surrounded the Endarian Continent and out onto the open ocean.

19

The upper deck was almost empty as the midnight watch took over. Alan Rafel leaned on the railing at the prow of the merchant vessel *Saimniece*, looking across the moonlit waves toward her sister ship, *Milakais*. Kat stood at his side, her left hand resting in the crook of his right arm. Her gentle touch sent a pleasant thrill through him that the beauty of the night and the taste of the salt spray on the wind amplified. He glanced at her profile, her shaved head glistening with an almost supernatural glow.

She had long made her feelings for him obvious. But Alan had resisted getting too close to someone under his command because he feared amplifying the loss that seemed inevitable for all of those who had pledged themselves to him. So why had he allowed her familiar touch beneath this midnight moon?

When she continued staring out at the sea and did not meet his gaze, he reached across his body, placing his left hand gently atop hers. The hint of a smile lifted the corners of her lips as her head turned toward him.

"Kat . . ."

Her soft kiss silenced him. The taste of her slightly parted lips sent fire coursing through his veins, burning his inhibitions to ash. Her arms moved up around his neck and he pulled her close. Her lean body pressed against his, firm and supple. Time froze as their moon shadows merged into one. Her taste, her smell, the soft moans that escaped her mouth as their caresses grew in urgency sent Alan's spirit soaring.

Suddenly he found himself very glad that the two ship's captains had insisted that all senior officers have cabins of their own. Alan released Kat to take her hand, catching the hunger in her gaze as he nodded toward the hatch that would take them into the aftcastle.

Alan ignored the arched-eyebrow look that Bill gave them as they passed between him and Quincy's lanky form to enter the hallway that led to the officers' quarters. Bill's lilting voice and the deep rumble of Quincy's chuckle followed them into Alan's cabin.

"Sleep well, Chosen."

Those sounds hinted at the ribbing Alan would have to endure going forward, but right now he didn't care. Sleep was not on his agenda.

—ɯ—

Arn awoke and reached out for Carol, only to find her gone. He sat up, rubbing the sleep from his eyes. What in the deep was wrong with him? Nobody had ever been able to sneak up on him, yet his wife had gotten out of the narrow bed they shared in the ship's aftcastle without rousing him. The last thing he remembered was waking in the middle of the night to sounds of a thumping bed and low moans issuing from the cabin across the narrow hall. Alan's cabin.

The roll of the galleon indicated that the seas had grown rougher during the night. The darkness in the cabin was almost absolute. The cracks around the closed door issued what little illumination there was.

Feeling for his clothes on the floor, Arn dressed, returning Slaken and his other knives to their customary places on his body.

Arn rose to his feet, leaning into the sway. He walked to the door, opened it, and stepped out into the dimly lit corridor. The hatch at the far end of the hallway was open wide, letting the morning light stream in. Climbing out into the sunlight, Arn blinked and allowed himself a moment for his eyes to adjust before looking around. The sun had just cleared the eastern horizon, and overhead, thin, wispy clouds filled most of the sky. They were the kind that whispered of strong winds aloft, presaging a coming storm.

A storm had filled Arn's dreams last night.

The way the crew scurried around the deck and up into the rigging meant that the captain shared his concern. As was his usual practice, Alan had the half of his Forsworn that had boarded this ship engaged in combat drills, taking advantage of the rough seas to add difficulty to the training. No doubt Kron would have the two dozen Forsworn aboard the *Milakais* doing the same thing. Galad was also aboard the *Milakais*, although he did not wield the time-mists to speed their journey, since the ships' crews would be unable to navigate surrounded by the fogs.

Arn climbed the steps to the top of the forecastle and looked around. There was no sign of Carol or Kim on the raised forward deck. He moved back down to the central upper deck and into the aftcastle. Ship's captain Kumstelis had graciously provided the *Saimniece*'s library for Carol's and Kim's study of the Scroll of Landrel, which is where Arn found them.

Daylight streamed in through the open shutters of the cabin's window. The two women leaned over the scroll spread out on the central table, which had been bolted to the deck. Their shadows shifted back and forth as the hanging lamp swung with the ship's motion. So immersed were Carol and Kim in their study that neither of them noticed him enter. When he approached the table they glanced up.

"Just the one I was hoping to see," said Carol, warming him with her smile.

"Any progress?" he asked.

She shook her head. "Aside from those that the scholar, Failon, showed us in Endar, we have not identified a single cipher within the scroll's text. Maybe we just need a fresh set of eyes to examine it. Someone familiar with secret writings and hidden meanings."

"I have already looked through the text," he said. "Nothing odd jumped out at me."

The disappointment on Kim's face was plain to see. Apparently Carol had given her false hope.

"If you don't mind," Carol said, "I would like you to work through it with us. In Misty Hollow you figured out that the wielder who penned the book on mind magic had written its exercises in reverse order. That intuition saved my life. Kim and I believe that discovering Landrel's masked intent is even more important."

The thought of spending the day inside a stuffy library instead of out in the sea breezes and salt spray did not excite Arn, but he nodded in acquiescence.

"Let me make a galley run first. I'll bring back something for us to eat while we work."

"Good idea," said Carol. "I just realized how hungry I am."

Kim smiled at him. "Excellent."

Arn turned and left the cabin, making his way down to the berth deck where hammocks had been slung for the crew and Alan's Forsworn and into the galley. He returned to the library carrying a loaf of bread, a jar of honey, several strips of venison jerky, a jug of water, and three metal mugs.

For several minutes, the two women set their work aside as the three broke bread. Then, putting the leavings on a shelf, they returned to the scroll. Kim volunteered to read aloud as Carol and Arn studied the careful calligraphy of the text.

As the morning gave way to afternoon, Arn found himself working harder to avoid staggering when the ship lurched at the behest of large waves. But despite the effort they applied to their study, Arn proved to be of no assistance. A big wave heaved the ship, causing Carol's white-knuckled grip on the table's edge to fail. She tumbled into Arn and they both sprawled, rolling across the steeply canted deck. The impact dragged Slaken from its sheath and sent the black knife sliding under a low shelf.

The galleon spun on its axis as it crested the wave, then rolled hard in the opposite direction. Arn slid across the deck toward the door. With his right hand he grabbed a table leg while he latched on to Carol's arm with the other. Kim had wrapped her arms and legs around a table support across from Arn, her eyes wide with terror.

Suddenly Arn felt the air in the cabin thicken around him, as if he were supported by a very large pillow. The look of concentration on Carol's face revealed the source of the magic that flowed to lift all three of them.

Arn felt the galleon right itself, recovering from the rogue wave to slosh through the rough sea with a much more normal rhythm. Carol released her spell's hold, and Arn grabbed the table edge, pulling himself and Carol back to their feet, focused on slowing his rapid breathing. His eyes settled on the scroll, which had fallen from the table, rolling itself back into its tubular shape.

"I'll put the scroll back where it belongs," Arn said, walking over to pick it up. "Then I'm going to step out and see how the ship fared from that battering."

But when he spread the lengthy scroll atop the table, the letters crawled across the parchment like worms wriggling from rain-soaked earth. The cabin faded into the background, Carol and Kim freezing in place, as he watched an aging Endarian lean over a white table, inscribing words on a lengthy sheet of specially treated paper. His long fingers positioned each letter so that they formed patterns that intertwined through the document.

The man's long raven hair draped his shoulders like a veil that shifted as he looked up. His black eyes glittered in the lamplight, locking with Arn's. He laid down his pen, his lips shifting into a knowing smile.

"Welcome, death dealer," he said, his deep voice mellifluent. "I've been expecting you. My name is Landrel."

—⁓—

Alan continued to press forward with the training despite the rough sea and leaden sky. His Forsworn expected nothing different from their leader. Violent bouts of nausea assaulted half his warriors, but they returned to their exercises after they emptied their stomachs.

"Look!" Bill yelled, pointing toward the prow of the ship.

Alan turned to see a monstrous wave approach the craft, towering above it.

"Grab the rail and hold on!" he yelled, matching his action to his words.

Katrin and Bill bracketed him along the railing as the rest of his Forsworn crowded together, wrapping their arms around the wooden beams.

To Alan's amazement, the *Saimniece* nosed up, climbing the wave until it was almost vertical, leaving Alan and his company dangling from the railing as seawater rained down on them. For a moment it seemed that the ship would capsize end over end. But the sturdy galleon crested the wall of water, falling forward and balancing with neither prow nor stern touching the sea. Rudderless, the *Saimniece* yawed clockwise, then slid down the wave's backside, returning to the white-capped breakers that Alan and his company had grown accustomed to.

As if on a signal from the sea gods, lightning stabbed the sea a hundred paces from the ship. Thunder cracked the sky, calling forth a downpour that made breathing difficult. Having regained his footing, Alan released the rail.

A new worry nipped at his mind. What had happened to the people aboard their sister ship? Looking up, Alan yelled at the crewman in the crow's nest.

"Crewman! Can you see the *Milakais*?"

The Endarian sailor pointed, and Alan climbed to the forecastle's top deck and looked off to his right, relieved to see through the driving rain that their companion vessel was still with them. Just as the captain of the *Saimniece* had ordered, the *Milakais* had lowered several sails prior to the storm. Alan did not see a distress flag, so he would not borrow trouble by worrying.

"Katrin," he said, "give me a roll call."

She reacted with the discipline he had come to expect of her, forming the company into two ranks, then moving among them, assessing each warrior's health.

"All present," she reported. "No serious injuries. Thirteen are sickly dogs, though."

Alan stepped forward and dismissed them, telling them to get what rest was possible. As he expected, half the group stumbled back to the rails, hugging them like long-lost lovers. Even Bill's face had a green cast to it, although he had not succumbed to the nausea.

"Remind me how I love the sea," Bill said as he ran both hands over his bald pate in a futile attempt to sluice away the rain.

"You've finally found a home," said Kat, her deadpan tone pulling a laugh from Alan.

Here he stood aboard a rolling ship in a drenching rain, chilled to the bone, yet somehow these two companions had reintroduced him to joy. It was an emotion that Alan realized was long overdue.

—◊—

Landrel!

The name filled Arn's heart with dread. His hand instinctively moved to Slaken, only to discover that the blade was gone. Of course. It had been torn from its sheath when Arn had fallen. Without its influence, a waking dream had enfolded him, plucking him from reality into this hallucination.

Landrel studied Arn's reaction, seeming to know what the assassin was feeling.

"Time sight is the most terrifying of the nine magics," Landrel continued. "It is easy to become lost in realities that were never meant to exist."

Landrel paused, as if considering what he would say next. Arn did not want to hear his words.

"You are just the third person in all of history," said Landrel, "whom I have known to possess the talent."

Landrel rose from his chair, standing a head taller than Arn. He turned and strode to a door in the far wall, opened it, then beckoned Arn to follow. Arn complied, taken aback by the scene he beheld.

There was no ship. There was no sea. He stared out across a vast, rolling plain.

Turning to look behind him, Arn saw only the house that he had just exited, a two-story structure of modest size. It was white and had a pitched red tile roof with a lone chimney on the right-hand side.

When Arn turned back, he saw Landrel staring out across that lonely plain as if he was seeing something far more interesting. Arn stepped up beside him, finally finding his own voice.

"Other than Slaken, I have no magic."

Landrel spoke as if he had not heard Arn.

"Many erroneously call this magic far-sight. It is possible to see both near and far, into the future or into the past. Looking back is easy, for there is just one path in that direction. Beholding the future is a very different thing. One path becomes many, and each of those becomes many more. For one with the talent, it is possible to discern the one trail that is the most probable way forward.

"But when one masters the talent, it becomes possible to nudge the path toward a particular future."

"I told you," said Arn. "I have no such talent. And you are a figment of my waking dream. Probably a sign of incipient madness."

"Ah," said Landrel, turning to face Arn. "You have been having a growing number of these hallucinations, as you call them. You think madness is growing within you?"

Arn clenched his teeth. "I fear it."

"And only the black blade can save you."

"Yes."

A veil of sadness draped Landrel's face.

"Because you are also of the talent, I cannot foresee which choice you will make with that mystic artifact. But know this. It is your salvation. It is the destruction of all you shall ever love. Only you can determine which of those futures you will embrace."

With these words echoing in Arn's mind, Landrel and the empty countryside faded away, leaving Arn staring down at the words that still crawled through the scroll.

The ciphers leapt out at him as if etched in blood.

—⚭—

Carol watched as Arn spread the scroll out on the table, her heart still pounding from the fear that the ship was capsizing. If she had been outside on the deck, she could have done something to prevent such a disaster. But she needed to see her target to cast a spell, either with her eyes or through those of a remote host. Fortunately, the ship had righted itself. And with calming breaths she would be able to return her pulse to normal.

Something about Arn's expression drew her attention. His eyes had a faraway look. He was staring down at the scroll as if he had never seen such a thing before, almost as if it were alive. He squinted, then blinked, as if he had just stepped out of bright sunlight into the dimly lit cabin.

She put a hand on his arm, pulling him from his trance. A glance at Kim's concerned face showed that she had noticed Arn's strange behavior too.

"What's wrong?" Carol asked.

The muscles in Arn's jaws tightened, but he did not look at her. With great effort he turned away from the scroll, walked across the room, knelt, and retrieved Slaken from beneath a low shelf, returning the weapon to its sheath.

When he stood and faced her, relief washed his face, as if he had just released a heavy burden.

"You had another vision," Carol said, surprised that she had not experienced it with him. "Tell me what you saw."

Arn glanced sideways at Kim, then inhaled deeply and met Carol's eyes.

"There was no vision. Just needed to catch my breath."

Carol felt her face flush. Arn had never lied to her before. But what she saw in his eyes was not deception. It was something else she had never seen in her husband's gaze.

Fear.

"I need to step outside for a bit," he said, awkwardly turning away.

Speechless, she watched him walk out the door, his left hand gripping Slaken's haft. The muscles in that forearm bunched so they threatened to burst through his skin.

For several moments she stared after her husband.

"What was that about?" Kim asked, stepping up beside her.

Carol felt exhaustion embrace her, dropping her into the nearest chair. This hadn't really been a quarrel, but it certainly felt like one. Something was happening to her lover, and Slaken was at the heart of the problem.

She felt Kim's hand on her shoulder and looked up at her. The concern in her sister's eyes released the tears she had not realized she was holding back. Carol angrily wiped the tears away. It was stupid to get mad at Arn. She knew he was struggling with a loss of control, and Slaken was just the cure he had chosen. Still, that solution felt wrong to her. Worse than wrong. Evil.

So, as she continued to ignore Kim's question, she vowed that, whatever it took, she would help Arn find himself again.

Or maybe for the first time.

20

Kragan didn't much care for being the merchant queen of Varjupaik. The daily duties bored her out of her mind. But to make this work, she needed to give the appearance of carrying on Lielisks's mandatory tasks, at least until getting the war with Rukkumine underway.

With two pieces of Landrel's Trident in her possession, her life magic was strong enough to destroy Carol Rafel, Blade, and the rest of those who accompanied her. Unfortunately, to channel the maximum power through the mummified fingers on her necklace, Kragan would have to return to her original body. That would subject the ancient sorcerer to more risk than she liked.

Wearing another's body weakened the connection to the artifacts, and with such a dangerous wielder hunting her, Kragan needed all the magical capacity the fingers could produce.

The assassin was another consideration. Blade had killed Kragan while the wielder wore Kaleal's mighty form. The man's immunity to mind magic did not extend to time and life magic. Still, Kragan would not underestimate his nemesis again.

Kragan's soft hands moved to the necklace from which the two fingers dangled. Her day's duties at an end, she intended to take her dinner in her own chambers. And after she had supped, she would link to Charna to see just how Carol and her band were progressing.

Once she confirmed that Carol was good and thoroughly dead, Kragan would be free to infiltrate war-torn Rukkumine to steal the third of Landrel's artifacts. With the expansion of her powers with each artifact acquired, retrieving the others would become easier and easier.

Kragan did not desire to make herself king or queen of anything. Not when godhood awaited.

—◊◊—

Charna awoke with a start, feeling Kragan touch her mind. She reached out, jammed her thumb on the bars of her cramped cell in the ship's brig, and growled. The stink of her vomit filled her nose and made her stomach lurch again.

"Ah, the joys of a seafaring voyage," Kragan said.

Charna's eyes adjusted to the dark. Her night vision was better than that of humans, but down on this bottom deck, there were many layers to the gloom. But since she had been alone for some time, it must truly be night. Fortunately, the howling wind and thunder had subsided, leaving the ship rolling through the waves much more smoothly.

"If you are wanting to know where we are, look around," said Charna. *"Because I have no idea. Someone comes down here a few times a day and asks me to point in the direction from which I feel your presence. They don't let me out of this cell."*

"Then," said Kragan, *"I think it's time you got a glimpse of the stars."*

"And how do you propose I do that?" she asked, rattling the bars that locked her inside the tiny space.

"The channel between us is too weak for me to wield any significant magic through you. But that does not mean I am impotent."

Charna felt her gaze shift to the lock. The skin of her right hand began to itch as if she had slept on it too long. Then, with a snap, the lock on her cell door popped open.

She jumped up, opened the door, and stepped out of her cell for the first time in days. Charna simply wanted to get to the upper deck without encountering anyone. With no need to patrol the ship, the night watch would be manning their stations, keeping the ship on course and watching for dangers from the sea.

Moving silently past the galley, she crept from the stern toward the cargo access hatch amidships. Charna made her way to the ladder that led to the decks above, careful not to overturn any of the stacked supplies stored down in the lower hold. She climbed to the first of the hatches through which she would have to pass and paused, pleased to find it open. She sniffed the air, accosted by the scent of people who had not taken the opportunity to bathe for days. Low snores sounded from above, so she poked her head through the opening.

The berth deck, with its dozens of occupied hammocks, filled the forward section of the deck, while a hall leading to what she assumed was the officers' quarters stretched toward the stern. Satisfied that nobody was awake here, Charna resumed her climb. Once more she stopped to peer out onto the main deck. A few sailors moved atop the forecastle. She could not see up onto the aftcastle's upper deck but knew that someone would be manning the ship's whipstaff to control the rudder.

Taking a breath to slow her rapid heartbeat, Charna climbed out onto the main deck and scrambled behind one of the longboats tied along the railing. For several moments she knelt there, tasting the salty spray on the cool evening breeze and hearing the crash of breakers against the ship's hull. She wanted to memorize this feeling of freedom, these smells and sounds. They would have to soothe her when she returned to the brig.

"Not at the sea," said Kragan. *"Look at the sky."*

Charna lifted her eyes to the heavens, pleased to see that, although the night was not cloudless, broad swaths of stars winked down at her on this moonless night. She leaned out of her concealment for a better view, feeling recognition in Kragan as she shifted her gaze fore, aft, and from side to side.

The sound of footsteps sent Charna scrambling back behind the boat. Three sailors climbed up into the rigging along the mainmast, their attention on the sails high above the deck. An oddly shaped lantern dangled from the end of a four-foot pole strapped to the back of the lead sailor, lighting his way but destroying any night vision the three might have otherwise had.

"Good," said Kragan, satisfaction filling his voice. *"I have the information I need. Now get back to your cell and lock yourself in."*

Then the wielder's mental touch was gone. Kragan's sudden breaking of their link pulled a soft hiss from Charna. She found the ancient one's concern for her well-being underwhelming. The warrior took several deep breaths of the refreshing sea breeze. Then, after several glances up and around, she crept back to the hatch and down. This time she did not pause between decks. If it was her destiny to be caught before she could return to her cell, then she would face the consequences of her brief escape.

After all, Blade and Carol still needed her alive.

PART IV

Death shall awaken to his true potential. Whether he shall embrace it for good or evil, even I cannot foresee.

—From the *Scroll of Landrel*

21

Arn tossed in his sleep as images crowded his unconscious mind.

Something was coming. Stare as he might into the predawn semi-darkness, Arn could not make out what concerned him so much that he held Slaken in a white-knuckled grip. He stood by the bowsprit, look-ing at the distant shoreline of the large bay they had just entered. The feeling of wrongness intensified, pulling his eyes toward the ship's stern.

The *Milakais* was dimly visible a quarter league behind the *Saimniece*. A strange froth churned the waters around the ship into tendrils of white foam that sprouted from the water to fall upon their sister ship. Men ran across the deck, swinging weapons as if charging living foes. Even from this distance, Arn could recognize two of these men. Alan's peg-legged Forsworn weapons master Kron whirled a war hammer at the large shapes that blurred through the sea spray to strike at them.

Galad fought alongside him, thrusting and parrying with his saber only to be knocked overboard and into the churning sea. Something tore through the *Milakais*'s mainsail, leaving long strips of it fluttering in the wind like a ragged banner.

Vision after vision formed in Arn's mind, but in none of them could the *Saimniece* close the distance to the *Milakais* in time to save her crew. And now, whatever was killing the *Milakais* was coming for Carol and her companions.

A gentle shaking pulled Arn from his dream, and he blinked up into Carol's concerned face, backlit by the elemental globe of light that floated in the air above their bed.

"I'm sorry to wake you," she said. "You were thrashing about, reaching for Slaken."

Arn sat up, swinging his legs off the bed and rubbing the dream remnants from his eyes. Carol moved to sit beside him, wrapping an arm around his waist and leaning her head on his left shoulder. Her ragged breathing raked Arn's ear like claws on glass.

"Did I hurt you, love?" he asked, taking her other hand in his.

"No," she said. "You would never hurt me."

"Not intentionally," he said, his voice thick with trepidation.

"I love you. Just as importantly, I believe in you. Whatever this is, I think you're meant to learn to control it, just as you control the deadly blades you wield."

Although he was tempted to argue, Arn made a decision he knew he might regret. But if he could not be honest with his wife, he would not be able to live with himself.

He shifted to face her, taking both her hands in his and looking into her russet eyes.

"Yesterday you asked me what I saw when I was staring into Landrel's Scroll. I lied to you, a mistake I promise I will never repeat, even if the telling causes you to lose faith in me."

She squeezed his hands, her nails threatening to draw blood.

"That," she said, "will never happen."

So they sat there, naked in bed, as he told her of the ciphers crawling through Landrel's Scroll, of how they had somehow transported him back through time, of his conversation with the ancient master of the nine magics. When he ended with his description of how the ciphers within Landrel's text had jumped out at him more clearly than the text within which they were hidden, Carol suddenly leaned forward and kissed him.

"What?" he asked when she pulled back, a broad smile on her face.

"Don't you see? Either you are crazy or, somehow, Landrel was telling you the truth you needed to hear. My darling, you are *not* crazy."

"And if you're wrong about that?"

She grabbed her clothes and began putting them on.

"Get dressed," she said. "The only way to verify or refute a hypothesis is to test it. You're about to validate my faith."

After dressing and strapping on his knives, Arn followed Carol to the ship's library, where dawn's first light filtered through the window, giving the great cabin a rosy glow. She retrieved the Scroll of Landrel and spread it on the table, leaving its two wooden rollers far enough apart to reveal the first several pages of the text. He studied the words for several minutes.

"I don't see any sign of a cipher on these pages," said Arn.

"Okay. Then let's look further in the scroll."

Carol curled the current pages onto the leftmost roller, then spread out the one on her right to reveal another set. But after more than an hour of study, Arn was unable to find any sign of what had jumped out of the text at him yesterday. He glanced up, his eyes meeting Carol's. The arch of his left eyebrow said "I told you so" as clearly as if he had spoken the words.

As she unfurled the scroll in the opposite direction to reveal the first several pages, Arn pulled Slaken from its sheath and set the black knife aside. When he returned his gaze to the words that Landrel had meticulously penned, the hidden patterns appeared, so quickly and obviously that Arn had difficulty believing that he had missed seeing them.

"So?" Carol asked.

When Arn began to read the ciphers aloud, Carol clapped her hands.

"Yes!" she breathed.

Then she went silent, focused on what he was saying. Page by page he worked his way through the document, reciting the missing pieces of Landrel's prophecy. And as he did so, Landrel's ghostly form appeared on the opposite side of the table.

"What's wrong?" asked Carol, her voice breaking the momentary trance into which he had fallen.

"Sorry," said Arn. "Landrel just peeked in to gloat."

Carol motioned impatiently at the scroll. "Please continue."

It was just past noon when Arn finished reading. He picked up Slaken and the pattern faded from sight. The words he had just spoken aloud remained invisible when he put the runed knife back in its sheath.

Carol finished rolling the scroll and placed it on a shelf, the document held in place by twin bookends. When she sat down opposite Arn, her eyes brimmed with a complex mixture of excitement and dismay. They now knew the names of the city-states where Landrel's sons and daughters had secreted the five mummified fingers, although the location of the sixth finger remained a mystery. They had been concealed within specially crafted time stones, meant to become the cornerstones of altars within temples to the deities worshipped by the people of the disparate merchant kingdoms.

Unfortunately, neither Carol nor anyone else aboard these two galleons knew the geography of Sadamad. More disquieting was the prophecy that Kragan would also learn where the fragments from Landrel's Trident were hidden.

Carol reached across the table to place a hand on Arn's left arm, drawing his eyes to hers.

"I think it's clear that Landrel wants you to put Slaken aside and focus on learning to control your time-sight talent."

"He didn't say that to me when he had the chance," said Arn. "He told me that Slaken was my salvation."

"Or the destruction of everything you love," said Carol. "He said that he couldn't foresee the choice that you'll make."

Arn gently took her hand.

"Even if Landrel is correct about my time-sight ability, its development cannot be as valuable to our mission as Slaken. With it, I'm immune from the magic that Kragan will wield against us. Without Slaken I cannot penetrate Kragan's defenses to kill him."

"Together," said Carol, "we can."

"Not if he acquires Landrel's artifacts of amplification."

Carol paused to ponder his statement, biting her lower lip.

"Then we'll just have to beat Kragan to them."

"He knows Sadamad," said Arn. "And he has a head start."

"We have your time-sight."

Arn laughed. "At this point, that's more of a hindrance than a help."

"And," said Carol, undaunted, "we have Galad to wield the mists of time."

"Let me make a bargain with you," said Arn.

"I'm listening," she said, rising to her feet.

Arn stood up to face her, a slow grin curling his lips.

"I will continue to put Slaken aside when we go to bed."

Carol narrowed her eyes, placing her fists on her hips.

"That's no compromise. You need to practice conscious control of the magic. You will never improve if you only let it choose your dreams."

Arn looked at Carol's determined posture and serious face, seeing some of her father in her. The beauty and power in that look took his breath away.

"Here's my offer," he said. "When we get on dry land, I promise to set aside some of each day to practice with you as we travel."

For several moments, Carol merely stared at him. Then she let her arms drop to her sides and nodded.

"We have a deal."

She led him to the door, turning to peer into his eyes before stepping out into the narrow hallway.

"I will hold you to it."

His smile returned.

"Of that, my love, I have no doubt."

22

Kragan, wearing a low-cut azure gown, sat in her study, looking at the collection of maps and star charts the merchant queen maintained on these shelves, some from the days before the time-mist barrier had closed the trade routes to Endar. She pulled forth the perfect memory of Charna's shipboard view of the moonless night sky over the Brinje Ocean. Her index finger drifted over the map, coming to a stop a little more than halfway between the Endarian and Sadamad continents.

"Got you," she said softly.

She envisioned the route the ship had made to this point, mentally extending it to Sadamad. True to her promise, Charna was leading them toward Kragan, here in Varjupaik. That would never do. True, Kragan could command her fleet to attack Carol before she reached Sadamad, but with her vast abilities, Carol would send the merchant queen's vessels to the bottom of the ocean. Besides, Kragan had already launched her fleet toward Rukkumine's harbor, where they would enter under the guise of normal trade. But there were no merchant goods in those holds, only fighters, their weapons, and other tools of war.

No. Kragan would stick with her original plan. Kragan ran her fingers over the lovely cleavage the gown exposed to draw the hungry eyes of the men who saw her. It was time for the assassination of the merchant queen whose body he had absconded with. The moment had come to make his escape from Varjupaik to return to the hidden crypt where he could assume his original form.

Kragan walked to the door and opened it. Varonis and another of the new guards whom she had raised from the dead turned to face her.

"Step into my chambers, both of you," she said. "And shut the door behind you."

The two guards did as she commanded. As the door closed, she bound and gagged the bearded guardsman in invisible strands of magic that the air elemental Ohk produced.

"Captain Varonis," she said, "draw your sword and slay this man."

Varonis's eyes widened, but, compelled by her will, as were all whom she raised from the dead, he drew his sword and slashed the other's throat. A fountain of blood spurted out and Kragan stepped into the spray, soaking her front, before she dismissed the tethers that held the bearded one erect. The body dropped to the floor at her feet.

She shifted her gaze back to Varonis and issued another command.

"Strip out of your armor and clothes. Then lie down faceup on my bed."

Again she felt the man's mind struggle to free itself from the iron grip of her will. And again those efforts failed. Varonis removed his armor and clothing, then lay naked as she had instructed. The captain had a rangy body, not heavily muscled but well defined. A long line of puckered skin ran from his right clavicle to his belly button, doubtless put there by the stroke of an edged blade.

"Do not move," Kragan commanded.

Then she climbed atop him and summoned the life magic through the mummified fingers between her breasts. Blood vessels burrowed from her form, burrowing into his everywhere her skin touched his body. Kragan's life essence squirmed from Lielisks into Varonis, returning the captain's soul to the land of the dead as Kragan stole his body.

The torment passed slowly, leaving Kragan weak and shaking beneath the merchant queen's corpse. With an effort he rolled Lielisks off him, arranging her faceup in the bed's center. He grabbed a fistful of her hair, lifted her head, and removed the chain with the two precious artifacts from her neck. He slipped it over his head, climbed from the bed, and dressed himself in Varonis's clothes and armor.

Kragan moved to the bearded guard, knelt, and arranged the body as if the man had been facing the door when he was killed. He stepped back to survey the scene, soon satisfied that it would confirm the story he was about to tell.

Holding his bloody sword, Kragan threw open the door and stepped out into the hallway.

"Guards, to me!" he yelled. "Our queen has been murdered!"

The sound of booted, running footsteps and the clank of weapons being unlimbered preceded a half dozen guardsmen answering their captain's call.

Kragan pointed, then led them into the queen's bedchamber, stopping to sweep his left hand out over the stage he had set. The guards stopped to take in the bearded guard lying in a pool of blood.

"I arrived too late to save our queen," Kragan said, letting his voice grow husky.

He turned to face the queen's guardsmen.

"You two," he said, indicating the warriors farthest to the left. "Guard this chamber. Let no one disturb this scene until instructed to do so by the high councillor. The rest of you, summon the senators so that they may bear witness to this latest act of treachery. I have no doubt that King Godus is behind this."

With a wave of his hand, Kragan sent the guards striding off to carry out his orders. He followed them down the hall at a far more leisurely pace, allowing himself a thin smile. Though he could have controlled the minds of these men who had recently crawled from the cemetery dirt, he had chosen to avoid making the links that would have accomplished that. If allowed their free will, they would believe the deception Kragan had created with these latest murders.

Now an outraged Captain Varonis would take a company of his reborn guardsmen and set out to hunt for any of Godus's other agents who would now be attempting to flee Varjupaik, a mission from which they would never return.

—◊—

Having traveled for two weeks from Varjupaik to the southwestern tip of the Kalnai Mountains, Kragan ordered a halt, making camp for the evening less than an hour's hike from his hidden crypt. He would soon unleash the life magic as he had done only once before. To restore his ancient corpse to life, Kragan would have to die.

As painful as stealing the body of another living soul was, revivification would make that suffering seem pleasant. Kragan would do this alone once he had returned to his buried tomb. Only when clothed in his real body would he have access to his full ability to channel life magic. Then the two fragments of Landrel's Trident would amplify that greater capacity, enabling him to summon from death the beings who would destroy the Rafel witch and her companions.

Charna would have to be sacrificed as well. The she-vorg was the only friend Kragan had ever known, and the thought of losing her saddened him. An unavoidable necessity. His latest link to Charna had revealed that Carol's two ships were less than a week away from the entrance to Whale's Mouth Bay, where Kragan, his company of soldiers, and the Zvejys people would be waiting to deliver a proper welcome.

Kragan issued commands that the guardsmen were to establish camp, post the normal night watch, and await his return sometime after midnight wearing a different body. He transmitted the vision of the diminutive physique with the large hands, feet, and head that was his true form. Having been recalled from the land of the dead, these battle-hardened warriors were not surprised.

He made his way up the forested hillside toward the cliff-lined summit. Kragan picked his way north through the undergrowth along the rock wall's western face. As the sun sank below the western horizon, the wielder found the narrow crack in the cliff that marked his tomb's location. Dalg answered his summons, giving the rock the consistency of air, forming a murky portal to a concealed passageway.

Kragan stepped through the stone and into a corridor that angled down to the east. He conjured a head-size globe of light and sent it moving down the hallway. He followed. Seventeen paces later, the crypt opened around him. He stepped past the gold mirror that hung on the tomb's southern wall to stop before the ancient sarcophagus that held his corpse.

Since he knew how weak what he was about to do would leave him, Kragan channeled the magic that lifted the heavy lid from the coffin and lowered it to the stone floor. The light revealed the withered body within. Mummified skin clung to the bones, some of it hanging in thin, hairy strips from the skull. Its right ear was missing, Kragan having cut it from his own corpse all those centuries ago. The skeleton stretched only a stride and a half from disproportionately large feet to the top of that head. The spectacle wrinkled Kragan's nose with disgust.

He shook his head at the irony of how moving his life essence back into that small form would grant him a far greater channel through which to funnel his life magic. Removing the chain necklace, Kragan looped it around his corpse's neck and stepped back from the sarcophagus.

While stealing another living body required a specific ritual, rising again in his own was a much simpler, if far more torturous, exchange. To restore a life, one must sacrifice another. Kragan pulled the dagger from Varonis's belt sheath, reversed it in a two-hand grip, and raised it high. The light from the mystic globe glittered off the razor-sharp edges, seeming to flow down to the tip that was slanted toward Kragan's upraised chin.

After taking two deep breaths, Kragan plunged the blade down into his throat. Pain blossomed in his mind and he dropped to his knees, feeling his warm blood coat his hands and arms. Then he toppled backward, spasmed twice, and lay still.

Dying was never pleasant. But resurrection was horrendous.

Time slowed as if Kragan were encased in one of the Endarian pomaly mists. As each muscle formed, new nerves sprouted throughout his body, wrapping Kragan in a seething blanket of fire. Skin knitted only to burst, then to meld once again. Lungs inflated in the previously empty chest, unready to breathe air. Veins, arteries, and a heart crawled into being, starved for blood to pump. A giant sat on his chest, holding Kragan's head underwater.

Kragan tried and failed to stifle the involuntary howl that shredded his still-forming vocal cords. His hands clawed at his chest, seizing the mummified fingers of power, as if they could somehow speed the healing or alleviate the pain. But this torture was the price of Kragan's immortality.

When he finally crawled from the sarcophagus, he collapsed on the cold stone, panting, harsh sobs of relief racking his small body. He rolled onto his back, wiped tears and snot from his face, and wiped his hands on the dusty floor. The blackness in the crypt was complete, the magical orb he had summoned having dissipated when he died. With an effort worthy of the gods, he sat up, panting and shaking with the effort. Once again his hands clutched the magical fragments of Landrel's Trident. But these were amplifiers of life magic, and there was no life within their reach that could be channeled to refresh him.

He did not know how long he sat there, leaning back against the coffin, waiting for the palsy to subside. When he recovered enough to summon a minor fire elemental to create an orb of light, he looked over at what remained of Varonis. The corpse looked as if it had lain there for millennia. But the clothes and armor that draped those ancient bones were unchanged, not that any of it would fit Kragan now.

That was okay. Kragan had disrobed when he had last slithered from this body, into that of the Varjupaik merchant marine. Before he had commenced the ritual of body stealing, he had folded his leather breeches and shirt, placing them alongside his socks, boots, and ceremonial dagger.

A glance confirmed that they lay, dusty but undisturbed, in front of the gold mirror that leaned against the chamber's south wall. All in preparation for this moment.

Kragan inhaled, pulling the musty air into his lungs. His belly rumbled in protest against its emptiness, and his throat ached with thirst, both things he could remedy as soon as he left the tomb.

Kragan walked to the mirror, taking several moments to study this form in which he had grown to manhood. The large extremities that had mortified him so when the woman sailor had rejected him now seemed to radiate power. These feet enabled him to move confidently through swamps that large people could not traverse without a knowledgeable guide. His oversize head cradled a brain capable of wielding the nine magics. And those hands with the long, dexterous fingers, especially the thumb, index, and middle fingers of his right hand, completed the magical channel, just as an iron tower funneled lightning into the ground.

Kragan ran his hands through the wild mop of hair that hung to his shoulders and hid his missing ear. Those were not the only extremities that displayed his masculine prowess. Perhaps if he had been nude when he confronted the woman, she would not have laughed at his clumsy advance.

Shrugging off the musing, Kragan retrieved his clothes and dressed, securing the sacrificial dagger in its belt sheath on his left side, ready for a cross-handed draw. He surveyed himself in the mirror one last time, drawing electrical energy from the air, letting it dance across his finger-tips, and smiled. It was time to collect his company of risen warriors and lead them to the Zvejys fishing village of Klampyne, built atop the bones of hundreds of long-extinct sea-dragons. There he would prepare his final welcome for Rafel and her companions.

Neither she nor Blade would ever reach land to threaten him.

23

Cradled in Carol's arms, Arn slept almost until dawn.

On this night Carol enjoyed the peaceful nature of her husband's dream, which wrapped her in wonderful memories of her childhood. The twelve-year-old boy who had become Rafel's ward after the high lord had rescued the lad from the gallows in Tal's capital city of Hannington had trained under Gaar's tutelage. Carol had often come to the training grounds to watch him. Arn had noticed her infatuation and befriended the high lord's daughter, five years his junior.

He had taken her on long rides, well beyond the boundaries that Rafel had set for her. And on each of those occasions, they had stumbled across something that happened so rarely that few ever got the opportunity to see the event. It was as if Arn's purpose for their outing had been for them to end up at the precise place and moment for the magical happening.

On one such outing, Carol had ridden a bay mare alongside Arn's pinto horse into a wooded basin that surrounded a grassy clearing with a large pond in its center. Arn dismounted near the water's edge and dropped his reins. Carol, having climbed from her saddle, did the same. He led her along the bank to where a rocky outcrop jutted out into the pond. His head tilted slightly to the side, as if he were listening to something she could not hear. Then he straightened and pointed to the muddy bank on their left.

For a moment Carol thought that the ground was moving. Then she saw them. Thousands upon thousands of tiny, multicolored vardez hatchlings wriggled from the mud. The little legs and webbed feet that would soon have them swimming beneath the surface of the pond to catch minnows and bugs were scarcely strong enough to propel them across the muddy surface toward the water. They glistened in the sunlight, forming incandescent shifting rainbows.

The flapping of many wings accompanied excited squawks as birds descended on the mire to greedily snatch up the helpless baby vardez. But even the winged predators were not sufficient to stop this mass migration. When the multihued tide reached the steepest part of the bank, it slid into the water in a brilliant fall that reminded Carol of glowing molten metal poured into a clay mold by a blacksmith.

Carol watched Arn's memory of the event, seeing her eight-year-old self standing beside him in awe of this occurrence, something that happened only every seventeenth year. He had smiled down at her, taken her hand, boosted her back onto her mount, and led her back to Rafel's Keep. The spectacle had lasted just a few minutes, but it had been one of Arn's many kindnesses that had made her love him as a brother, a fondness that eventually morphed into a wholly different form of adoration.

A sudden jerk of Arn's body startled Carol awake, though it did not break her mental link with her husband.

A new vision exploded into her mind. It was the same coastline she had seen in Arn's earlier nightmares, densely overhung, swamplike shores that surrounded a wide bay. The *Saimniece* tacked hard, struggling through the whitecaps to get to the *Milakais*, as beings she could not quite make out swarmed the *Milakais*'s decks and shredded the ship's sails and rigging. Kron fought amidships, his thick arms whirling his war hammer as he waded into the seething mass of attackers, each blow spraying fountains of green slime.

A tentacle wrapped itself around Kron's waist, pulling him over the rail and into the boiling sea before Galad could reach him. Galad's mouth opened in a furious yell that she was not close enough to hear. Carol saw herself rush to the *Saimniece*'s bowsprit, casting the spell that lensed the air into a far-glass, trying to resolve the combatants so she could cast spells to help them. Her vision self cried out in horror as something within the sea spray that washed the *Milakais*'s deck pulled Galad into the waves.

The raging ocean around the *Milakais* suddenly calmed. A wedge of frothing water speared out toward the *Saimniece*, leaving the dead ship *Milakais* in its wake.

Arn stepped up beside the other Carol, Slaken in his hand. The horror on Carol's face transformed into fury. She gestured with her right hand toward the sky, ensnaring Lwellen and blasting the writhing ocean with chain lightning. But that failed to stop the things that churned the sea's surface from beneath. Whatever had just killed everyone aboard the *Milakais* was now coming for them.

Beside her in bed, Arn sat up straight, the vision dissolving as quickly as it had appeared. Carol huffed out a ragged breath, stunned by the tension that swathed every muscle in her body. Arn's dream had felt so real that she had unconsciously tried to reach inside it to change the dreadful outcome.

Her husband turned to look down at her, his eyes filled with concern.

"So," he said, "you still think that digging deeper into this time-sight magic is a good thing?"

She suppressed a shudder and took his hand. "If Landrel and his scroll prove anything, it is that there is no single future. The outcomes you see can be altered. Your visions provide you with knowledge of things that we can change."

"How many different versions of this dream have you experienced with me?" asked Arn. "Dozens. No matter what we do within them, we are never able to reach the *Milakais* to save it. Those monsters, whatever they are, kill everyone aboard and then come for us."

Carol paused to ponder the truth of what he said. "By the time we first saw the bay, it was too late to change the outcome. What if we lash both ships together now, while we still can?"

"That will slow our progress," said Arn. "And having the two ships lashed together presents dangers of its own."

"True. If I'm wrong, we will suffer a delay for my foolish fears. But your visions of that bay are becoming more distinct. We should not ignore them."

She saw his jaw muscles tighten.

"You truly believe that I am seeing our future," Arn said, his voice filled with incredulity.

"A future, yes. One that can be avoided if we act now."

Arn got out of bed and began dressing. "Then I guess we better talk to the captain before we get to that bay."

Carol slipped into her own clothes, her eyes drawn to Slaken as Arn strapped the blade to his waist. He caught her look. His arched eyebrow invited her challenge to his taking up the runed knife. She placed a tender hand on his arm, leaning in close enough to whisper in his ear.

"My love, I am not asking you to give up Slaken, only that you consider letting me help you take small steps to develop your magical talent. Your intuition will guide you to the right decision."

Then she pulled back to look at his stern face. For several moments his eyes locked with hers. Then he gave a slight nod and turned toward the door.

That nonverbal signal, small as it had been, funneled hope into Carol. Maybe she could yet overcome Slaken's hold upon her husband.

Then, as they stepped out into the hallway, she noticed how tightly Arn's left hand gripped the knife's haft.

The warm glow that had flowered in her chest faded away, leaving a wintry chill.

—⁂—

"Chosen."

Alan turned to see Bill hastily stride across the deck toward him, the man's mischievous grin having been replaced with a look of agitation. Kat also noticed the change, as evidenced by the way her hand moved to the hilt of her long knife.

"What is it?" Alan asked.

"Lorness Carol sent me to summon you to the captain's cabin. She, Arn, and Princess Kimber are on their way there now."

"Did she say why?" asked Kat.

"No," said Bill. "But from the looks on her face and Arn's, it is serious."

"Okay," said Alan, slinging his ax across his back. "When we get there, you and Kat wait outside."

His curiosity aroused, Alan led the way to Captain Kumstelis's cabin. When he arrived at the captain's door, he knocked twice. Arn opened it and ushered Alan inside. Kat and Bill moved to either side of the entry, as if they were royal guardsmen, as Arn closed the door behind Alan.

The room was sparsely furnished. A bed on the wall to Alan's right was neatly made. Chart-filled bookshelves lined the walls. In the center of the room stood a round table with only a single chair, both bolted to the floor. Captain Kumstelis leaned back in the chair, and Kim, Alan, Arn, and Carol gathered around the table.

Although all the Endarians Alan had encountered wore their hair long, Kumstelis's tresses draped the back of his chair to actually touch the floor.

"Ah, Lorness Carol," said Kumstelis, "it appears our mysterious discussion has a quorum. Perhaps you can now tell me why you have requested this meeting."

"My apologies for the cryptic nature of my request, Captain," she said as Arn moved to stand beside her. "But I prefer to have all the major players present so I just have to do this once."

"Very well," said the Endarian captain.

Alan watched his sister glance at Arn, almost as if she were seeking validation. Whatever support she wanted from that glance she failed to receive. The assassin's face remained impassive.

What was going on between these two, who had loved each other almost as long as Alan could remember, long before they both admitted it? Alan had felt growing tension between them ever since they had boarded this ship and set sail for Sadamad. Arn had become increasingly withdrawn, almost sullen, as if he shouldered a burden that increased with each passing day. On more than one occasion Alan had been tempted to confront his brother-in-law. Perhaps he could shake some sense into the brooding man. Then again, brooding was a habit Alan had grown way too familiar with. His father's death at the hands of their enemies had not helped.

Carol straightened, her face regaining the authority that he had grown used to seeing in her manner. When she began to speak, the tale that flowed from her lips transported Alan into another world. His sister described what it was like to share Arn's dreams while he slept and, as she did, visions formed in Alan's mind. They plucked him from this cabin and onto the windswept deck of the *Saimniece* as it struggled through the surf to reach its distant sister ship. The sight of the ferocious assault that left the *Milakais* dead in the water had him seething.

Alan realized that this was not the work of a master storyteller. Carol was wielding her mind magic on everyone in the cabin, transplanting Arn's dreams into each of her companions' heads. Though he had felt his sister enter his mind before, this experience raised gooseflesh on Alan's arms and neck.

When Carol released her companions from the hallucination that had pulled them from this world into another, Captain Kumstelis leapt to his feet, backing up against the far wall, his sword drawn.

"What dark magic is this?" he rasped.

Arn moved between the wide-eyed Endarian and Carol, Slaken in his right hand.

Princess Kimber spoke, her voice steady, commanding.

"Captain Kumstelis, sheathe your sword!"

The captain's eyes shifted from Carol to his princess. He blinked twice, took a deep breath, and did as she ordered. The well-honed saber made a smooth hiss as it slid into its scabbard, but a mixture of anger and fear still shone in Kumstelis's eyes.

Alan could not blame the captain for his response. Despite the length of Alan's experience with his sister's magic, what she had just done had left his heart pounding as if he had been in battle. He saw Arn step back to Carol's side, returning his knife to its sheath on his left hip.

"I am sorry to startle you, Captain," said Carol, exuding an aura of authority that impressed Alan. "But if I merely described what Arn has foreseen, the vision's impact would have been insufficient to portray the depth of the incoming threat."

To the captain's credit, he recovered his equilibrium, pausing to consider Carol's words and the apparitions he had just beheld.

"Princess Kimber," he said, "do you believe the truth of this prophecy?"

Kim's confident eyes met the captain's, her gaze unblinking.

"I do."

Kumstelis stroked his chin with his right hand. His unfocused eyes looked off into the distance, and Alan knew that he was reliving the horrible imagery that he had just experienced. When his attention returned to Carol, he straightened.

"Then we must turn aside, make landfall somewhere besides that mouth-shaped bay toward which you say we are headed."

The idea of turning away from the target they pursued rankled Alan.

"Bad idea," he said. "Never let your enemy turn you away from your objective. I say we adjust our tactics to meet this threat and stay on target."

"Usually, Lord Alan," said Kumstelis, "I would agree with you. But we have all just experienced a prophecy of our impending destruction. To continue into that trap would be folly of the worst sort."

Arn spoke, his low voice thick with emotion.

"We hunt the wielder who destroyed Tal and killed thousands of Endarians. He killed High Lord Rafel. He murdered my family," Arn said, pointing toward the ship's bow. "Out there, Kragan awaits us. To turn aside would show that we fear him. We will make him fear us."

"We don't even know what killed everyone aboard the *Milakais*," said the captain. "Why could we not see the things Prince Galad and his warriors were fighting?"

"My brother was wielding the time-mists against the attackers," said Kim. "The miasmas masked the enemy beings from our sight."

"If Galad swathed the *Milakais* in the mists," said Carol, "why could we see the ship?"

Kim glanced down, collecting her thoughts. "Galad did not swathe the *Milakais* with the time-mists because the crew needed to steer the ship. So he wove rychly and pomaly mists to separate his enemies into manageable waves. Had we been but close enough to support his efforts with the rest of Alan's Forsworn and our own magics, Galad might have succeeded."

Arn placed his hands upon the round table and leaned in, eyes set in determination.

"I say we fight."

"Yes," said Alan, rolling his shoulders as if loosening them in preparation for wielding his great ax. "Let these foul things taste the fury of my Forsworn, fighting together as one."

All eyes shifted to Carol, a gentle breeze stirring her shoulder-length brown hair. The flame in the storm lamp over the table guttered.

"Captain Kumstelis," she said, "bring us alongside the *Milakais*. From here on out, we shall sail side by side, staying to the course the she-vorg points out."

Once again the captain caught her nod of approval.

"As you command, Lorness Carol," said Kumstelis.

"Up ahead our enemy awaits," Carol said, "and there we will defeat him or die."

Alan watched his sister, felt the magic swirling about her, and grinned. He had no doubt that, in the land of the dead, their father was proud of the young woman he had brought into this world and raised. Come the battle, Alan would seize his own slice of glory. If it was his fate to stride alongside these companions into the Dread Lord's realm, so be it.

Perhaps he was the Chosen after all.

24

Zvejys Fishing Village of Klampyne, Whale's Mouth Bay,
Continent of Sadamad
YOR 415, Mid-Summer

Kragan stared out across the town square of Klampyne, the village in which he had been born. His company of guardsmen had assembled the 327 Zvejys people in the center of the open space. Their lone magic wielder lay dead upon the cobblestones. Men, women, and children gazed upon the imposing armored warriors who ringed them, their eyes wide with distress.

Kragan stood over the body of the wielder, looking down at the Zvejys woman who had dared challenge him. She lay on her back, her tawny eyes open wide in death, seeming to stare up at her killer in shocking recognition of her mortality. Her face looked so familiar. His reflection in those glistening orbs thrust him back into a vivid memory from his childhood.

—⁓—

Kragan had just finished a wonderful meal of fish cake and sugarcoated ryziai fresh from his mother's woodstove. He was celebrating his seventh birthday.

"Ah, you liked that," Motina said, smiling at her son and running her hand through his wild tresses. "Run along and play now."

Pushing back his chair, he stood to hug her, grabbed his fishing pole, then darted out the door before she could change her mind and decide that he needed to help with the dishes.

"Stay close," she yelled after him, and he waved his hand in acknowledgment.

His favorite fishing hole lay just a short distance from their hut's front door. The wispy branches of an ancient glousnis tree draped this fingertip of swamp that touched the southwest corner of the fishing village. Kragan pulled up a large glob of mud, baited his hook with a fat worm, and tossed his line into the pool.

He propped his pole in the fork of a branch he had previously stuck in the muddy ground for this very purpose and moved to the water's edge to wash the mud from his hands. His hands had no sooner touched the water than its surface exploded, spraying him with green slime. A tooth-filled maw snapped a handspan from his face, sending him scrambling backward up the bank and pulling a terrified scream from his mouth.

Kragan's left heel caught on an exposed root and he fell backward, the impact knocking the breath from his body. The green-scaled kroko-dilas scrambled up the bank after him, its black-slitted red eyes siphon-ing what little strength his fall had left him. He kicked out, catching the beast on the tip of its open snout. The jaws snapped shut, making a sound like the boatbuilder's mallet striking a board.

A terrified mewling crawled from Kragan's throat as he clambered back against the tree trunk, unable to break his lock with the oncom-ing creature's eyes. Something blurred into his peripheral vision. His mother flew through the air to land on the back of the krokodilas, her butcher knife plunging into the thing's neck.

"Run!" she yelled as the beast whipped its head and tail, then rolled.

Kragan scrambled to his feet and ran. He did not stop until he reached the cottage door, ducked inside, and slammed it behind him. He stood there, back braced against wood, panting. When his breathing subsided, he sank down to the floor, praying to hear his mother's voice telling him that everything was okay and to let her in. As the minutes dragged by, he waited. Dread wrapped him in its deathly cold grip, leaving him curled into a ball, weeping on the floor.

Unable to stand not knowing any longer, Kragan climbed to his feet, his eyes drawn to the half-finished pile of dirty dishes beside the washbasin. He sniffed, wiped away his tears, walked to the door, and opened it. As theirs was the last house on this side of town, nobody else had heard his scream or seen his mother's flight toward the swamp. Neither did they observe Kragan's dragging footsteps carry him back to his fishing hole.

When he reached the glousnis tree, he approached it from the back as tremors racked his entire body. He touched the trunk, leaned his forehead against it, then peeked around the right side. At first he saw no sign of his mother. Then he saw it. A slick, red track through the mud, deep finger marks clawed into the muck. With a howl of misery, Kragan sank to his knees, squeezed his eyes closed, and tried to blot out the horrific images his vivid imagination painted in his mind.

—∽—

Kragan blinked away the vision that the sight of the dead woman at his feet had pulled forth. That small body, face, and tightly braided hair fastened close to her scalp gave her an eerie resemblance to the mother he had been unable to save. He had not even tried to help her. Powerless.

His lips curled into a sneer. Who was powerless now?

Even though he was a member of the Zvejys race, he now wielded power beyond that of any other.

He scanned the frightened, whimpering crowd, feeling revulsion at the peaceful timidity of the people who had spawned him. They had counted on the surrounding swamp to protect them from the large mountain marauders. But Kragan had guided his band of warriors here along paths that only a Zvejys could identify.

He looked up at the high clouds that shrouded the sky, filtering the sun's illumination into a gray half light that suited his mood. His link with Charna had been growing noticeably stronger for days now. At this point Kragan no longer needed to make direct contact with the she-vorg. From the rate at which the clarity of that connection increased, she was just hours from entering Whale's Mouth Bay.

When he had first begun planning his response to Carol Rafel's pursuit, Kragan had considered summoning a storm to destroy her ships at sea. But Carol would have little difficulty in countering such elemental mind magic. A grin curled his lips. The wielder would have no such luck in dealing with what he was about to unleash.

Kragan turned to look up into the bearded face of his subcommander, Captain Nieksas. "March these villagers onto the fishing piers. Pack them tightly together."

"Yes, Lord Kragan."

Kragan stood back and watched as his company of once-dead guardsmen herded the terrified mass out of the square and through the narrow street that led to the harbor. His right hand moved up to grasp the shriveled fingers on his necklace. His mind focused on the artifacts, gathering to him the mystic power that would soon allow him to channel his life-magic in greater quantities than he had ever before attempted.

Then he strode forward, his short legs carrying him toward the place where he would unleash his wrath on the one who had tortured his dreams since he had killed Landrel all those thousands of years ago.

—ᴍ—

Carol stood beside Arn, to the right of the bowsprit on the *Saimniece's* forecastle. Her shoulder-length brown hair whipped around her neck in the chill wind. The call from the watch basket high on the mainmast had brought the ship's captain and Carol's companions to the forward rail. All eyes scanned the horizon for the land that the high watch had seen.

Carol lensed the air into a far-glass, magnifying her view. Still, she saw only sea on the horizon. Motion on the periphery shifted her gaze upward. Several gulls soared beneath the gray clouds overhead. She shifted her concentration, stilling her thoughts to establish a link to one of the seabirds.

The water swept away below, her eyes drawn to the two sailing vessels cutting through the waves just a dozen paces apart. Large fish leapt from the water around the craft, a joyous challenge to race.

She looked out toward the northwest. From this elevation the gaping bay at the southwestern tip of the broad peninsula looked like the mouth of a gigantic sea creature. As she focused her sight, the details became recognizable. This was the bay she had seen in Arn's dreams, and its entrance lay slightly to the west of where the ships were heading, perhaps only an hour or two away from their current position.

That made sense to Carol. Since the *Saimniece* was following the straight line that Charna had pointed out, their route did not take into account the fact that the bay stretched from southwest to northeast. Kragan would be awaiting them not at the mouth of the bay, but at its gullet.

Releasing her connection to the gull, she turned to Captain Kumstelis and informed him of the required course correction. He gave the appropriate command, which was promptly relayed to his first officer, and the ship tacked left, a maneuver that the *Milakais* replicated.

Carol lifted her eyes to the watch basket high atop the mainmast, a new determination resolving into a decision.

"Captain," she said, "I will take the high watch from here on."

Kumstelis raised an eyebrow as he looked down into her face, judging her resolve.

"As you wish, Lorness. Have a care with the ship's roll up there. I trust that you have a strong stomach."

Carol gritted her teeth at the thought but nodded.

The captain issued another order to his first mate. "Signal the high watchman to climb down."

Carol felt Arn's hand touch her elbow and turned to look into his concerned face.

"I cannot protect you up there," he said.

"You know I can take care of myself," she said. "I need you down here, working your own special magic in the coming battle."

Arn's mouth twisted into a frown.

"I cannot fight while distracted by hallucinations. I cannot set Slaken aside until this fight is done."

She placed her left palm on his cheek.

"You always find the right path, my love. Live or die, nothing shall shake my faith in you."

Carol kissed him, feeling herself swept into his arms in a grip that threatened to rob her of breath. He reluctantly released her, his obvious fear that this might be their last embrace bathing her in dread. But she managed to keep that emotion buried deep inside, forcing a hopeful smile as she stepped back. It would not fool Arn, but she hoped the gesture would give her husband some solace. When she met his eyes, she saw what she needed. The ice-cold assassin Blade.

Carol made her way down the steps that led from the forecastle to the main deck, and from there to the mainmast. From this position the rigging seemed to stretch up to touch the sky. She considered summoning the air elemental Ohk to carry her up to the watch basket, but immediately discarded the idea. The roll of the ship was magnified in the upper reaches of the mast, and she had no faith that she could compensate sufficiently to keep herself from being struck by the sails, ropes, and rigging.

With a gulp she reached out, grabbed the rope ladder that formed the pathway to the apex, and began to climb.

—⚲—

Kragan summoned Ohk, forming an invisible staircase that led up to a platform of solidified air, thirty feet above the mass of Zvejys people crowded onto the pier. When he reached the pinnacle, he stood looking out across the deep bay, still unable to see the approaching ships, hidden as they were by the ridge of land that formed Whale Mouth Bay's southern lip. Within the coming hour, those twin ships would make the turn around that point and enter the maw of death that awaited them.

He looked down at the frightened crowd. Small children huddled in their mothers' arms, the men standing protectively between them and Kragan's warriors. As far as Kragan knew, this was the last living enclave of the Zvejys, the descendants of the people he had once known and loved. Now they stared up at him in dismay. In those eyes he saw terror, but also revulsion that one of their own would treat them with such disdain.

A stiff breeze blew in from the bay, ruffling Kragan's shoulder-length wheat-colored mane. He imagined that, for those looking up at him standing on air, it enhanced his aura of mystic power. For several moments he stood there, savoring the terror that radiated up from the small people below. Then his left hand reached up to cradle the mummified fingers that hung from his neck chain, unleashing the power he had previously stored within them to open wide the channel for his life magic.

Hundreds of smoky tendrils radiated outward from the three primary digits of his right hand. Half the strands of life magic crawled among the Zvejys, each selecting a different target, entering the body through nose and mouth. An equal number of vaporous offshoots dived into the water beneath the pier, burrowing into the muddy soil of the bay's bottom.

And as those tentacles reached their targets, Kragan found himself transported millions of years into the past, to a time when the sea's most deadly hunters had made their spawning ground within this bay, long before the cataclysm that had swept them into extinction.

The size of a sea lion, each uzraudze had winglike fins, a head like that of a horse, a mouth filled with several rows of finely honed teeth, and a long, prehensile tail. That appendage propelled them through the water with such speed that they could take to the air and glide above the surface of the water for several hundred paces. Pack hunters, the uzraudze used their tails like tentacles to seize their prey and pull the victims into their rending maws.

The bay began to boil, pulling Kragan from the vision that had engulfed him. Atop the pier the Zvejys clutched their throats, their mouths open as they convulsed upon the wood planking. Dozens rolled off the pier in their death throes to plunge into the froth.

Hundreds of alien minds assaulted Kragan's with hunger such as he had never known, nearly breaking his hold on the air elemental that kept him aloft. But his grip upon Landrel's ancient artifacts tightened, establishing his mastery over those who stole the life and flesh from his Zvejys sacrifices. And as the bodies atop the pier ceased their struggles, they withered into dust. Of the 327, only ancient bones remained. A like number of uzraudze launched themselves toward the mouth of the bay, propelling themselves through the water with such speed that a spearhead-shaped wake formed around the swarm.

From his lofty perch, Kragan transmitted into his new pets' minds the image of Carol's two ships and the tasty morsels that roamed their decks. As he made his way back to the ground, Kragan's thoughts turned to Charna, a thin web of regret momentarily dampening his excitement.

Every victory had its cost. Like the bones that littered this pier, his commander would forfeit her life for a great cause.

The birth of a god.

25

Whale's Mouth Bay, Continent of Sadamad
YOR 415, Mid-Summer

The entrance to the bay hove into Arn's sight as the *Saimniece* crested a wave, several minutes after Carol had called down from the watch basket high on the ship's mainmast. The view pulled forward his memory of the dreams that had haunted his sleep for the last several nights. Oddly enough, his last sleep had been dream-free. Perhaps it was because the captains had brought their two ships together, sailing into danger side by side. Or maybe his peaceful rest had been pure coincidence. Not that it mattered. Every member of Carol's company was about to find out what awaited them in that vast cove.

"They come!" Carol's cry from the high basket was accompanied by a lensing of the atmosphere forward of the twin ships, pulling the distant sight forward for all on the decks to see.

The wake that churned the sea's surface generated within Arn's breast a sense of otherworldly dread despite his inability to see what sort of creatures swam beneath the roiling waters.

Captain Kumstelis bellowed orders, and his crew responded with the professionalism and alacrity to which Arn had become accustomed during this voyage. The Endarian sailors swarmed the rigging, furling the sails on both the *Saimniece* and the *Milakais* and hurling grappling hooks between the ships. Crewmen set their backs to wheels that turned the winches, hauling the ships together and lashing them to one another. The sailors lowered gangplanks, providing walkways between the ships, turning the two vessels into one becalmed fighting fortress.

Alan's Forsworn arranged themselves in combat formation along the double perimeter of the two hulls, weapons at the ready. Alan moved among them, clapping his left hand on backs, speaking words of encouragement as he rested Ty's great crescent-bladed ax on his right shoulder. Kim stood beside her brother, having joined him atop the upper deck of the *Saimniece*'s aftcastle.

As much as Arn wanted to set Slaken aside to allow himself to share Carol's thoughts and emotions, he would need the magic-damping blade in the coming fight. As his right hand reached across his body to draw Slaken from its sheath, a new thought occurred to him. All these years, he had given himself to his intuition whenever the need had called. Knowing what he now understood of his innate time-sight talent and the way his runed knife blocked that magic, he marveled at how the nudge of his intuition still managed to influence him even while he wore or wielded the blade.

Could his magic be penetrating the knife's shielding? The elemental runes carved into its haft had no effect on Kim's life magic or on Galad's time-shaping. But it blocked mind magic, of which control of elementals was just a small part. Perhaps that accounted for the partial blockage. Even though Arn's foresight was time magic, it was also of the mind.

Arn focused his thoughts, returning his attention to the approaching danger. He surrendered to the intuitive tug that positioned him amidships along the western railing. He allowed himself a single upward glance to where Carol stood in the watch basket, high up on the mainmast. With all the sails lowered, her leather-clad body stood out against the gray sky. She reached out with her hands, summoning arcane energy that produced a translucent shimmer in the air around her.

Pride for this woman swelled Arn's chest, filling him with determination. He gritted his teeth and looked toward the churning foam that had now branched into multiple spearheads just a few hundred paces from the ships. Then, as he had done so many times before, he opened himself to his Blade persona, becoming vengeance incarnate.

—⁂—

Carol watched the approaching swarm as the conjoined galleons rocked in the waves, having lost all forward momentum with the furling of their sails. Over the last hour, she had grown used to the stomach-churning sway of the *Saimniece*'s mainmast. But now she was thankful that lashing the two ships together had reduced the side-to-side motion.

The creatures that churned the sea surface so violently had split up, approaching the ships along multiple paths. If only they would break the surface, Carol could target them. But whether they sensed danger via natural intelligence or Kragan's will directed them, they did not provide her the glimpse she needed to launch her attacks.

She summoned the water elemental Glajus, transforming the sea surface before the monsters into thick sheets of ice. Despite the raw power she channeled into that sending, her efforts failed to impede the swarm's progress. They just swam under or around the impediments. If only she could see the creatures, she could use her magic to attack them directly.

And Carol did not dare conjure such jagged ice chunks anywhere near the ships. Like the fighting men and women who lined the decks far below, she was forced to await the coming onslaught.

Her eyes were drawn to the distant shorelines that bounded the bay. Somewhere out there, Kragan awaited. How he had generated this attack escaped her. While she could take control of individual beings or spread emotions such as fear or rage through a large gathering, she did not have the mind magic to control a large collection of individuals such as the foul beasts that Kragan hurled at them. How was he doing it?

The thought that the wielder might have already recovered one or more of the fragments of Landrel's Trident sent a chill through her body that she angrily banished. Kragan had killed her father. Carol would not allow that bastard to destroy all whom she loved. Not on this day. Not ever.

She recalled a scene from Arn's dream. The sea monsters had launched themselves over the ships, ripping through sails and pulling warriors from the decks. If she could not kill the beasts beneath the sea, she would deny them access to the open air. Summoning a half dozen air elementals, Carol wreathed the ships in glittering shields of crystallized atmosphere.

"Come on, beasties," she breathed, adding force to her visualization. "Let's see how you like that."

As if in answer to her call, the water a hundred paces to the left front of the *Saimniece* erupted with leaping bodies. Although Carol had grown familiar with the large fish that often leapt into the air alongside the ships, these ugly creatures did not dive back into the sea. Instead they spread their winglike fins and glided through the air toward the vessels. Their extended jaws opened wide to reveal row upon row of wicked teeth. Each had a twenty-foot-long tail, as thick as a man's leg, that ended in a clawed, vertical flipper. The bulbous red eyes had slitted pupils like those of a giant cat.

The first wave of these slammed into her shields, only to tumble back into the waves. The second swarm of attackers swung wide, testing the strength of her defenses all around the perimeter. When they failed to get through, they and the scores of their fellows changed tactics, diving beneath the waves to disappear. A low-pitched grinding sound pulled Carol's eyes down to the main deck. Captain Kumstelis, accompanied by a score of his Endarian crewmen, rushed to the central hatch and scrambled down into the ship's interior.

A sudden revelation hammered Carol. Those things were attacking the ship's hull from below. Despite the strength and thickness of the planks that had been used to build these galleons, she doubted they could withstand an organized attempt to tear one or more holes in the lower deck. And these damned creatures were smart. Carol considered following the crew down to help them patch any damaged spots before real holes could form, but that would require her to drop her shielding and leave her family and friends to defend the upper decks unaided by her magic.

New groups of the sea monsters launched themselves into the air to renew their testing of her shields, some from straight overhead. Carol called forth lightning, frying three of the things before the others dived back beneath the surf. Before the last of these disappeared, she made a mental link to the monster.

An overwhelming need to rend and kill washed her with desire. She did not fight the feelings. Instead she amplified those emotions, targeting the group of horse-heads that attacked a spot near the *Saimniece's* bow a dozen feet above the keel. The horse-head tore into its fellows, taking the first two by surprise. Agony speared Carol's side as others in the swarm ripped at her surrogate body. She lashed out with her tail, wrapping its tentacle-like length around the torso of the nearest attacker, pulling it free from her side to bring it to her maw.

As that enemy died, she shifted her link to an uninjured horse-head and renewed her assault. The savagery of its longings frayed her sanity, causing her to lose focus on the shielding that protected the upper decks of both ships.

The mainmast shuddered as a heavy body smashed into it, two paces below the watch basket within which Carol stood, the impact breaking her mind link and restoring her wits. She launched a dozen ethereal bolts into the thing's snapping mouth, loosing the hold of its tentacle on the mast and sending the big body tumbling to the deck, where desperate combat reigned. But the damage was done. The crack in the mast that the horse-head's impact had created widened, sending Carol's basket tumbling forward.

She leapt from her perch, using a burst of air to cushion her impact on the forecastle's upper deck. Carol's feet slipped on the wet deck and she fell into the railing. Pain lanced her vision as her shoulder popped from its socket, dragging a shriek from her throat. The sound attracted the attention of a horse-head that soared onto the deck two paces from where she lay. The beast lashed out with its tail, the clawed fin at its tip latching on to her left ankle. Then, with a jerk, it yanked her toward jaws that unhinged to form a maw capable of swallowing her whole.

—⁂—

Alan saw the translucent shielding shimmer and vanish, unleashing a discordant screeching that he had heretofore never heard.

"Be ready," he yelled.

A fresh swarm of the fiends erupted from the sea to glide toward the deck. His Forsworn raised their weapons to meet them. Three of the beasts crumpled into the waves, one crashing into the side of the ship, a spear shaft jutting from its right eye. Then the others swooped down on them.

Alan's first stroke severed a head, drenching him in acrid-smelling green blood. But as he whirled into his next blow, a prehensile tail wrapped the haft of his ax. It lashed about, trying to wrest the ax from his grip or pull him from his feet. Something bright glittered, and more of the stinking blood splattered Alan's face as Kat's long knife severed the tail. His weapon free once more, Alan bounded forward, cutting away one of his attacker's gaping jaws and opening its chest cavity to reveal its beating heart.

To Alan's left, Bill slipped on the blood-slicked planking, falling into the snapping jaws of another beast. It ripped open the ranger's throat. From the corner of his eye, Alan saw Kim gesture and watched Bill's fatal wound knit itself closed while a matching injury formed in the neck of the startled monster. Alan did not give the thing time to bite down again. His ax descended with the full force of his double-handed grip, severing the beast's spine and dropping its limp body atop Bill.

All around him, his Forsworn fought and died faster than Kim could heal them. A berserk fury swept all thought from Alan's brain. The world misted green as his ax screamed its wrath at the universe.

—ᴍ—

Kim swallowed the bile that crawled into her throat from her gut as she funneled the bite wound in Alan's side through her own body and into the sea-worm that had inflicted it. As always happened when she used this necrotic form of life magic, she felt the thirst-hunger as her health drained away followed by the ravenous euphoria as she refilled herself, drinking in the life essence of her enemy. Somehow the creature sensed what she was doing and uncoiled its powerful tail, launching itself through the air toward her. A spear passed between the gaping jaws through the back of the creature's head. The dying beast flopped to the deck two paces in front of Kim, its death throes knocking her onto her back.

She kicked at the snapping jaws, her booted right heel hitting the thing's snout and sending her sliding across the wet deck. Kim scrambled back to her feet just in time to see Captain Kumstelis ripped asunder by two more of the monsters.

Alan's enraged bellow rang out above the insane screeching. Fighting in a tight knot beside Katrin, Quincy, and Bill, he cut a swath of destruction through the beings that surrounded them, his bald head and face so coated with a mixture of red and green that it seemed only his eyes shone through the slime.

Kim's pain-and-pleasure-filled moan merged with the shrieks of the monsters, the battle yells of the Forsworn, and the screams of the dying all around her. For a terrible instant, she was tempted to fully immerse herself in the heady rush of life transference, taking bigger and bolder doses. Why not finally join her husband in death? But then she saw Galad, wielding the time-mists even as he fought, the sword in his one good hand slashing his attackers despite wounds that wept down his right leg.

With a shuddering breath, Kim straightened and formed the channel that pulled Galad's injury into her on its way into one of her brother's opponents. She would master the powerful urges that bombarded her. Such was the price she would pay for failing to keep John within her healing range during the battle for Endar. She still had a brother and sister to save.

—◊—

Arn heard Carol's scream of pain and spun to see the horse-head creature wrap its tail fin around her leg, jerking her toward its hyperextended jaws. His left hand snatched a throwing dagger from its sheath and hurled it at her attacker. It spun through the air to bury itself hilt deep in the sea-beast's right eye. Then Arn was on it, severing the tail with his first stroke. His second strike cut the thing's throat as it turned its snapping teeth on this new enemy. The severed tail released its hold on Carol to lash blindly about the deck. It struck Arn across his right wrist, knocking Slaken from his grip and sending the knife sliding through the nearest hatch.

As his blade tumbled down into the ship's interior, reality frayed around him. And for Arn, time ceased to have meaning. He strode from dream to dream, each playing out around him over the course of moments. Within those nightmares where he retrieved Slaken, he fought his way through a whirling maelstrom of death and destruction, only to emerge as the lone survivor, his thirst for vengeance against Kragan unsated. In some of those visions, he killed Charna, but in none did he reach his real target.

Arn turned his attention to the paths that opened before him should he decide to let Slaken go. Buried within these equally dismal sequences, he found options with some small chance of saving the woman he loved. With the weight of a thousand worlds suffocating him, a new realization dawned upon him. His next actions would determine the path along which Carol and her expedition would make their way forward.

Having found no perfect course, nor even a good one, he made his choice.

Arn stepped from his timescape world back into the life-and-death struggle aboard the linked ships. The screeching of the creatures that swarmed the decks had risen to a deafening level, but this suddenly diminished as Carol and Arn disappeared within the time-mists that Galad wielded. Apparently the prince had seen Carol fall and channeled a rychly fog to hide her and Arn from the swarm of attackers. This allowed Arn to race to her side as Carol struggled to sit up on the wet deck.

The dead beast's claws had torn through her leather pant leg and opened a hand's-length gash in her left thigh. But she clutched at her dislocated left shoulder, her face contorted in a grimace. As he knelt beside her, a fresh sequence of visions raced through his mind.

Reaching out, Arn grabbed her injured arm above the elbow and yanked hard, pulling a fresh scream from his wife's throat. Her eyes widened in shock and anger as he hauled her to her feet. But her expression softened when he released her, as she realized that he had popped her shoulder back into its socket.

"We have to get out of this mist and back to the others," she said, gasping the words out through teeth clenched against the pain. "I cannot cast spells through the time boundary."

Arn nodded, relief flooding his body. Then, as he had seen in his latest waking dream, he plucked his dagger from the dead monster's eye, turned, and pushed his way through the mist barrier and back into the timescape within which their companions battled. And his bloodied and battered wife strode at his side.

—⁓—

Kragan stood amidst the desiccated corpses of the men, women, and children who had been all that remained of his Zvejys people, staring out across the bay toward the distant sea battle. The far-glass that the elemental created from the air brought it into partial focus. Although amidst the thrashing sea spray he could not make out the fine details of his sea-dragon assault, he did observe the upper section of the mainmast on one of the twin ships topple to the deck. And when it fell, it spilled a female body that, by the light color of her skin, could only have been that of Carol Rafel.

His mind touched that of a sea-dragon, directing it at the fallen witch, but Blade leapt into the fray even as Kragan's resurrected beast reached her. Then a dark miasma swirled up from the distant ship, hiding Carol, her assassin, and the monster from his view.

Kragan hissed with frustration but shifted his focus to the fight raging on and around the twin ships. With Carol out of the action, he summoned Lwellen, using the air elemental to pull thunderheads into the heavens above the galleons. But before he could channel the lightning, a pale time-mist that the Endarians called pomaly churned into being, sweeping the ships and the sea-dragons into a region where time passed more slowly, blocking Kragan's attack before it could begin.

Growling a curse, Kragan balled his fists, then opened them to stare down at the hands that seemed too large to fit his diminutive body. His frustration at his inability to channel enough mind magic to penetrate that barrier caused him to run those fingers through his unruly mop of hair.

He turned to Joresh, the new captain of his troop of nearly five-score guardsmen.

"Depending on the outcome of yon battle, I will lead us out through the swamp. Should my enemies emerge from the conflagration I have unleashed on them, they will be depleted and in need of time to recover. If they try to follow, I will let the treacherous marshes kill them. Make ready to depart."

"Yes, Lord Kragan."

Kragan returned his attention to the eddying mists just beyond the mouth of the bay. That they did not dissipate meant that the Endarian time-shaper and some of Carol's troop yet survived. His right hand moved to the bony thumb and forefinger that hung from his necklace onto his chest. The wielder let his gaze wander over the remains of the hundreds of Zvejys he had sacrificed on this day, surprised at the heaviness the sight generated in his chest. He had thought their martyrdom would be sufficient to free him from his prophesied nemesis.

Releasing his grip on the ancient artifacts, Kragan turned away from the docks and the dozens of moored fishing boats. Whatever the outcome of today's sea battle, he would remain here to witness it. Then it would be time to gather the remaining fragments of Landrel's Trident.

—⚶—

Charna yanked at the bars that sealed her inside the tiny cell on the *Saimniece*'s lower deck, the muscles in her arms cording with effort, sweat drenching her bare shoulders. Her frantic growl rumbled through the hold, ignored by the Endarian sailors who struggled to shore up the thick planking that spewed seawater, already ankle deep. With a loud crack, the ten-foot beam they used as a brace splintered into two pieces. A misshapen head slid through the opening as more planking gave way, the toothy maw closing on the head of the nearest sailor even as its thick, gray-skinned body plugged the hole.

The other ten sailors attacked the monster with swords but, with a mighty effort, the beast heaved itself through the rip in the ship's side. Its bulk, propelled by the pressure of the seawater, swept the crewmen aside.

"Deep-spawn!" Charna cursed, redoubling her efforts.

The wood that anchored the bars, top and bottom, creaked. Charna leaned back, bracing her feet against the wall as her growl morphed into a wild howl, spittle flying from her fangs. The bars broke free, spraying Charna's face with splinters and sending her splashing to the floor. She scrambled to her feet, grabbed one of the steel bars, and squeezed out through the opening and into the hold.

Ignoring the screams, yells, and maddening screeches, she rushed through the now-knee-deep water and climbed the ladder up through the open hatch to the next deck. To her amazement she found that she was the only soul on the ship's berth deck. A noise from the hatch pulled her head down. She kicked the sailor on the top rung of the ladder in the face, knocking him back down atop some of his mates, and then slammed the hatch. She slid the steel bar through two rings, locking the hatch closed.

She spotted a weapons rack and armed herself with a heavy ax just as the flopping body of another of the sea monsters crashed into the berth deck from above, ripping several hammocks from their moorings. Charna launched herself at the writhing creature, ducking beneath the grasping tail, putting all her weight and strength into the blow that buried the ax blade in the monster's neck. She pulled it free with a snarl, her next blow taking off half the thing's head.

The beast dropped limply to the deck and Charna leapt over it, intent on climbing up into the shrieking madness that sounded from the main deck. Even though the thought occurred to her that she was safer down here, she could not bear the thought of dying within the bowels of the ship in which she had been kept prisoner. Blade had known that all vorgs hated caves and confined spaces. If there had been no brig down in the ship's hold, he would have built one in order to imprison her down there.

Then she saw it, its tip embedded in a deck plank, its black blade and handle barely visible in the shadows. The magical knife that Blade called Slaken. The sight of the legendary weapon sent a thrill through the she-vorg's body that caused her to catch her breath. It was the weapon that legend said only Blade could grasp. The knife would consume anyone who had not made the blood bond to the four elementals bound within its runed haft. For it to be left here could mean only one thing.

The dreaded assassin was dead.

If Charna could survive the creatures that Kragan had sent to destroy these ships and make her way to shore, she could follow her link to the wielder. A scowl twisted her lips. She would have to ask her old friend why he had made so little effort to ensure that she might survive this assault. Another thought softened her anger. If the Endarian prince was wielding the time-mists around these ships, as surely he was, Kragan's mind magic would be unable to reach her.

Charna redirected her gaze to the ladder leading up to the main deck. Blood and green slime ran down through the hatch to drench the rungs and pool upon the planking beneath the ladder. Her ax in her right hand, wearing just her leather pants, jerkin, and boots, she began to climb toward the conflict that raged above.

She poked her head out of the hatch and into mayhem. Rather than the salty smell of the sea that she remembered from her midnight excursion, the air was thick with the stench of death and the acidic smell of

244

sea-monster blood. A gray tail lashed out at her, and she ducked below the deck. Charna reacted with the ferocity that had served her so well in battle, leaping out of the hatch, her ax whistling along an arc that severed the tentacular appendage near its base.

The creature twisted, its distended jaws snapping closed on the ax handle, breaking it in two. Charna jammed the jagged tip of the shaft into the thing's left eye, swung her body onto its back, and wrapped both legs around its throat without losing her grip on the impaling handle. She wrenched the wooden spike violently, breaking through the beast's skull. The monster thrashed twice before collapsing, belly-up atop Charna, pinning her right leg beneath its bulk.

She struggled to free herself, but the creature was heavy and the deck was slick with blood, entrails, and slime, denying her anything she could grip. Another of the monsters disemboweled a human warrior, lifting the woman's body in its jaws and shaking her as a dog would shake a squirrel. It hurled the woman's corpse to the deck, sending it sliding into Charna. Then the beast turned its eyes on the she-vorg.

Charna kicked at the slick gray body that pinned her but failed to free herself. Then, with rising dread, she saw the monster that had just shredded the woman lunge toward her, its powerful tail undulating like a snake to propel it across the deck.

The jaws dislocated and distended, revealing row upon row of bloody teeth, as it screeched its chilling hunting cry. Knowing that she was about to die, Charna opened her own jaws wide, baring two-inch canines, growling her fury at the world.

—∞—

Another vision staggered Arn when he emerged from the time-mist onto the main deck, a dozen paces from the mast where Alan, Katrin, Quincy, and Bill fought back-to-back in a tight diamond formation. In this waking dream, a horse-head closed its maw on Charna's snarling face, crunching down with such force that her head shattered like a melon struck with a hammer. The idea that this beast had destroyed the vorg that was reserved for his own vengeance enraged him. Worse was his premonition that he would yet need Charna to guide him to Kragan.

His sight cleared and he spun to see one of the creatures propel itself toward Charna, whose lower body was pinned to the deck beneath another dead monster.

A guttural yell issued from Arn's throat. "No!"

He dived forward, his knife rising and falling as his shoulder struck the side of the thing's neck. The jaws snapped closed, missing Charna's face by a handbreadth.

Twin magical bolts of light streaked into his opponent's head, tearing out its eyes and burning their way into its skull. With a loud *pop*, its head burst. And then a fresh wave of hallucinations consumed him.

—⁂—

Carol summoned the magical bolts that exploded the monster's horse-like head even as Arn's dagger repeatedly plunged into its neck. Her mental link to her husband formed of its own accord, the strength of his visions pulling her into the alternate realities that blossomed all around them. She watched herself and Arn die again and again. And in those near futures, none of her party survived. Dizziness assailed her such that she almost lost her balance.

But then she found a thread of hope. Instead of fighting her way out of her husband's fugue, she changed tactics. For the first time she realized why Arn was so frightened of his talent. Just as her mind had gotten lost within her links to animal minds in Misty Hollow, it would be easy to permanently lose oneself within these all-too-real visions. Nevertheless, she willingly stepped into his madness. Carol guided her consciousness to the centered state of concentration that underlay all her magical training, allowing herself to be swept along through the ever-changing dreamscape, an emotionless observer of chaos.

Rather than fight Arn's time-sight's influence upon her, Carol embraced it. A pattern emerged before her eyes, one that connected her thoughts and actions with how these immediate futures progressed. Anything she did, no matter how subtle, produced some changes in the timelines that spun out from this moment. Carol picked her path, seeing the impending movements of all the attacking monsters, and acted.

Her mind reached out to simultaneously ensnare elementals from the planes of air, fire, earth, and water, making them dance to a tune that only she could play. With an effort that made her heart throb, Carol wielded her arcane servants to unleash a superfluity of destruction upon Kragan's foul swarm. And as she wielded her mind magic in conjunction with Arn's, a growing sense of exultation filled her. This was wielding arcane might as she had never imagined.

—⚏—

Standing with her back to the *Saimniece*'s mizzenmast, Kim saw a seafiend aboard the adjacent sister ship rip Alan's weapons master Kron apart, the one-legged horse warrior's wound instantaneously fatal. With a leap that carried him onto the deck of the *Milakais*, Alan cleaved the monster's head from its neck, his blow a moment too late to save the first of his Forsworn. Sick to her soul, she was wrung out. Right now she just wanted to join her husband in the land of the dead.

Then her gaze was drawn to Arn and Carol. Arn rose from atop a beast's body, dripping green gore. But he did not assume a fighting stance. His knife hand dropped to his side, and he stared out into the distance, his eyes unfocused. Beside him Carol froze, seemingly unaware of a fresh wave of attackers that leapt from the sea to sail toward them.

Carol spread her arms wide, unleashing an apocalypse such as Kim could not have imagined. Fireballs crackled through the air as lightning, wind, and hail the size of melons pummeled the new swarm. The deck and hull of the *Saimniece* and the *Milakais* distorted. Thousands of needle-tipped pikes sprouted from the wood, forming protective barriers around the small groups of survivors. But those magical spears did not remain motionless. Like the spines on the back and tail of the porcupine, these thrust themselves into the monsters that had survived the journey through the supernatural cataclysm to reach the ships, directed by Carol's borrowed visions of the moves the sea monsters would make. Three of these beings dived at Kim, only to impale themselves upon the living pikes.

Kim became aware of several wakes streaming out and away from the ships. It became clear to her that whatever sea monsters still survived had determined that their chance of victory had vanished and their survival now depended upon retreat.

It had been years since Kim had heard her brother's laugh, but as the monstrous screeching of the horse-heads died away, Galad's hearty guffaws turned her head toward him. The Endarian prince stood tall amidst a forest of wooden spears, his sword lowered, laughing, the time-mists around the two battered and misshapen sea vessels dissipating.

But since she had knelt by John's corpse inside the Endarian palace, no mirth or relief could find purchase in her soul. Kim merely hung her head and wept.

26

Zvejys Fishing Village of Klampyne, Whale's Mouth Bay,
Continent of Sadamad
YOR 415, Mid-Summer

Kragan stood at the end of the pier, watching as the distant storm clouds parted to reveal a sky of royal blue. Even the time-mists that had blocked his view of the two Endarian galleons dissolved. The quantity of magic he had felt Carol unleash had put a tremor in his hands that he had failed to still. Despite the inner voice that told him that she must have exhausted herself in the destruction of his resurrected swarm of sea-dragons, he dared not confront her. Not now, without Kaleal's might to augment his. Not until he had acquired more fragments of Landrel's Trident.

Kragan noticed that he had been rubbing the scar of his missing right ear and lowered his hand, a scowl curling his lips. Turning away, he walked back toward the shore, where his company of guardsmen awaited him.

Then Kragan led his company of warriors through the deserted streets of the dead village and out into the marshes. It was time to make the long journey north to the seaport city-state of Vurtsid to retrieve another fragment of Landrel's Trident.

—Ⱳ—

Arn's visions dissolved, although his reentry into reality left him wondering whether he was still living inside a dream. The sky was brilliant blue, the time-mists were gone, and the twin ships had sprouted spiny branches that held the impaled bodies of the sea monsters. Even the stiff breeze and the sea spray failed to drive the cloying stench from the remains of the dead.

Beside him Carol lowered her outstretched arms and, as she did so, the spikes that had grown from the hulls and decks of the twin galleons retracted, depositing the bodies of the creatures on the upper decks. Arn took a single step forward and turned to survey the scene, not bothering to brush at the goop that covered him from head to heel. From where he stood, he had a clear view of both ships. Whereas the original crews from both galleons plus the company that had accompanied Carol and Alan aboard had numbered 107, Arn now saw fewer than half that number, although some additional crewmen might have survived belowdecks.

Of Carol's party, only Carol, Arn, Alan, Kim, Galad, Katrin, Bill, Quincy, and perhaps three dozen more of Alan's Forsworn remained standing. The torn body of Captain Kumstelis lay where it had fallen from atop the aftcastle onto the main deck. The *Saimniece* slumped low in the water, threatening to overturn the battered but seaworthy *Milakais* should the *Saimniece* succumb to the call of the depths. It was time to gather the survivors aboard the vessel's sister and scuttle the *Saimniece*. But before he joined the others, Arn had one more task to accomplish.

"Gather everyone aboard the *Milakais* and prepare to cut the *Saimniece* free," Carol called to Alan. She gestured toward the spot where Charna lay pinned beneath the bulk of a dead horse-head. "And take the she-vorg with us."

"I will be along shortly," said Arn.

Seeing a frown of concern furrow Carol's brow, he placed a gentle hand on her forearm. "Trust me."

Then he walked to the hatch, scraped the bottoms of his boots on the second rung, and climbed into the semidarkness below.

—◊—

"Trust me."

Arn's tone, the intense blaze in his eyes, and the tension in the muscles of his lower jaw placed a doubt in Carol that those two words could not counteract. She watched Arn disappear through the hatch into the ship's interior, her heart catching in her throat. Knowing that what she was about to do was a violation, Carol shoved aside her revulsion and did it anyway.

With a subtlety that she had mastered through long hours of practice, she touched Arn's mind. Not at a conscious level, which would have made him aware of her presence, but with a technique that let her access his senses and feel his emotions.

She felt his boots slip off the bottom rung to land with a thump on the decking in the ship's berth deck. The sunlight filtered in from above to cast shadows that moved with the motion of the wounded ship. Arn surveyed his surroundings, studying the corpses of dead horse-heads and the remnants of the hammocks they had destroyed as they plunged down from the upper deck. Aside from the creak of the wood and a sloshing sound from the closed hatch that led down to the ship's hold, silence reigned.

Arn's gaze settled upon the spot where Slaken had stuck in the deck's planking. Carol sensed the way the black haft called to her husband, felt his need for the weapon that would shield him from the vision-storm that threatened his sanity. When his fingers curled around the knife's handle, Carol's connection to her husband's mind winked out.

The sense of loss that accompanied the sudden separation leached a chill into Carol's breast. Holding back the tears that tried to breach her resolve, she set her jaw and magically cleared a path through the gore that covered the *Saimniece*'s upper deck. Then she strode to the hatch that led into the aftcastle. She walked into the great cabin, plucked the Scroll of Landrel from its place on the shelf, then returned to the cabin she and Arn had shared.

Arn met her at the door, Slaken in its sheath at his side.

When he enfolded her in his arms, she returned his embrace and kissed him. Despite the filth that covered them, it felt almost as it had each time in the past. Almost, but not quite. Carol felt the black knife's handle press against her, as if it were trying to push her away.

They entered the cabin, gathered their two bags of belongings, and carried them onto the *Milakais*, where they met Captain Tekelas, her blue eyepatch covering the socket that was missing the eye she had long ago lost to a fishing hook. As soon as they were across the gangplank and safely aboard, she signaled for three of her surviving sailors to cut the *Saimniece* free and shove off. Carol summoned a water elemental, altering the currents to propel the dying ship to a safe distance away. Then she snapped the *Saimniece*'s keel, breaking the ship in half.

For several moments Carol, Arn, and the other survivors of the sea battle watched as the once-proud vessel sank beneath the surface and disappeared into the depths.

"Captain," Carol said, turning to face the Endarian, "take us into the bay. I need to go ashore."

The captain yelled, sending a handful of sailors scurrying up into the rigging to unfurl the sails. As the ship tacked into the bay, Carol led Arn, her two siblings, Galad, and four of Alan's Forsworn up onto the forecastle of the *Milakais* to stand at the ship's prow. Two more of her brother's followers ushered Charna forward, the she-vorg's wrists and ankles in chains.

Despite having survived what Carol knew had been Kragan's best shot, Carol took no chances, standing ready to shield the craft from magical attacks.

Arn turned his attention to Charna. "Where is Kragan now?"

"Ah, my protector," the she-vorg crooned. "It must make you feel good to have saved my life?"

Carol saw Arn's eyes narrow.

"I can change that at any moment," he said. "Where is Kragan?"

Charna, a smile curling her lips, lifted her manacled arms to point north, toward the mouth of the bay. "He has been moving away from us for some time. You are far too late to catch him."

Carol detected no deception in Charna. The she-vorg believed everything she said.

Lensing the air, Carol brought the distant shore into focus. The houses of a good-size village stretched out along the shore, with narrow streets stretching inland. Dozens of fishing boats were docked along a lengthy pier that stretched out over the water. Odd piles of rubbish lay along the docks and on the pier, but she was too far away to make them out.

What stood out most starkly was the lack of any movement within the town. It appeared bereft of life. Had Kragan held the villagers hostage prior to taking flight? That would just slow the wielder down.

Carol wondered what form Kragan had now taken. Without Charna they would have little hope of finding him. Charna's eyes said she was counting on that advantage to keep her alive until an opportunity for escape presented itself.

Off the port side of the ship, the sun sank lower in the west, partially masked by billowing thunderheads on the horizon. The *Milakais* should just make port before sunset. And if the harbor was deep enough, they would anchor a short distance from the fishing village docks.

Once again she looked around the ship, making a rough count of the survivors. Roughly twoscore of her original party, Charna, Captain Tekelas, and seventeen sailors. Seeing Kim leaning against the rail, her head bowed, her brunette hair draping her face, Carol moved over to put her arm around her sister.

Kim stared off into the distance, her eyes unfocused, feeling as stiff as if she had been carved from ice. Carol's sense of her half sister's loss shamed her, making Carol's worries about Arn seem pitiful in comparison. Kim pulled away, wiping her tear-streaked face with both hands as she turned.

The princess glanced at Galad, who stood looking out over the bowsprit at the distant village, his matted waist-length hair swirling around his shoulders in the wind. With that look, Carol felt her sister gather her strength, her face slipping into a mask as stoic as that of the Endarian prince.

Carol's thoughts turned to her responsibilities to her people, and not just the ones she had led upon this daunting quest. The company had known the risks involved and had all volunteered. But she sometimes felt that she had abandoned the people of Areana's Vale and the remainder of Rafel's legion. Her decision to appoint Hanibal as steward and place him in charge while she was gone had angered Alan. She had even had second thoughts about that choice. But Hanibal had been the best commander left alive after the battle, and the legion respected Battle Master Gaar's son.

With the sun sinking below the western horizon, bathing the fishing village in orange, Carol found her attention pulled to the lakeside hamlet the *Milakais* was approaching. Rather than being desolate, the quaint village glowed with a warm color. She found the eerily welcoming scene disconcerting.

Perhaps her interpretation of the sight was affected by the knowledge that, despite their losses, they had beaten Kragan once again. Her attention was drawn to the scroll in her right hand, and she noticed that it had also picked up that sunset glow. As she hefted the twin dowels around which the parchment was wrapped, she had the strange impression that, despite all that Arn had already learned from this document, more of Landrel's secrets remained hidden within.

Carol felt Arn slip his hand into hers. Whatever their individual traumas, tonight she would sleep with this man in that empty village, thankful for whatever brief respite might await them.

She squeezed Arn's hand, feeling the strength and determination in his gentle response. With the salt breeze in her face, she could almost ignore the blood and gore that coated their bodies. Yes, there was good reason for the empty village they were approaching to welcome their arrival. There they would rest, recover, and reorganize for their continuing mission. In the days to come, this little town would launch Carol, Arn, and company to find Kragan and end his reign of terror, forever.

If need be, they would chase him to the end of the world.

ACKNOWLEDGMENTS

I want to express my deepest thanks to my lovely wife, Carol, without whose support and loving encouragement this project would never have happened.

I also want to thank Alan and John Ty Werner for the many long evenings spent in my company, brainstorming the history of this world, its many characters, and the story yet to be told.

Many thanks to my wonderful editor, Clarence Haynes, for once again helping me to refine my story.

ABOUT THE AUTHOR

 Richard Phillips was born in Roswell, New Mexico, in 1956. He graduated from the United States Military Academy at West Point in 1979 and qualified as a US Army Ranger, going on to serve as an officer in the army. He earned a master's degree in physics from the Naval Postgraduate School in 1989, completing his thesis work at Los Alamos National Laboratory. After working as a research associate at Lawrence Livermore National Laboratory, he returned to the army to complete his tour of duty.

Richard is the author of several science-fiction and fantasy series, including The Rho Agenda (*The Second Ship*, *Immune*, and *Wormhole*); The Rho Agenda Inception (*Once Dead*, *Dead Wrong*, and *Dead Shift*); The Rho Agenda Assimilation (*The Kasari Nexus*, *The Altreian Enigma*, and *The Meridian Ascent*); and *Mark of Fire*, *Prophecy's Daughter*, and *Curse of the Chosen* in the epic Endarian Prophecy series. Richard lives with his wife, Carol, in Phoenix, Arizona. For more information, visit rhoagenda.me.